Farew

to the

Coffee Shop of

Kabul

Also by Deborah Rodriguez

DEBORAH RODRIGUEZ
with Ellen Kaye

Farewell
to the Little
Coffee Shop of
Kabul

SPHERE

SPHERE

First published in 2023 in Australia by Bantam,
an imprint of Penguin Random House Australia
This paperback edition published in 2024 by Sphere

1 3 5 7 9 10 8 6 4 2

A CIP catalogue record for this book is available from the British Library.

ISBN 9-781-4087-2811-6

Printed and bound in Great Britain by
Clays Ltd, Elcograf S.p.A

Papers used by Sphere are from well-managed forests
and other responsible sources.

Sphere
An imprint of
Little, Brown Book Group
Carmelite House
50 Victoria Embankment
London EC4Y 0DZ

An Hachette UK Company
www.hachette.co.uk

www.littlebrown.co.uk

To Heather Haslam, Richard and Feyza Shipley, and the Shipley Foundation. You showed unconditional love and support to the people of Afghanistan; you are what genuine kindness is all about.

And to refugees around the world. You are a reminder of the power of the human spirit and an inspiration to never give up.

1

Monday, July 26, 2021

Sunny sat wedged between Halajan and the back door of the old Mercedes convertible, the large pink elephant slumped on her lap as if it were a petulant child. There had barely been room for her luggage, what with the entire family insisting on coming along to greet her at the airport, showering her with flowers and balloons and kisses and more than a few tears. Fitting everyone in the car to go home was like trying to put toothpaste back into the tube. Despite the dust clogging the skies, they'd had to open the top to accommodate everything she'd brought—most of it gifts, including the stuffed animal for little Aarezo that was now blocking Sunny's view of the city.

After twenty-nine hours in the air, from Seattle to London to Doha to Kabul, the jetlag was taking its toll. Things felt a little surreal. Landing once again in Afghanistan, being with her friends, not having Jack by her side—it seemed weird and familiar, happy and sad, all at the same time.

The hot summer air felt like a blow dryer set on high, aimed smack at Sunny's face. She could feel the moisture being sucked right out of her skin. The balloons were batted around by the breeze, making her feel as though they were aboard a float in some sort of bizarre parade. Halajan was downright giddy, holding Sunny's hand in a tight squeeze, jabbering away like a magpie. They had barely left the parking area when she'd launched into a rambling story about how she'd outsmarted an unscrupulous vendor at the Mondai-e, the city's largest market, by pretending to be the mother of the chief of police. "And do you think that man's prices suddenly turned to half of what they were? You bet your ass!" she cackled. The old woman seemed to have barely aged in the eight years since they'd last seen each other. They'd video chatted regularly, but in person, somehow, Halajan seemed more vibrant. Sunny was relieved.

Halajan's husband, Rashif, was seated on the other side of his wife with eight-year-old Aarezo on his lap. What little hair was left on Rashif's head had gone completely gray. He looked distinguished, grandfatherly. In the front seat Halajan's son, Ahmet, was behind the wheel sitting straight and proud. Sunny couldn't help but think of the tortured young man Ahmet had been when they first met, struggling so hard with his traditionalist views in a changing world. Since then he had become such a loving husband and father, a man dedicated to standing up for what's right, committed to supporting his wife, Yazmina, in her efforts to help those who couldn't help themselves. There she sat, right by his side, that naive girl from the mountains, who had landed on the Kabul Coffee Shop doorstep scared and alone so many years ago. But that girl was long gone, and in her place was a woman bursting with confidence, which was only right considering how much she had accomplished. Next to Yazmina was her younger sister, Layla, balancing her twelve-year-old niece Najama on her lap.

Sunny wrestled with the head scarf that kept slipping off her in the gritty wind. How the Afghan women always wore the chador so effortlessly remained a mystery to her. Halajan reached in to help, looping the cloth into place in one quick move.

"Hey, Hala, why aren't you the one driving?" Sunny asked. Halajan had taken great pride in secretly learning how to drive not long before Sunny's last visit.

"He says I'm too old to drive." She pointed her chin toward Ahmet as she spoke. "Ach!"

Sunny peered around the elephant's ear as they passed some of the new, massive wedding halls that had gone up in recent years. *Las Vegas* was what the road had come to be called, due to the mirrored glass and bright neon lights that far outshone the starry Afghan night skies. The traffic was still heavy, the smell of diesel and the blaring of horns as familiar as her face in the mirror.

It wasn't long before they found themselves in gridlock, stranded in the open car like sitting ducks for the constant flow of beggars and peddlers desperate for a little cash. A small hand thrust a rusty tin can billowing with smoke into Sunny's face. *Espand bala band!* the little boy pleaded. A *spandi*, one of those many children spending hours a day working to bring home a few afghanis to help feed their mothers and siblings by trying

3

to sell the burning herb thought to ward off evil spirits. The boy eyed the balloons with envy, and Sunny's heart broke. "Give him some coins, would you please, Yaz? I haven't changed any money yet."

They finally inched forward, but again had to slow to a stop as they approached the police checkpoint near the American embassy, to wait their turn for inspection by the K-9 unit. Sunny felt herself stiffen. The mere sight of dogs sniffing around the tires and the swarm of men in full uniform and bulletproof vests, wielding rifles almost as big as they were—weapons they seemed to be itching to put to use—was enough of a reminder of just how dangerous a place Kabul could be. Horns honked. Tempers were on edge. Sunny watched as a pair of police wove through the chaos, sweeping mirrors on long poles under the cars' chassis to check for explosives.

The Mercedes was almost through the mess when there was a commotion up ahead. A battered red Toyota had tried to back up. Guns were drawn. A man and a woman were dragged from the car. There was shouting, lots of confusion. The man yelled back then was suddenly on the ground. The woman looked frightened. Sunny held her breath. She knew how unpredictable the police could be. Suddenly a loud pop sent her diving toward the floor of the car with the pink elephant clutched tightly around her head. And then, silence.

"Did you drop something down there, Sunny jan?" Hala howled after a beat.

Sunny sat up to see her old friend laughing, a lifeless piece of blue rubber tied to a string dangling from her knobby fingers. The Toyota was waved through and Ahmet pulled forward.

Sunny settled back into her seat, embarrassed. It had been so long since she'd lived in a warzone that she'd forgotten how normalized situations like this could become for people; when you live every day among chaos and destruction, you barely notice it. Even Sunny had found herself somewhat inured after a couple of years of living in Kabul, but she never became quite as accustomed to the havoc as the Afghans did. She remembered the day she heard a blast not far from the coffeehouse, strong enough to make the cups rattle on their shelves. By the time she went past the spot where the explosion had occurred, not more than an hour later, the shopkeepers were already sweeping up the broken glass from the blood-stained street, carrying on with business as usual.

They were now approaching Massoud Circle, where a new high-rise had sprouted from the ground. Mohib Towers.

Rashif raised his voice to be heard over the noise. "Stores, apartments, offices. It is impressive, is it not?"

It was. Kabul had changed. It struck Sunny that she was seeing less of the big-ass SUVs that used to hog the roads ferrying UN workers and NGOs around the city. It seemed as though the last of the foreigners had already left. Either that, or those who remained were locked in their compounds waiting for the clock to tick down. But what she did see were lots of women. Afghan women, walking in groups or even alone, carrying books or briefcases with their heads held high, their eyes ready to meet those of anyone who might try to challenge them. "So many women out and about. It's nice to see."

"I have heard there is even a woman who became a mayor out in the Wardak province when she was just twenty-four years old," Ahmet spoke over his shoulder toward Sunny. "She was one of the first. There are a few."

"Back in the old days, when your mother was a girl," Layla explained to Najama as they pulled up to a stop sign, "the only jobs women could have outside their homes were in women's prisons and hospitals, or at checkpoints at the airport. Anywhere they would not have to mix with men. Now you see women who are lawyers and journalists and politicians. Always remember, you can be anything you want, if you work hard enough."

An awkward silence filled the car, the growing uncertainty surrounding Layla's declaration remaining unspoken. Sunny rushed to change the subject as they finally pulled forward.

"Will you look at that," she said, craning her neck to see. They were driving adjacent to one of the concrete barricades that ringed the city. Staring back at Sunny was a pair of giant eyes that had been painted by someone with obvious skill.

"It's a message of anti-corruption. The words are *Man Tora Mebinm*, which means 'I see you,'" Ahmet explained. "There are graffiti artists who have done things like this all over Kabul. They call themselves ArtLords."

"Ha! ArtLords. I love it."

"Sometimes the murals have messages about women's rights or anti-terrorism, things like that," Ahmet continued.

"There is a really good one that shows streetsweepers," Rashif added. "It is meant to celebrate the everyday people who are heroes, instead of those with guns or swords."

"That's fantastic." Sunny swiped at the dust that had settled on her face with her free hand. She couldn't help but think of the blast wall she'd worked so hard to cover with paint over a dozen years earlier, back when the Kabul Coffee Shop was hers. It stood thirteen feet tall against the street, a monstrosity required to get the compliance that would allow UN personnel to frequent the café. After many fits and starts she'd finally settled on a scene that had been etched in her brain ever since a life-changing visit to Mazar-e Sharif—thousands of white doves soaring across a clear, cobalt sky. It was just after that trip when she'd realized she was truly in love with Jack.

They wound their way through the tangle of cars and motorbikes in Shahr-e Naw, downtown Kabul, past tall shiny buildings that housed offices, hotels and banks. There seemed to be many more beauty salons and supermarkets than before.

"Oh my God, what is *that*?" she asked as they slowed near an odd vehicle that looked like a hot dog on wheels.

"It's a food truck. Hot dogs and hamburgers," Ahmet explained.

"Oh, wow. I sure wish we'd had that when I lived here. And all these stores!" Sunny couldn't wait to hit the shops and markets, even though she'd promised herself to return home with far less than she'd brought. What surprised her was the number of places she recognized—Clark shoes, a Subway sandwich shop, even an Apple store on the ground level of the huge City Center Mall. "An Apple store," she said out loud. Jack would have never believed any of this.

"It is not a real Apple store," Yazmina explained. "It's unofficial. A lot of those big-name stores are."

"Fakes?" Sunny asked.

Yazmina shrugged in reply.

7

"You see over there, Sunny jan?" Layla pointed toward a trendy, glass-fronted café. "That is the café where I go now. You will love it. It's where all my friends meet. We have some very interesting conversations with men, women, everyone saying what they think."

"Really? That would never have happened when I was here."

"And maybe it should not be happening right now," Ahmet said.

"*Laalaa*, big brother, you worry too much. You yourself have always talked about the importance of discourse, the voicing of opinions. That is all we are doing there."

"*I* know that. But perhaps there are others who don't look at it that way. I just want you to be safe. You know what I always tell you—you can never trust anybody but your family."

"I am always careful," Layla replied. "I have eyes in the back of my head like Hala, and ears as big as that ridiculous elephant behind me."

Najama giggled.

Sunny could not believe what a formidable young woman Layla had grown into. Well, actually, she could. When Layla had first arrived in the States as a sixteen-year-old with a one-year student visa, she had clung fiercely to her traditions. She'd stayed at Sunny's place, on Twimbly Island off the coast of Washington, where things had started out rough. There Layla was a fish *way* out of water. But when the year was up, she'd returned to Kabul a changed person. Not that she'd given up an ounce of her identity—she'd simply expanded it with a mind that embraced new thoughts and a voice unafraid to question everything.

It wasn't long before they entered the Qala-e-Fathullah district, where the old coffee shop sat. "They paved the roads!" Everyone nodded. Jack had had a point when he'd insisted, some sixteen years ago already, that it was time to give Afghanistan back to the Afghans. The progress that had been made, against so many odds, was undeniable.

But just around the next corner Sunny was met with a harsh dose of reality that made the hair on her arms stand on end, despite the sweltering heat. Shahr-e Naw Park, with its tall, old pine trees and patchy lawn, had in her time been a place for locals to gather for games of chess and *carrom*, and, sadly, to buy and sell drugs—especially after dark. Back then it was mainly men who wandered the park's walkways or stretched out on the scrappy ground, but what Sunny saw now was what appeared to be a new population. Dozens of burqa-clad women were balancing babies on their hips and shepherding little ones around makeshift shelters strung between the trees and pop-up tents that rose from the ground like big neon mushrooms.

"What the hell is going on there?" she asked. "Who are they?"

"Refugees," Yazmina replied softly. "From the provinces in the north—Takhar, Kunduz, Badakhshan. Many have run from homes that have been taken or burned to the ground by the Taliban. Their towns and villages have been destroyed, their men killed. Some have been sent by their husbands and fathers, who have stayed behind to protect their homes. They have nowhere to go, and their numbers are growing by the day."

Ahmet had slowed, as if in respect for these women and their children. Once again the car grew quiet.

9

"Stupid Talib idiots," Halajan muttered as they made the next turn. Here, the street was as full of pedestrians as ever, the *chokidors* at their posts dressed in black with their weapons slung across their puffed-out chests, as if they'd been standing guard ever since Sunny left.

And there it was. The turquoise gate, that crazy wall. The little coffee shop of Kabul. Sunny was home.

2

The heavy metal door to the roof swung open under the weight of Kat's shoulder. There she found a jetlagged Sunny asleep in a chair, silhouetted against the fiery sky as the sun began its descent behind the mountains. Kat smiled at the sight of her friend. She'd missed Sunny over the course of the year she'd spent here in Kabul helping Yazmina and Ahmet with their work, and was looking forward to returning home with her friend to Twimbly Island.

Sunny stirred as the door banged shut.

"It's my favorite spot too." Kat placed two cups of steaming *sheer chai* on the plastic table next to her friend, the sweet odor of cardamom mixing with the smoky scent of kabobs drifting up from the street below. She pulled up a chair.

"I know, right?" Sunny yawned. "I used to come up here all the time to hide from the craziness of the coffeehouse. It was the only place I could hear myself think."

11

"Seriously. Sometimes I think these guys need a referee for their family discussions. So many opinions under one roof."

"Yeah. And imagine adding to that all those pushy foreigners wanting everything just so, exactly like they used to have it at home, always saying *gimme this, gimme that, make it snappy please*." She sighed. "I still miss it."

Sunny had opened the Kabul Coffee Shop in the complex owned by Halajan after she'd followed an old boyfriend to Afghanistan. It became *the* place for the missionaries, mercenaries and misfits who were as oddly energized as she was to be living in the middle of a war zone. Kat had heard all the stories. To Sunny, Kabul had been a place where anything was possible, and anything could happen. And it did. She'd met Jack and fallen head over heels in love, for one. And if it hadn't been for his insistence that they leave Kabul and move back to the States, Kat had a feeling that perhaps Sunny never would have.

Kat took a sip of her tea. "Speaking of home, how are things going back there?"

"Oh, you know, the usual." Sunny swept up her wavy hair into a clip on the top of her head, a few strands of gray now evident among the brown. "Pretty quiet. Covid really did a number on the tasting room when we had to shut down for so long. But things seem to be picking up again, and the takeout and delivery business is still crazy busy. Thank God people haven't stopped boozing it up."

If there was one thing Kat could say about Sunny, it was that the woman worked her butt off. Inheriting a winery without wine, saddled with a crappy house and a crumbling barn, and here she was, eight years later, having turned what Jack left her in his will into a business that supported her, and the handful of locals she employed, quite nicely. Kat could only hope to have that kind of energy when she reached Sunny's age.

She thought about when she and Sunny had first met, not long after Sunny had arrived in the Pacific Northwest. Kat was barely eighteen and working at that dentist's office in Seattle. She'd been angry at the world back then, and had barely wanted anything to do with anybody. Sunny, on discovering that Kat was originally from Kabul, had coerced her into teaching English to Layla while she was living with Sunny. One thing had led to another, and before Kat knew it she was practically living out there in Sunny's house on Twimbly Island as well. It wasn't long before Sunny became privy to Kat's story, and the reasons behind her determination to distance herself from everything Afghanistan. Sunny had worked hard at turning that around, too.

"I sure wish they'd let me help down there," Sunny said. Yazmina had shooed her away when the dinner preparations began.

"*You* were the one who taught me that a guest is never supposed to offer help in an Afghan home, right?" Kat responded. "You told me it was considered an insult."

"A guest? Me? Ouch."

The crackle of loudspeakers signaled the beginning of *Maghrib*, the evening prayer. Soon the skies were echoing with the staggered melody ringing from the highest minaret of every mosque in the city. The muezzins' call to prayer reminded Kat of when she was a very little girl, before she and her mother emigrated to the States, before things in her family became so complicated and got so ugly. The tinny sound of their amplified voices never failed to make her miss her mother, dead ten years now. She had not, herself, prayed since that dreadful day.

Kat waited for the sadness to pass. "How are things with Brian?" she asked as the din faded away.

"Good," Sunny said. "It's all good."

To Kat's ears, Sunny didn't sound convinced. Kat really liked Brian, whom she'd introduced to Sunny not long after he'd arrived at Kat's university as a visiting lecturer. She thought Brian was perfect for Sunny, with his background in Islamic Studies. They seemed to hit it off pretty well and were spending a fair amount of time together, but Kat always got the feeling Sunny was holding back. Just the fact she wasn't elaborating on her answer made Kat wonder. But she wasn't one to pry.

"Layla seems to be doing well." Sunny shaded her eyes against the setting sun. "I love that you two are so close now. I remember the days when you fought like cats and dogs."

Sunny was right. When they'd first met, Kat and Layla were constantly challenging each other's beliefs. "Yeah. Who knew she'd grow up to be such a loudmouth? She must have learned it from you."

"Very funny. But I think it's great she's out there speaking up for women's rights. I see all the stuff she posts on Instagram, Twitter, YouTube, Facebook. She's got tons of followers."

Kat shrugged.

"What? You don't like what she's doing?"

"No, of course I do. She's awesome. Really dedicated. But, you know, sometimes she can get a bit cocky, like she believes her own press a little too much."

14

"No shit. Seriously?"

"Yep. And Ahmet is always freaking out because he thinks she's not careful enough, that she's too out there for her own good."

"Well, he always was the cautious one."

"But maybe he's right. There are plenty of people around here who would love to shut up people like Layla. And it's only going to get worse."

"I know. I have to say, it all feels kind of weird. I get here, I see all the new buildings, Afghan-run businesses that are doing well, women doing the news on TV, others up there in politics. It's like there's a whole new generation ready to take risks, to fight for their freedom, and to keep this country going in the right direction. And I've been listening for months now to Yaz and Ahmet telling me how great everything is. But you've been here, you know what's going on. Don't you think they might be painting too rosy a picture?"

Kat placed her empty cup on the table. "Of course they are. Things are *never* great in Afghanistan. But they don't want you to worry. And the truth is, things are actually relatively okay right now, at least in Kabul."

"Well, of course I'm going to worry. Who wouldn't? And things being 'relatively okay right now' doesn't really bring me any comfort. The US troops will be out of here in just six weeks. And then what?"

Sunny's concern was nothing new to Kat. Her friend had squeezed in this visit to make sure she'd have an opportunity to see everyone in person while she still could, before the troops' departure possibly made travel to the country difficult. Kat also knew that Sunny wanted to get a feel for herself about what the family might be facing once those troops were gone. And, perhaps, to encourage them to leave. "Yeah, I know what you mean," Kat replied. "But you know how tough these guys are And the Taliban have been here, like, forever, right?"

"Sure they've been here, circling like wolves stalking their prey. But you can only keep the wolves at bay for so long. Once the foreign troops leave and the Taliban gain control again, all bets are off. Who knows what's going to happen?"

"I don't think they really believe the Taliban *will* gain control again, at least not as the sole authority. And, besides, what are they going to do? They'd never leave. You know that."

"When I lived here, I never wanted to leave either. But Jack convinced me that it wasn't safe for me anymore. I know it's different for someone whose roots go back hundreds, maybe even thousands of years, but the writing is on the wall. I think they may need to start preparing for the worst."

A sudden gust of wind traversed the rooftop, bringing a blast of dust with it. Sunny put down her cup and wiped her eyes with the hem of her T-shirt. "And you?" she asked Kat. "Are you ready to go home?"

A burst of backfire from a car below made both women jump. "Boy, am I." Kat laughed. "But don't get me wrong. This year has been incredible, in more ways than I ever imagined. Working with Yaz and Ahmet has taught me so much more than I ever learned at school." Kat brushed the grit from her jeans. "Seeing what they've been able to accomplish with the shelters and meeting so many of the women who've been helped has me really jazzed to start something of my own. At least eventually. But I do miss my Popeyes spicy chicken."

Sunny laughed.

"And going to the movies. And running out of the house in my yoga pants and T-shirt, without having to even think about it."

"And C.J.? I'm sure you must miss him a ton."

Kat felt the color rise in her cheeks. "Of course I miss him."

"Well, if it makes you feel any better, he misses you too."

Kat's heart melted at the mere thought of her boyfriend. He was another thing to thank Sunny for. Without her, Kat would have never met Jack's son—a guy as warm and funny and smart as his father must have been. The way everyone around the coffee shop talked about Jack it seemed as though C.J. had some awfully big shoes to fill. Kat truly wished she'd had the chance to meet him.

"Wait until you see the gorgeous—" Sunny suddenly clamped a hand over her mouth.

"What?" Kat asked.

"Oh, nothing. I was just thinking about how nice the sunsets have been back home."

"Yeah, right." Clearly something was up. Sunny had always been a lousy liar.

"By the way, love the hair."

"Thanks." Kat brushed the blue-streaked strands away from her face.

"Is that new?" Sunny pointed to the tattoo on the inside of Kat's forearm. It was a rose, her mother's favorite flower.

"It is. There's this amazing woman who has a mobile business. They say she's the first female tattoo artist in the country."

"Well *that's* ballsy."

"Yep. That's why she doesn't have a permanent location. She's gotten death threats, not just because tattoos are considered unacceptable here, but also because she's divorced, an unmarried woman working with men."

"Wow." Sunny slipped a pair of reading glasses from the pocket of her shirt and took a closer look. "Well, she did a good job."

They sat for a moment, silent under the darkening sky, as the lights popped on across the city around them. In the compound next door, a woman was singing, her reedy voice accompanied by the clattering of pots and pans. Kat imagined the woman's face as her mother's, in an alternate reality, one in which they'd never left Kabul.

"Are you still planning on seeing him before you leave?"

Sunny's voice jolted Kat right out of her thoughts.

"Who?"

"Your dad."

Kat paused before answering. "I think so," she replied quietly. "I'm not sure." Kat had not laid eyes on her father since she was sixteen years old. For ten years she'd done everything possible to erase him from her memories. But being in Kabul had really done a number on her. Here, she couldn't help but think about the man, and about everything that happened after she and her mother had been in the States long enough for her mother to become a permanent resident and have a good enough job to sponsor her husband's immigration. Kat and her mother had been happy, living in Seattle with the uncle who had been *their* sponsor, who had encouraged her parents that America would hold greater opportunities for their futures.

However, in the seven years the little family was apart, things had changed. She'd always felt her father's disappointment in her— simply for being a girl—and had always felt more of an inconvenience to him than a joy. But this was different. Her father had been disgusted by a teenage daughter who dared to talk back, who insisted on wearing clothes so tight that nothing was left to the imagination, who ran around with a rowdy band of long-haired cousins dressed in backward baseball caps and jeans that were more holes than fabric. What had been even more offensive to him was a wife with a job, who dared to talk to men other than her husband. The shouting matches between her parents were brutal and kept Kat away from home as much as possible. At the time, she thought her father was literally crazy. Now she had a better awareness of the cultural dynamics that drove the acts of that fateful day. Her father, proud, steeped in tradition, his manhood taken away by his English-speaking wife becoming the provider for the family. Her mother, knowing that the perceived shame she'd brought on her husband—simply by adapting to her new country—would never be forgotten, leaving her devastated that she'd never be allowed to live the life of freedom she'd dreamed of.

Kat would never be able to forgive her father for what happened. Though there were no witnesses, her mother's death had clearly been a brutal one. Her charred body had been burned beyond recognition. A suicide? Or a horrendous crime in the name of honor? Either way, her father was not innocent. He'd fled back to Kabul immediately, no doubt knowing that in the US, the blame would have surely been put on him, no matter what.

Kat, left behind in Seattle, had pretty much shut down after that. That is, until Sunny came along. It was thanks to Sunny that she was here in Kabul, a place she'd never in a million years dreamed she'd want to spend time in again. Not after what happened to her family. But she'd come to love the city of her birth and, as she had confided to Sunny, was determined not to allow the ghosts of her past ruin that bond. Kat wanted closure.

"Well," Sunny said, "the clock is ticking, girl. We'll be leaving in a few weeks."

"I know, I know." Kat sighed. "Honestly? Part of me really wants a confrontation with him, but the other part is petrified of running into him around every corner. And every time I think I'm going to go do it, I chicken out. I psych myself up, and by the time I walk out the door my heart starts beating so fast I think it's going to leap right out of my chest."

"Are you scared of him?"

Kat shook her head. "Not really." She slumped against the plastic slats of the chair and dragged a toe across the baked-mud roof. "Maybe a little. But it's more like I'm scared of what *I* might do, what *I* might say. I don't know. The whole thought of it kind of freaks me out."

"Well do me a favor, would you? Promise me that if and when you do go to see him, you won't go alone, okay? I'll come with you."

Again the wind kicked up, and the dust along with it. Kat rose to gather the clothes that had been left on the rooftop line to dry. Sunny stood to help. And then, poof. Darkness and silence, as if someone had pulled a plug. Cursing replaced the singing next door.

"Seriously?" Kat asked. "Again?"

"Some things never change, right?" Sunny said as the familiar noise of the household coming back to life—appliance by appliance—began. "Thank God for those generators," she added as the water pump started up once again. "A day like this without a shower at the end of it? Not gonna happen." Sunny wandered to the edge of the roof, her gaze settling on the front courtyard with its hyacinth vines in full bloom. *Shangri-La*, she told Kat she'd always called it.

Kat wished she could read her friend's mind, see what Sunny saw. So much had happened here in the old coffeehouse over the years. So many memories, some good, some bad, some downright horrific. Kat had heard the stories, had felt the ghosts of times past kicking around the place. Who knew what the future would bring? Kat shuddered despite the warmth of the wind and hurried to head downstairs.

3

The look on Sunny's face when she saw the room made all the hard work worthwhile. It had been Yazmina's idea to hold their welcoming dinner for Sunny inside the old coffee shop, as opposed to atop the rugs and *toshaks* on the floor of Halajan's house across the courtyard, where the family was all staying to accommodate Kat and Sunny in the bedrooms upstairs. That meant clearing the downstairs of laptops and phones and pens and piles of paper, pushing the tables together in the center of the room, digging out the old napkins and gathering whatever remained of the cups and saucers, the plates and spoons and forks, until it finally looked like a proper dining room instead of the office that it was today. Rashif had even polished the copper espresso machine for the occasion, using the juice of a lime and a soft rag to do the job, just as Sunny's barista, Bashir Hadi, had done so many years before. Yesterday Yazmina had purchased an extra-large maroon *distarkho* for covering all the tables to make them look as one. It was said that one can tell a generous man by the length of his dining cloth. Looking at two rows of dark wooden chairs and the place settings stretched out before her, Yazmina felt more grateful than generous to be surrounded by this many friends and family.

"I cannot believe you guys actually did this," Sunny said as she wiped a tear from her cheek. "I feel as if I've gone back in time, or like I'm dreaming."

"Sit, sit." Ahmet pulled out a chair at the head of the table. "The place of honor for you, Sunny jan."

"Stop already! I'm not used to being the one waited on. It's too much."

Yazmina laughed. "Did you really think you would arrive here without being welcomed with a special meal? You know better than that." Yazmina could feel the pride swelling in her chest. She had been planning and preparing this dinner for days—the *mantu* dough made from scratch, the lamb for the kabobs procured from the best butcher on Butcher Street, the fruits fresh from her favorite vendor up the road, and the bread still warm from the ovens of the women's bakery a few buildings down. How happy she was to be able to do this for Sunny, to show her appreciation for all Sunny had done for her. She'd been a young woman on the run—penniless, scared, and pregnant, her parents and husband all dead—when Sunny took her under her wing. When she had arrived in Kabul from the mountains of Nuristan she hadn't had much of a clue about anything, but here she was, running an American-backed NGO, helping women in situations like hers or even worse, keeping them from the fate that befell so many here in Afghanistan. And it was all thanks to Sunny.

Yazmina smiled as she watched her two young daughters circling the table with the *aftahbah wa lagan*, the copper basin and pitcher with water used to wash one's hands before a meal. Layla and Yazmina followed, serving from the platters, heaping Sunny's plate high with the steaming *qabili palau* Yazmina had made with lamb, the *sabzi* and two types of *boloni*—leeks, and potato with onion—chunks of kabob from the skewers, and the little *mantu* dumplings stuffed with beef and onion that she knew were Sunny's favorites.

"What are you trying to do to me? My hips are already as wide as a truck."

"A plump woman is a healthy woman," Halajan scoffed.

"Well, if it can help keep Covid away, I'm all in."

Sunny was seated between Halajan and Rashif, the guest and the elders placed the farthest from the door, as was the custom. Once everyone was served, the *dua* was said. *B-ismi-llāh-ir-rahmān-ir-rahīm.* In the Name of Allah, the most Beneficent, and the most Merciful. Then the attention turned to Sunny.

"What?" she asked, her eyes darting from person to person.

"You must be the first to start eating. You are the guest."

"Enough with the guest thing already. We're family, right?" Despite her protest, she tore off a piece of *naan* and popped it into her mouth. Even Sunny was familiar with the tradition of beginning with the *naan*, to symbolize that bread alone is enough food for man.

24

For a few moments the room was empty of words, the only sounds were the groans of hunger being sated. The children eagerly scooped at the food with their hands, thrilled to be up so late with a roomful of adults. In his very own chair, next to little Aarezo, sat the pink elephant, who had been given a name that sounded like Phil, which Sunny was told meant elephant in Persian. But it wasn't long until the chatter resumed. It was a luxury to be able to communicate face-to-face instead of through the screen of a computer.

"So, Hala," Sunny was saying. "Tell me. What kind of trouble have you been into lately?"

"Me?" the old woman replied without lifting her eyes from the plate. "I don't do trouble."

A sharp laugh rang out from the other end of the table. "Are you kidding me?" Kat asked.

"Katayon, what I say to you out in the courtyard stays in the courtyard."

"*Katayon?*" Sunny looked incredulous. "You're going by Katayon now?"

"She only uses that name to piss me off," Kat replied.

"Ach, that is not true. There are plenty of other names I would use if I wanted to anger you. Like—"

"*Maadar!*" Ahmet interrupted. "Will you never learn to act your age? How many times must I ask you to please try to set a better example for the children?"

"And why would I want to act my age? I don't even know what that means to act my age. Should I have to swallow my words just because I have lived for so long? Am I right, Layla?" she asked, deliberately drawing the young woman's attention away from the phone she had hidden on her lap.

25

Yazmina quickly glanced at her husband to see if he had noticed. "Please, Sunny jan, eat some more food." Yazmina jumped up and ladled another portion of *mantu* onto Sunny's plate before she could object.

"So what is new with our friend Candace?" Halajan asked between bites. "Is she still bouncing all over the world shaking money out of people's pockets to play Robin Hood?"

Though the idea for taking in women at risk at the coffeehouse location—once it had ceased being a coffeehouse—had originally been Ahmet's, it was Candace Appleton who had helped them expand the organization into one that ran two fully operational shelters, one now located elsewhere in Kabul, and one in Kunduz. Through Candace, who had years of experience and plenty of contacts, Ahmet had learned the business end of running an NGO, and Yazmina had been taught the logistics of overseeing the shelters. And, somehow, between them, they'd been able to succeed in helping hundreds of desperate women.

"The last time I saw Candace she breezed in and out of my house so fast I barely knew she was there," said Sunny.

"Hurricane Candace." *The Candace Show*, as Sunny used to say. *Princess Candace* had been what Halajan first called her. Yazmina thought about the first time she saw Candace, entering the coffee shop with those boots that came all the way up to her knees and hair so light it almost glowed. She remembered watching with envy the way Sunny and Candace used to tease each other without consequence, as if they were sisters instead of just friends.

"Oh, I almost forgot!" Yazmina rose and scurried behind the counter, returning with a chipped teapot that had survived from the old days. Into Sunny's cup she poured the red wine, now almost brown, that she'd been saving for years. "I hope it is still good." She turned to the children. "It is your Auntie Sunny's special juice."

Sunny took a cautious sip. Yazmina saw her lips pucker, her eyes begin to tear. "It's perfect, Yaz. I've never tasted better."

"Just the way we used to serve it. Right, Sunny jan?" Yazmina remembered how uncomfortable she'd first been among the foreign customers in the café, alarmed at the men and women sitting together, drinking contraband alcohol. Now she followed Sunny's gaze as it slowly circled the room, as if she, too, were thinking about the old days. She tried to see the coffeehouse through Sunny's eyes, imagining the flood of memories that must be coming in strong from the place she'd worked so hard to build—a home far from home for so many, a place where they were welcomed with the aroma of freshly baked cookies, the comfort of voices ringing with a million languages, the warmth between the walls of ochre, orange, green, and mauve, now faded and scraped from years of wear and neglect.

As if reading her mind, Sunny pointed toward the bullet hole in the counter. "You leaving that there for posterity?"

Yazmina was ashamed. Along with putting off the badly needed paint job, Ahmet had also never gotten around to filling the marks left by the gunman's bullets that horrible day eight years ago, the last day the coffeehouse had actually operated as a coffeehouse.

Halajan jumped in. "The marks are there to honor Bashir Hadi." The barista had been a hero that day, putting himself

27

in harm's way to prevent even more carnage. Sunny had been gone from Kabul for four years by then, having left the coffee shop in the hands of Ahmet and Yazmina, with Bashir Hadi as their partner. They'd worked hard to keep it going, until it was shut down for good by the bullets of a lone gunman out to seek revenge on behalf of a man whose honor had been challenged.

"What's up these days with Bashir Hadi?" Sunny rested her fork on her plate. "I haven't heard from him in a while."

"He is now in India, with his wife," Rashif said. "They went for medical treatment."

"Is everything okay?"

Rashif shrugged. "I think so. Sharifa had to get her knee replaced. It was better to go to Delhi for the surgery. You know they have better care there and, besides, it is a lot less expensive. But it will take some time for her to heal."

"Well, I sure hope I get to see him before we leave."

"*Inshallah,*" Yazmina said. God willing. "Sunny jan, you have barely eaten. Please, have some more *boloni.*"

Sunny smiled weakly as Yazmina topped off her plate. She'd forgotten the cardinal rule of eating slowly and steadily to avoid finding your portions generously replenished by an eager Afghan host. The salty, oily food was delicious, but she could already feel her jeans cutting in at the waist, and there was still plenty more food on the table. She was happy being in this room, thrilled to be with her friends, yet missing those who were no longer there. Especially Jack. She could almost hear his booming laugh bouncing off the walls, could almost feel

28

the touch of his hand grazing the small of her back, could almost see those steel-blue eyes that could pierce straight through to her soul.

"Auntie Sunny!" The sound of Najama's voice snapped Sunny back into the present. "*Aya khodit hamesh enja ba maa mebashi?*"

Kat answered the child in Dari, swiftly and deftly. Sunny was lost. "Well, *your* language skills have certainly improved," she said to her friend.

"*Alay ghaibat Sunny ra peshroi'sh kada metanem,*" Hala said.

Kat translated. "She said we can now do the back-biting of Sunny in front of her."

Everyone, save for Sunny, laughed.

Then the sound of the legs of a wooden chair being pushed across the marble floor rang out as Layla stood and flicked her long black hair behind her shoulders. "I am so sorry," she said, directing her words to Sunny, "but I must go to the university campus to meet with my study group. I have a huge exam coming up."

"You are leaving *now*, Layla?" Yazmina asked, embarrassed by her sister's rudeness.

"A million apologies to you, Sunny jan. I would do anything to stay here with you, but I cannot afford to get a bad mark at this point." She stood in place, her head bowed slightly. "I am so very sorry to have to go."

"No worries, Layla," Sunny assured her. "We'll catch up soon enough." Then she saw a look cross Kat's face, one that said she knew something about Layla that she wasn't saying. Sunny made a mental note to ask the girl about it.

But it was Ahmet's face that concerned Sunny more. "That girl," he said as soon as Layla was out the door. "She spends more time working on that graduate degree than she should. There is plenty of real-life learning to be had around here with her so-called job that she barely pays attention to." He sat quietly for a moment, staring at his plate, as if he were sorry to have spoken such words out loud.

Yazmina forced a smile. "But, Ahmet, you know how important it is for Layla to study. We agree on how important it is for her to get an education."

"Yes, that is true, my dear wife, but we also both know that the work is a valuable experience, and perhaps one that needs more of Layla's focus. Maybe it would be better for her to spend more of her days here, with us."

"I remember a son who could once work and study at the same time," Halajan said. "Tell me why it should be different for Layla."

"Please, I only have the girl's best interest in mind. You have heard what's going on at the university with the fundamentalists, Mother. It's not safe for Layla there."

"What's going on?" Sunny asked, turning from one to the other.

"Ach," Halajan said, "the same that has been going on forever. Layla can handle herself."

Ahmet shook his head. "But it is different now. It's not just about some girl being harassed for not properly wearing a scarf. The universities have become recruiting spots for the extremists looking to radicalize people. It's dangerous to be in that atmosphere, especially for someone like Layla. She is at too much risk there with those types who are just looking to find fault in others."

Sunny sat back in her chair, stuffed. "And, unfortunately, things are about to get worse. I think we need a plan. I think *you all* need to have a plan."

"A plan? A plan for what? They come, they fight, they stay, they fight some more, they go. And life goes on."

"Come on, Hala. You, of all people, know exactly how things will go down with the Taliban in control. You once told me that life under them was like a prison sentence, remember?"

It was Rashif who answered. "The Taliban have been living among us all these years. And, yes, there will be trouble, but the war will stay in the provinces, where it's already full of Taliban. Not in Kabul."

"The Afghan army has been trained," Ahmet added. "The warlords have been polishing their rifles, eager to fight again. The Taliban will have no chance at Kabul."

Yazmina, quiet, busied herself with the fruit on the table.

"You can't be so sure of that, Ahmet," Sunny disagreed. "Some people are saying that the republic could collapse as soon as six months after the American forces leave. And then what?" She had heard Brian's opinion on the matter, and it echoed what Jack's son, C.J.—who had numerous ties to intelligence—had shared with her. She feared for her friends if they were right.

"Our government will not collapse, Sunny jan. We have more men and more weapons than they do. Our forces will pull together for our survival," said Ahmet.

"How can you be so positive? You know how much corruption has screwed up your government, how quickly people can change sides." Sunny shook her head. "It won't be safe here."

31

"Did you not hear President Ghani's speech when he promised to stand and fight? 'This is my home and my grave,' is what he said."

"Yeah? Well, rumor has it that Ghani's family and those of his whole administration are already out of the country. What does that say about loyalty?"

A sudden clatter stopped the conversation in its tracks. The fruit bowl had slipped from Yazmina's hands. Everyone scrambled to catch the apples and pomegranates that were now rolling across the table.

"Perhaps we can talk about other things, and enjoy our meal together without talking about matters we do not control?" said Yazmina.

Sunny could see the tension etched in the fine lines around Yazmina's mouth. She felt badly for upsetting her friend. Especially on her first night back.

It was Halajan who answered. "Come," she said as she reached for the platter of sweet *firni*. "We should be welcoming Sunny with joy and happiness. You know what they say: *A frown of a host is like the gatekeeper's stick.* Let's try to enjoy, like Yazmina says. After all, this is a celebration, not a funeral."

4

Layla hurried through the busy streets of Shahr-e Naw toward the bright yellow sign of the sleek café. She felt terrible about lying, though her excuse didn't even seem to matter. Ahmet appeared to disapprove of everything she did lately. She could understand that her sister's husband was on edge. Everybody was. Yet did he have to take it out on her? She also felt bad about running out on Sunny so soon after her arrival. But they'd have plenty of time to catch up later, *inshallah*. She paused for a selfie in front of the café's heavy glass doors. *#afghanistanwomen #dukhterAfghan #womensrights* she typed before hitting 'Share'.

The place was packed, the open room vibrating with chatter and laughter and the whir of espresso machines churning out their dark, thick brew. Layla stood for a minute inside the doorway, scanning the tables to see who she recognized and to also—if she were honest with herself—see who might recognize her. It sometimes surprised her when complete strangers, mostly women, approached with words of admiration and encouragement for her efforts, but she was getting used to it. It felt good to have the power to influence others.

In a corner of the café she spotted her friends from the university. She signaled to them and went to the counter to put in her order. "One large latte, please. And also a brownie." The brownies here were almost as good as Bashir Hadi's, and Layla could never resist. As she waited for her coffee she took in the scene around her—men and women together, some casually conversing, some playing chess, others pecking away at their phones—and thought how this must have been how it felt in Sunny's coffeehouse, before the Taliban began their attacks on the places where Afghan men and women mingled with Westerners.

The worst attack had happened at the restaurant Taverna du Liban, where twenty-one customers had died from the suicide bombing and gunfire. Afterward, many establishments shut down, fearing their very existence would elicit more violence. It was around that time that Sunny headed back to the States and it wasn't until a few years later when new places like this one began to pop up, providing a haven for young Afghan men and women who were intent on socializing together in public. Kabul was still a place where a woman could get cursed at—or worse—simply for strolling and chatting with a man. It had happened to Layla. But in the café, nobody blinked an eye.

Layla paid and thanked the barista then went to join her friends, pulling up a chair to the two glass tables they'd pushed together. Haliah was there, and so was Needa. She kissed them both three times on the cheek. At the other end of the table were the guys. But no Haseeb. She was tempted to ask where he was, but didn't. Layla loosened her head scarf and let it fall to her shoulders. In here, she could relax.

The brownie was as tasty as always. She blew lightly on the steaming latte and listened to the lively chatter of her friends enjoying an evening together. "Haseeb!" someone called out. With the mere mention of his name Layla's skin began to tingle. Then she saw Haliah watching her. Layla did her best to remain casual as she turned in her chair, and there he was, all square chin and stubble, his thick hair parted on the side and tumbling onto his forehead like a movie star's.

Haseeb made his greetings around the table, kissing the men, offering a nod of the head and a hand over heart for the women. Layla smoothed back her long, dark hair. Though the draw of the café had always been the opportunity to gather and discuss and debate with her friends, this was also as close as she and Haseeb could come to having a date. Sure, they communicated non-stop on WhatsApp, but real-life encounters were way less frequent. It was frustrating. To Layla, being friends with a guy felt normal. Perhaps it was because of her time in the States, where she eventually—thanks to Kat—got used to the casual ways of men and women together. Or maybe it was just that this—men and women together—was simply the way things were supposed to be. She wasn't so sure anymore.

What she was sure of, what she kept hidden from the rest of them, was how she felt about Haseeb. It was as though nothing else mattered when he was in the room. And if he didn't call, or didn't respond quickly enough to her messages she'd find herself aching inside, constantly checking her phone. Here she was, a grown woman, a woman who was known for her devotion to women's rights, and admired for her skill in getting others to rally behind the cause, and a *man* could make her react this way? Was this what love was? Sometimes it made her feel like an idiot.

How she wished she could talk to her sister about this. Yazmina, of all people, should understand; her love for Ahmet was like a rock in a swirling tide. But even in a progressive family like hers, it was still not acceptable to date. She wondered what Yazmina would think of Haseeb. Surely she would be impressed by him, with his good looks and intelligence and manners. And she wouldn't wish for Layla to be alone. Lately, with the completion of Layla's graduate degree in sight, her sister had been making sly comments about it being time for her to think about marriage. Of course Yazmina would say that. At Layla's age, Yazmina had already been widowed and remarried, had already given birth to Najama. But also at this age, Yazmina had never known what it was like to feel as though you had the freedom to choose what your life would be. She had not tasted the sweetness that comes with power, had not seen herself as someone who might use her voice to change the world.

Haseeb was talking. The others around the table were laughing at what he was saying, which made him laugh as well. Someone asked her a question, but Layla was lost in Haseeb's smile and had to fumble for her response.

Just then something out of the corner of her eye caught Layla's attention. She could almost feel it, a man she didn't recognize standing near the door, staring at them. In particular, he seemed to be staring at her.

Needa had noticed as well. "Do you know him?" she asked.

Layla shrugged. Another fan, was her first thought. Now he was crossing the café toward them. She sat up straighter as he approached. Before she knew it, the man was practically in her face.

Haseeb stood and flung back his chair, placing himself in front of Layla, towering a head above the intruder. "Excuse me, but do you know her?" Haseeb asked, before the man could speak.

Layla peered around him to see. The man's eyes narrowed.

Haseeb stiffened; Layla held her breath.

"I know who she is, all right. And I know what a big mouth she has." His eyes remained on Layla as he spoke.

"You cannot disrespect anyone in here like that!" Haseeb said, his volume rising.

"Tell your little whore that she is being watched, and that the words she is using to brainwash our women will only end up getting her silenced in the end."

"How *dare* you threaten me!" Layla shouted.

The café went quiet. Her heart was beating a million times a second. The man shifted his gaze to the other tables. All eyes were upon him.

"Mikael!" Haseeb called to the owner of the café. "What kind of people are you letting into your business?"

Mikael signaled to the guard, who appeared by Haseeb's side in a flash. He grabbed the man by the elbow, but the intruder pulled away and left on his own, though not without first spitting loudly and crudely onto the sparkling blond-wood floor of the café.

The whole incident had lasted only a minute, but it took a while longer than that for the atmosphere of the place to return to normal.

"Who do they think they are?" Layla asked once the clatter of dishes and the humming of the espresso machines could be heard again. This wasn't the first time she'd been confronted for her outspokenness. Some of the comments on Instagram were outrageously graphic. Those she deleted in a flash. The death threats on her phone were even more disturbing. How those creeps ever got her number in the first place was a mystery, especially after she'd been forced to replace the SIM card so many times. She'd had to come up with some crazy excuses to explain to Yazmina and Ahmet why she changed her number so often.

"Who do they think they are is right," Needa agreed. "Invading our space, turning a place of comfort into a minefield."

"Even now, twenty years after the Taliban has been toppled, and we're still putting up with this shit?" Haliah added.

"At least we're not smothered by burqas, or locked up in our homes," Needa said.

"Sure, but you know what they say about history repeating itself." Haseeb pushed his hair off his face.

"It can't go back to like it was. We won't let it. It's the Taliban who must change, not us." Needa looked to the others for affirmation.

Haliah nodded. "Personally, I'd rather live with war than live with the Taliban in charge."

"And I would rather live in a Kabul where women don't need to be afraid of their own shadow," Layla said. "Where people like us can speak our minds without fearing retaliation. Where little girls can grow up with confidence and hope. Where all the good that comes from hard work will be appreciated and valued and encouraged by all."

"And that," Haseeb said, beaming with pride, "is why she is a star."

Layla laughed. "Come on, everybody. Squeeze in." She arranged the plates of sweets in front of her lineup of friends and squatted beside them. "Smile!" she said, although her phone was aimed carefully to avoid showing their faces.

She tapped in *#kabulcafelife* and the photo was shared. "This café?" Layla said. "*This* is what we want our country to be."

5

Thursday, July 29, 2021

Halajan hurried past the guardhouse and across the front courtyard with her canvas tote bag—the one printed with the words *Stay Calm and Eat Pizza* that Sunny had left behind on her last visit—pressed to her belly. She headed straight through the coffee shop to the smaller courtyard in the back before anyone could notice she'd arrived home. It was getting trickier and trickier to come up with excuses for her Thursday-afternoon absences. Today she'd told Rashif she was going to the market. Of course he had wanted to accompany her, but she had hurriedly made an excuse about having to meet a friend who needed some advice. Now, hot and out of breath, she unwrapped her chador, leaned back against the concrete wall and pulled the pack of Marlboros from her pocket.

Today's session had been exhilarating, with over twenty women attending. Halajan had come forward to recite one of her poems, one she was motivated to write after a particularly annoying encounter with a vendor on Butcher Street. The others seemed to have liked it, which made her feel as proud as a rooster strutting around the yard. She was grateful to Layla for having introduced her to a friend who was in the group. Halajan loved belonging to something bigger than herself, being a part of the tradition of Afghan women who had been secretly handing down their poems for hundreds of years. How she wished she could share her newest creation with Rashif, or with the others in her family for that matter. But Halajan was too embarrassed to expose herself like that. It was hard enough with strangers. Besides, she was well aware of how alarmed and concerned her family would be for her safety, considering the topics she and the other women chose to write about.

Her group had been inspired by the Pashtun women who wrote *landays*—two-line poems that spoke the truth, centering on five main topics: war, separation, homeland, grief, and love. Some of the *landays* were funny, some sad, others angry. Most, like the poems Halajan's group wrote, would be considered blasphemous by the fundamentalists. A lot could be said in twenty-two syllables. There were women and girls who had paid with their lives simply for writing these poems. One young girl in the provinces had been caught by her family as she was reading a love poem over the phone. Though it was actually a group not unlike the one Halajan belonged to that was on the other end of the line, her brothers assumed it was a boyfriend and beat her brutally, threatening to kill her if she kept on writing. Shortly after that the girl took her own life by dousing herself with cooking oil and lighting a match. The family claimed she caught fire while warming herself after a bath. The girl was sixteen years old.

Although Halajan would never have to face that kind of brutality from within her family, to her, whatever risk she did face from others was worth it. Poetry had opened up a whole new world for her, one in which she finally had an outlet for her voice. Of course it was Rumi who had always been her favorite poet, but the words coming from these women—every one of them at least thirty years younger than she was—were different.

Halajan flicked the purple plastic lighter and inhaled deeply, tilting her face back to allow the blazing sun to soak into her leathery skin. All was peaceful, quiet, until—

"It's good to see that some things never change." Sunny's big, whooping laugh bounced across the courtyard.

Halajan quickly kicked the tote bag behind the trunk of the little pomegranate tree. Looking down, she could see the corner of her notebook poking out from the top. She hoped Sunny wouldn't notice.

"Got a spare?" Sunny pointed with her chin to the cigarette dangling from Halajan's fingers.

"Your new boyfriend, does he like you smoking?"

"I don't smoke. And I don't have a boyfriend. Who told you that?"

Halajan shrugged. "I hear things." She handed Sunny a cigarette from the pack.

"Besides, I'm too old to have a boyfriend."

"Pfft. A woman is never too old for love. Look at me."

"True. How old are you anyway, Hala?" Sunny leaned in to take a light.

"Who knows? Fifty? A hundred? We don't celebrate birthdays in our part of the world."

"Right. Well, at least you don't have a turkey-neck, like the one I seem to be getting." Sunny flicked at the loose skin under her chin.

"Ach, look at me. My face looks like a lizard's. An ancient lizard."

"Actually, you're looking pretty good, Hala. You're wearing a bra now?"

Halajan laughed. "I have to do something to keep these over-ripe melons from sagging down to my toes."

"And your clothes. Am I wrong, or have you upgraded your wardrobe?"

"What, you are missing the old rags I used to wear under my chador?" Halajan thought fondly of the blue-jean skirt she'd held onto since the pre-Russian, pre-Taliban times, way back in the 1970s. That skirt, and her closely cropped hair, though carefully hidden from view, had been her last vestiges of freedom, her cherished symbols of defiance. Now she knew she could hold onto her independence with her mind. And her poetry.

"Well, you're looking kind of tame to me, Hala. Where's the rebel I used to know?"

Halajan laughed. "Don't worry. She is still here."

"Well that's a relief."

The two women stood leaning against the wall, lost in their own thoughts, the sounds of the purring generators drowning out the sounds of city life around them.

Sunny crushed the half-finished cigarette under her shoe and sighed. "What are we going to do, Hala?"

"Well I don't know what you are doing, but I'm planning on taking a nap before dinner."

"I meant what are we going to do about all this, all that is happening around here?"

"We? You, Miss Sunny, are going to get on an airplane in a few weeks and go back to your home. And me? I will stay here in mine."

"You *can't* be serious, Hala. This isn't your first rodeo. You've seen first-hand what it's like when the Taliban swoop in. What happens when they want to put you back in the burqa? Then what?"

Halajan shuddered inside. After the last sentence under Taliban rule, she had vowed she'd die before being hidden in the darkness again. Death in life is how she remembered that time. But the memories only served to fuel her furor. "Why should we have to be the ones to leave? It is *our* country, not theirs. They're just a bunch of punks. Besides, who is going to bother an old woman like me?"

"But, Hala, leaving doesn't have to mean forever. All I'm saying is that you guys need to be prepared to protect yourself should the shit hit the fan."

Halajan looked at her, puzzled.

"Should the worst happen," Sunny explained. "Go somewhere to sit it out, just until things settle down."

"And abandon the country I love? This is my home. Why would I do that?" Sunny was right. This was not her first rodeo. Halajan had been here in Kabul when the Russian fighters had dropped down from the skies like rain, when the mujahideen had fought back with missiles that lit up the night as if it were day, when thousands were scrambling to leave for Iran and Pakistan, and others were flooding into the city already so crowded that there was no room left to breathe. Back then—like now—they had no idea what was coming next. But she had stayed. And things did get worse. And then they got a little better. Then the darkness threatened again. The people of Afghanistan had been living with uncertainty for so many years that it had become a way of life. Halajan had survived this long, why would she give up on her country now? Sure, there were things she encountered every single day that made her blood boil, that made her long for the Kabul of her youth. All the people without work forced to beg in the streets, the heroin addicts wallowing like pigs along the muddy riverbanks, the drug lords and the government working hand in hand, the suicide bombings and kidnappings. These had, sadly, become normal. But Halajan was old enough to remember what this country could be. And she had never given up whatever sliver of hope she held for its future. Nor would she ever.

Sunny wiped the perspiration from her brow with the sleeve of her T-shirt. "Would you and Rashif ever consider joining your daughter in Germany?"

"And what would we do in Germany? How would I even speak with anyone?" Aisha had been living in Berlin ever since leaving Kabul for university there. Now she had two degrees and a very good job. For years she'd been urging Halajan to visit, but Halajan preferred to stay put and experience Germany through Aisha's eyes, through the pictures she sent to her phone, and stories she shared on their weekly calls.

"I get it, Hala. I really do. This place gets under your skin," said Sunny quietly.

"Hah! Like a wooden splinter."

"Yeah, or like a man you can't forget."

"I miss Mr. Jack too, Sunny jan."

"Sometimes I think I'm crazy, Hala. He's been dead almost ten years already, and I can't stop thinking about the guy. And being here? Oh my God. I keep imagining I hear that laugh coming from the next room. Everywhere I turn, I think I see his face."

"Love can do funny things to a person. And your Jack, he was like a shining star in a stormy sky. But that doesn't mean your love had to disappear along with him. There is always more to go around."

"But no one is Jack."

"Pfft. Of course not." She took a long drag and blew out the smoke slowly into the air. "Now, tell me something about this new man."

Sunny thought for a minute. "Well, Brian's smart, but more like book-smart. Not street smart like Jack."

"Not everyone is a superhero. What else?"

"He's a good-looking guy, if you like that type."

"And what type is that?"

"You know. Lots of dark hair, sharp dresser, works out a lot."

"You mean the not-Jack type. What else?"

"He's nice. But sometimes I feel like he's a little *too* nice. That always makes me wary."

Halajan dismissed her with a wave of the hand. "Maybe you are not being fair. I will tell you what my Rumi says about all that.

If you are looking for a friend who is faultless, you will be friendless."

Sunny didn't seem convinced. To Halajan, she just looked sad.

"I don't remember this tree ever bearing this much fruit," her friend said in an obvious attempt at changing the subject. "That's amazing."

"It is no miracle." Halajan pushed off from the wall to place herself between Sunny and the trunk, and the tote bag below. "The tree is new. Only a few years old." Rashif had bought the tree as a gift for Halajan, to replace the one that had grown old along with her.

"It's a beauty." Sunny leaned in and plucked a ripe red orb from a branch. "What's that, Hala?" She pointed to the notebook, clearly visible behind Halajan's feet. "You journaling? Writing your memoirs?"

"It is nothing." Halajan could feel her face turn even warmer than the afternoon sun as she tried to kick the bag back toward the wall.

"You can't fool me. You're up to something, aren't you?"

"I am up to nothing."

"Seriously, Hala. I can read you like a book."

"It is nothing important."

"Come on, don't be modest." She tried to reach around Halajan. "Let me see."

"All right, Miss Bossy. If you must know, I am in a group. A women's group where we share things."

"Like what?"

So Halajan ended up letting Sunny in on her secret Thursday outings, explaining to her the history of the *landays* and their importance to so many of the Afghan women who felt silenced

47

and invisible, and how they inspired her group of women to write and share their own poems.

"That sounds awesome, Hala. Can you read me some of yours?"

"Mine?" She shook her head. "No. But I *will* share with you some of my favorite *landays*, written by others." Halajan leaned back against the wall and closed her eyes, struggling to best translate the poem for her friend. "Okay," she finally said. "Here goes. *When sisters sit together, they're always praising their brothers. / When brothers sit together, they're selling their sisters to others.*"

Sunny nodded knowingly. "Tell me another."

Halajan had to think for a moment. "There is one from a fifteen-year-old girl. It goes like this: *You won't allow me to go to school. / I won't become a doctor. / Remember this: One day you will be sick.*"

Sunny laughed a little. "I love the attitude."

"And here is another. This is a poem I say to myself a lot." Halajan drew a deep breath, thinking of that young girl who had taken her own life. This was one of her last verses. "*My pains grow / as my life dwindles. / I will die / With a heart full of hope.*"

"That is beautiful." Sunny took Halajan's bony hands into hers, and the two women stood together in the hot summer air that was swirling with shared memories of the past and unspeakable fears for the future.

6

Fawiza held tight to the edges of the hard seat beneath her as the bus bumped over the rutted road. For the hundredth time she twisted herself around to look through the window to make sure no one was following. All she could see was the cloud of dust being left behind by the turning wheels. She sighed and allowed her eyes to close for a moment. Never had she felt so tired, or so frightened. She'd heard stories of others who had tried to escape—some even younger than her, maybe eleven or twelve—only to be arrested and sent back to face the wrath of the local mullahs, forced to endure brutal floggings from a leather strap for daring to run away from their husbands. But Fawiza would rather die than go back to the life she'd just fled.

How long had she been on the road? From the feel of her empty stomach, it had to be more than a full day and night already. She had been able to steal only one piece of bread and a fistful of afghanis before she snuck out of the house of her new husband and his first wife. That, and some clothes belonging to their son, which now hung loose and lumpy on her body. Eyes still shut, Fawiza tugged on the scarf wrapped like a turban around her newly shorn head. Had she slept at all since boarding the bus for Kabul? Her nightmares were so vivid it was hard to tell if they were dreams or simply memories still fresh enough to make her quake.

The day she'd been handed over by her father was a sunny one. When the final payment was made by the gray-bearded man from another village there wasn't a cloud in the sky. Two hundred thousand afghanis—in land, sheep and cash—was what she was worth. Enough to care for her entire family, less one mouth to feed, for a good, long time. She could not blame her father for what he had done. What was his choice? For them all to starve? But that did not make her pain any less. Fawiza had been in tears as the old man and his first wife dragged her away from her family, from the two sisters she loved so very much. From her mother. *Take care of her* were the last words she'd heard her father say.

She did not last long under her new roof. The thought of the old man's dry, bony hands touching her body repulsed her, and she'd fought back like a tiger. She was beaten for that. And though she didn't mind hard work, the man and his first wife and his brothers and sisters-in-law all treated her worse than a servant, striking her and doling out lashes for the slightest faults. Each night she'd pray for her father to appear from nowhere and steal her back, away from that house and those horrible people. Every morning she'd wake on a pillow damp with tears. But, of course, her father could do nothing. So there had been no choice but to take the matter into her own hands.

Fawiza opened her eyes to the sight of the family seated across from her—a father, mother, and their three young children. Just looking at them made the pit in her stomach grow larger, though she wasn't sure if it was due to her missing her own family, or because of the potatoes and boiled eggs they were sharing. The mother must have caught her staring, because before Fawiza knew it she was being offered an orange. She lowered her gaze and shook her head no. But the woman persisted, leaning across the aisle, her hand extended. Fawiza accepted the fruit, taking hold of it quickly, before the woman noticed the smallness of her hands and the rough, reddened skin that came from scrubbing laundry and washing dishes.

"*Tashakur.* Thank you," she said, her voice coming out soft.

"What is your name?" the woman asked, her eyes gentle and kind.

Fawiza hesitated. "Esmael," she finally said.

The woman nodded and then, thankfully, left her alone.

She watched outside the window as they passed through endless fields of wheat, the monotony of it making her sleepy. Fawiza could not even imagine what lay ahead. All she knew was that it could not, in any way, be worse than what she was leaving behind.

When the bus ground to a stop Fawiza woke with a start. She had no idea how long she'd been asleep. It was not yet dark. Were they already there? But a quick look out the window told her otherwise, and what she saw made her begin to sweat.

A police car was parked in the dirt off the side of the road. She pulled the baggy *shalwaar kameez* away from her chest to hide the breasts that were beginning to bloom and smoothed the pants that were many sizes too large for her. Two policemen were making their way down the center aisle, asking questions, peering into faces. She thought she might faint. Soon one of the policemen was speaking with the family opposite. The other turned to Fawiza, whose heart was pounding so hard she was certain he could hear it. He opened his mouth, about to ask a question.

"That is our son. Esmael." The woman across the aisle had stood and was handing Fawiza an egg. Her husband looked confused but did not say a word. "Go sit with your sisters," the woman said, pointing to the little girls across the aisle. "I will take this seat for a while, to try to get some sleep."

The policemen had to move out of the way as the two exchanged places, the woman busily moving bags and pieces of clothing back and forth. Then they continued, searching for who knows what, and finally left the bus without incident.

"You will come with us," the woman leaned across and whispered once the bus driver had restarted his engine. "I know of a place you can go. You will be safe there."

7

The rainbow hues of the amusement park were a stark contrast to the drab, muddy backdrop of Kabul's cluttered hillsides. Sunny felt as if she were in that scene in the *Wizard of Oz*, the one when Dorothy enters the Technicolor dreamworld right outside her black-and-white Kansas doorstep. "Toto, I have a feeling we're not in Kansas anymore," she said.

Only Kat laughed. The girls ran ahead, Najama holding her little sister firmly by the hand, their brightly colored dresses blending with the vibrant swirl of their surroundings.

"Do not go too far!" Halajan called after them.

"We won't, Nana!" Aarezo yelled back, using the name Sunny had adopted for Halajan back when Najama was born.

53

"This is crazy," Sunny said as she took in the jam-packed scene. "Who would've thought?" The place was a wonderland of fun—an oasis nestled between the polluted Kabul River and the Hindu Kush mountains. If she squinted, it might look as though she were at an amusement park just about anywhere back home.

"We want to go on the Ferris wheel!" the girls chimed in unison once the others caught up. "*Lutfan,* please, Nana? *Lutfan,* Auntie Sunny?"

"We will all go," Rashif said, handing out tickets.

"That's okay," Sunny said, "I'm good. I'll hold your stuff." She held out a hand to take Phil, the pink elephant, that Aarezo had been insisting on carrying everywhere.

"What, you are willing to navigate the streets of Kabul alone, yet you are afraid of a little machine that goes around in a circle?" Halajan asked.

Sunny sighed and took a ticket from Rashif's hand. She squeezed into the purple car next to Aarezo and Kat and across from the others. The contraption lurched forward before coming to rest to allow the next group to board the car behind them. A few more jolts, and they were off. Sunny clung tightly to her seat and closed her eyes as they rose. The thing was going to break down, she just knew it. *Everything* broke down in Kabul. Why should the Ferris wheel be any different? What if the accelerator got stuck? What if the power went out? Her stomach dropped as they began the descent of their first revolution, before they were propelled back into the sky. And then they slammed to a stop, the car swinging back and forth like a pendulum. Aarezo squealed with delight. Sunny opened her eyes. The jagged mountaintops were faintly visible through the dusty sky. She took a breath and looked down. The park was a sea of motion, the rides spinning and dropping and swinging, the crowds churning. She felt as though she were going to puke. "It's fun, is it not, Sunny jan?" Hala asked with what Sunny read as a smirk.

"It's all good. I'm good," Sunny answered as the wheel began to turn again. It was a lifetime before the damn thing slowed to its final stop. Sunny exited on shaky legs, vowing it to be her last ride of the day. They wandered a bit, the girls debating which ride to go on next. Sunny walked with Kat, who seemed quiet, reflective. She had to wonder if the girl was thinking of her father, her mother, her childhood as the scores of families passed them by. In front of them were Hala and Rashif, strolling hand in hand. The old woman laughed loudly at something her husband said. Sunny was envious of their ease together, the obvious joy they found simply by being in each other's company. It reminded her of the way she used to be with Jack. It also made her think about how much longer people like Hala and Rashif would be able to live with such abandon, how much longer they'd be allowed to express themselves so freely.

The girls finally settled on the carousel. "Come with us, Auntie Sunny!" they begged.

"Kat will go," she said, nudging her friend forward. The damn thing was spinning just a bit too fast for Sunny's taste.

"What? Surely you can handle a little carousel? Or are the painted ponies too scary for you?" Hala laughed.

Sunny chose to ignore her and headed to a bench to wait. Hala and Rashif followed close behind. Rashif smoothed his brown vest and settled in next to Sunny. Hala, grasping her tote bag, sat on Sunny's other side.

"I am a lucky man, happy to be among all you women." Rashif chuckled, gesturing toward the two of them and the other three waiting in line for the ride.

"We're the ones who are lucky," Sunny corrected him. "To have men like you who believe in us, stand up for us."

He swatted away the comment with the back of a hand. "Please, I am just an old, retired tailor now. My fighting days are long gone."

"But it's your attitude that counts, Rashif. You will always remain an activist at heart, right?"

"I will always remain true to my own thoughts, if that's what you mean."

Beside them, Halajan pulled a notebook out of her bag and began to write, holding the pages close and shielded from their view.

They both looked at her quizzically.

"What?" she said. "I'm just jotting down some reminders for myself. My old brain can never remember a thing anymore."

Sunny turned her attention back to Rashif. "So what do you think is going to happen?"

"Who knows?" Rashif shrugged. "Everyone is saying that Kabul will remain safe."

"But what if it doesn't? Then what?"

Rashif looked at the sky, as if trying to find the answer hidden behind the clouds.

"Do you ever think about trying to get to New York, to your son and grandson?" Sunny continued.

"What is an old man like me going to do in New York? And can you imagine Halajan unleashed upon a city like that? Those poor people." He laughed.

"Aren't you worried?"

Rashif sighed. "I have spent so many years of my life worrying. I am tired of worrying. And, you know, maybe there isn't so much reason for worry. Some people are saying that the Taliban of today are not like the 'old Taliban,' that they are now more concerned about the image they show the rest of the world."

"Yeah, but it's the Taliban who are the ones saying it. Do you believe them?"

"Maybe. One can only hope."

"I hate to say it, but to me it feels sort of like sheep waiting for slaughter."

"Well, I guess all we can do, no matter what does or does not happen, is watch out for each other. Perhaps I can dust off the old sewing machine from my shop in the Monadi-e and help clothe the refugees as I did the last time around." He raised two bony hands and rubbed at his arthritic knuckles. "But should the worst happen, I know life will be different for me as a man. In the end, I will do whatever Halajan wants. Her happiness is what matters most to me."

Sunny glanced at the old woman, who was deep inside her writing. Behind her Sunny could see the ride that drops you down from an impossibly tall tower. The platform was inching its way to the top. She held her breath. Suddenly, the air exploded with screams as the platform plummeted, slowing to a soft-landing mere seconds before impact. All Sunny could do was shake her head. Why people should feel the need to seek

57

out fake thrills when there was real, live danger staring them in the face every single day was a mystery to her.

The girls were back, tugging at the tail of Kat's shirt, pleading to try another ride. Rashif doled out more tickets, and off they went. Sunny thought back to the day, eight years ago, while Layla was staying with her, when her octogenarian neighbor Joe had taken them all to the state fair in Puyallup. Kat had led the way for Layla, riding the rides, sampling all the food. That was also the day when old Joe had shared the fact that he had once lived there, right on the spot where they sat, imprisoned as a Japanese detainee in an internment camp that was built on the fairgrounds during World War Two. Sunny had to wonder what past atrocities had occurred here on the site of the Kabul Family Park. During the over three thousand years of the city's existence, she had to assume it had seen plenty of conflict. And yet, she thought as the crowd flowed like a river before them, life goes on.

Next they strolled past the carnival games lining the broad walkway. Sunny shivered as a rifle, looking way too real, was handed to a boy no bigger than Aarezo. *Sniper* was the name emblazoned on the sign above the booth. *Really?*

Lunch was on the lawn, next to a fountain—an optical illusion of a running faucet suspended in thin air. Aarezo found it particularly perplexing, circling the fixture over and over, trying to figure out where the water was coming from. Lunch was followed by ice cream, pumped into a cone with meticulous care until it reached a peak not quite tall enough to topple over. Hala tackled hers from above, coming away with a big white dot on the tip of her nose. Sunny snapped a photo with her phone. For a while, she realized, she had forgotten where she was.

And then it was time to head home. "But wait!" Najama protested, pointing to the bumper cars. She took Sunny by the arm.

Sunny laughed. "Oh no you don't."

"Come on!" Kat urged. "It'll be fun."

"We'll all go," Hala said as she gathered her skirt around her and headed to an open car.

"Shit," Sunny muttered to herself. She watched as Halajan, grunting and groaning, slowly folded her skinny legs into the little car. The girls ran to choose one to share, Rashif not far behind.

"Need help?" Kat asked.

"Smartass," Sunny responded, sliding across the slippery surface toward a small black coupe with red wheels. "Okay, suckers," she shouted back to them, "buckle your seatbelts. Sunny Tedder's behind the wheel!"

They slid and spun and raced around, bouncing off each other like a bunch of reeling drunks. Hala was brutal, with tactics that would rival a demolition derby champ. Turning the wheel hard, she'd make her car go backward somehow, before slamming down on the pedal to ram full force into whichever of them was in her path. Kat howled. The girls squealed. Rashif had a proud smile plastered across his face. Sunny wiped the tears from her eyes and realized she had not laughed that hard in years.

8

Thursday, August 5, 2021

*S*alam eshqem.

Hello Love. Layla's heart leaped as the words appeared on the screen of her phone. It never failed to amuse her how she and Haseeb could say things in a text that they would never say to each other's face.

Salam eshqem, she answered. *I was just thinking about you.*

And what were you thinking?

That I am looking forward to seeing you. I literally cannot wait. It will be a fun party.

Do you know this guy well? The one with the apartment?

Well enough. Don't worry. It won't be wild. You are sure you will come?

Of course.

Please. I know you wouldn't break my heart :D

Don't be crazy. I cannot wait to see you.

The door to her room flew open.

"You don't knock?" Layla said to her sister, tucking the phone deep under her leg. It was a stupid reflex reaction, one that she knew made her look as guilty as she was.

"It is just me. Why should I knock?" Yazmina was carrying a pile of towels.

"You are right. I'm sorry." Layla smiled sweetly. "You look nice today."

Yazmina looked down at the dress she wore practically every day of the week. "And why do you say that, *khowar*? Is there something you want from me?"

Layla laughed awkwardly. "No, there's nothing I want. Why would you say that?"

"Well, I have something I want from *you*. Please can you come with me? I need to take these towels to the shelter."

"Now?"

"Yes now. And perhaps while you are there you could spend some time trying to talk with the new girl. She has barely spoken a word since she arrived."

"I will go tomorrow, or perhaps Monday."

"But, Layla, you have not been there in days."

Layla felt bad about saying no to her sister. Yazmina worked so hard to help the women in the shelters, doing the intake, supervising the staff, and organizing the services that were offered. But there were so few opportunities to get together with Haseeb in a situation where they could just be themselves—a couple of young singles who simply wanted to spend time together in a place with others like them, where no critical eyes were watching and no tongues were wagging. She had really been looking forward to this party and knew that if she agreed to accompany her sister to the shelter it would likely be hours before they'd return. "I am just too busy between my schoolwork and the planning left to do for the rally next week," she said, the lie catching in her throat. "I promise I will try to get a lot done this afternoon so that I can get to the shelter. Tomorrow. I promise."

Yazmina looked disappointed, but simply nodded and closed the door.

Kat was settled in a plastic chair in the shade of the old acacia tree, her legs curled underneath her, her phone in hand.

Miss me? she typed.

Are you kidding? I'm dying here.

Kat smiled at C.J.'s words. *Only eleven more days. But who's counting?* ☺

Not soon enough. All okay there?

I'm going to see him today. My dad.

No shit? You set something up?

Nope. He still has no idea I'm even here. At least I don't think he does.

Kat had been a little worried about her cousin's big mouth. Hanifa had found her on Instagram not long after Kat had arrived in Afghanistan. Seeing Kat's selfies in Kabul, she'd reached out from her home in Chahar Asyab, south of the city, and began what became a months-long back and forth via WhatsApp. Hanifa seemed nice enough, but when she started obsessing on gossip about other cousins that Kat didn't know and didn't really give a shit about, Kat kind of wished she'd never shared anything about herself with this girl. Yet without Hanifa, Kat would have never known that her father was still living in the very same house Kat had lived in until she was nine.

So you're just going to show up?

I guess.

Maybe you shouldn't go by yourself.

Kat paused before answering. Despite Sunny's plea, she felt as though a meeting with her father was something better faced alone.

No, I'm good.

The truth was, though, that Kat was not good at all. She was petrified. And she couldn't even tell the others at the coffee-house what she was doing. Sunny would flip knowing Kat was planning on going without her, and Ahmet, Yazmina, and Halajan had all tried in the past to discourage her from seeing her father. They didn't know him and they didn't trust him. Who knew how he might react to her, a fully grown woman who was way more American than Afghan? Only family were to be trusted, they said, and in their opinion, her father gave up that privilege when he destroyed his so many years before. Kat didn't understand, they claimed, they did. Nobody knew the Afghans better than the Afghans. But Kat had woken up resolved that today was going to be the day. She'd spent all morning psyching herself up, and nothing was going to stop her.

Hearing the crunch of footsteps crossing the pebbled patio, Kat looked up to see Yazmina standing over her, a pile of folded towels in her arms. She looked tired and stressed, with little lines that Kat had never noticed before sprouting from the corners of her mouth. *Gotta go. Later*, she typed to C.J.

"Are you busy?" Yaz asked.

Caught off guard, Kat shrugged.

"I need someone to take me to the shelter. Can you come?"

"Oh. Well, I wish I could, but I—"

"So you have something else you need to do?"

Kat nodded. She felt terrible turning Yazmina down but knew that if she did not go to see her father today, she might never be able to gather the courage again. "I'm so sorry. It's just not a good day." Silently vowing to do something special for Yazmina to make up for her deception, Kat stood and headed inside to prepare for the trip to her father's neighborhood.

Halajan was almost out the door when she ran smack into Yazmina, causing her daughter-in-law to drop the ridiculously large pile of towels she'd been carrying.

"*Maadar*. Just the person I was looking to find." Yazmina bent down to gather the towels.

"And why is that, *dokhtar*?" Halajan scrambled to help her, anxious to get going to avoid being late for her poetry group.

"I need someone to go with me to the shelter."

"Layla cannot go, or Kat?"

"Apparently not."

"What about Ahmet?"

"Ahmet has a phone meeting set up with a donor from Italy."

"Then Rashif will do it. No problem." She tucked her tote bag under her arm and turned to leave.

"Rashif has promised to take Najama and Aarezo to get ice cream."

"But I am too old to drive, am I not?" Halajan said with a smirk.

"Please, *maadar*. Besides, it has been over a week since you've helped the women with their reading. How are they supposed to make progress when you hold class so seldom?"

A wave of guilt washed over Halajan. She would never forget what it felt like to finally learn to read. And without reading, she would have never known the joys of writing. And that was all thanks to Yazmina who, years ago, had taken it upon herself to share her knowledge with Halajan. But she really did need to get going. "You are a much better teacher than I am," she said to her daughter-in-law. "Who better to learn from than the teacher's teacher?" She began to inch her way out the door. She was running out of excuses. The other women would be waiting for her.

"Come." Yazmina took her arm. "You will be happy once you are at the shelter. You always are."

Halajan, desperate, grabbed at her stomach with her free hand and let out a moan.

Yazmina tightened her grip on the old woman's arm. "What is it? Are you all right?"

"I'm not sure." Halajan moaned again. "Perhaps it was something I ate. You had better go ahead without me."

"Absolutely not. Come, take a seat inside."

"I'll be fine. Don't worry about me."

Yazmina led her to a chair. "Can I get you some water, *maadar*? Some tea, or perhaps some *kapaa* to settle your stomach?"

65

Halajan tried to wave her away. Just then she saw Sunny coming down the stairs. Sunny took one look at Halajan, and another at the tote bag now resting at her feet.

"What's up?" Sunny asked.

Yazmina turned to answer. "I need to get to the shelter, but everyone is busy, and now Halajan seems to be ailing."

Halajan slipped Sunny a wink.

Sunny tried not to laugh. "I'll take you, Yaz. Let me first get Hala some tea. She looks okay to me. And Ahmet will be here, right?" Ahmet was sitting at his desk, laptop open, headphones on.

"You are our guest, Sunny jan. I cannot ask you to be my driver."

"Would you stop with the guest thing already? I've been here sitting on my butt for over a week now. Please, let me do *something* useful."

"This thing must be held together with spit and glue by now," Sunny said as the old Mercedes jerked into gear.

Yazmina held on for dear life. "Turn left at that corner," she directed her friend. Once again she looked behind them to make sure they weren't being followed. It was crucial that the location of the shelter remain a secret, not only from any of the irate husbands or fathers the girls had fled from, but also from those who wrongfully branded safe houses like theirs as brothels, or who blamed them for breaking up families by encouraging women to act up at home, knowing they had a place to escape to. The original shelter in the old coffee shop had housed a very small group of women. But the location had been too public, and the building already had a reputation in the eyes of the fundamentalists. So an undercover location was secured, which was right now housing ten women and three children, and the new girl. Later, the second shelter, the one in Kunduz, was added. Yazmina was proud of what she and Ahmet had accomplished with the help of their old friend Candace. At the shelters women could access legal advice, healthcare, and mediation. There were literacy courses and vocational training, even a psychologist who regularly visited to help counsel the women through their trauma. The goal was to prepare the women to be active in society, to be independent or, if they wanted, to return to their families.

They'd had some successes, but now, despite the brave face she put on day after day, Yazmina was worried. Her nightmares were something she'd not mentioned to anyone, as if saying them out loud might make them come true. In them, the Taliban would come bursting into their office at the old coffee shop, rifling through their documents for the names and locations of the women they were protecting. What would happen to women like these in the hands of the Taliban? Would they be sent to prison? Or, even worse, sent back to their abusive families, where they could be killed in the name of honor for the crime of leaving their homes? Yazmina was a wreck inside. This was why, despite what Sunny had been saying about leaving Kabul, she didn't feel as though she had a choice. She could never abandon those she had promised to help. It was good Sunny was coming with her today. She would see the shelter, meet the women. Perhaps then she would understand why Yazmina needed to stay in Afghanistan.

9

"It is there, on the left." Yazmina pointed. "At the end of the street. The one with the green gate."

Sunny slowed to make the turn into the driveway.

"No! Wait! Keep going. Around the block."

"What?" Sunny was confused.

"There is a car behind us. We cannot be too careful."

Sunny did as told and circled the block. "Now?" she asked, checking the rearview mirror before turning the wheel.

Yazmina nodded. "Quickly." She waved to the guard as he emerged from the gatehouse and seemed to take a breath only after they'd pulled in and the gate was shut securely behind them.

Sunny turned off the ignition and took in the yard around her. In the center was a swing set and slide. Around the perimeter, three women were taking a slow jog dressed in their everyday clothes. They smiled at Yazmina as she exited the car, and continued to circle the small courtyard, one behind the other.

"Well that's something you don't see every day. I used to love it that women around here weren't obsessed with exercising like they are at home. Women after my own heart."

"These women have to move," Yaz explained. "It's like being in prison, living in a shelter." Yazmina was greeted at the door with a kiss on the cheek from a plump, motherly woman in an apron. "*Salaam alaikum*," Yazmina greeted her back. "Sunny, this is Feba. She is one of the caregivers for the women here, and a true hero to me."

"*Salaam. Khob asten?*" How are you? "*Man Sunny astm.*" I'm Sunny.

Feba answered with something Sunny couldn't quite understand.

"She says she's heard a lot about you," said Yazmina.

"Uh-oh. Should I be worried?"

Yazmina handed the pile of towels to Feba and laughed. "I only speak of good things, Sunny jan."

Sunny took a look around. The place was neat and clean, with dozens of pairs of shoes lined up by the door, the floors covered with rugs and pillows. She could hear the sound of children's voices coming from another room. "It's nice, Yaz. You've done a great job."

"It's not big, but it is big enough. This is the room where the women relax, take their meals and do their studies, or meet with whoever comes in to help. There are two other rooms where everyone sleeps."

Sunny followed her into the kitchen, where two women were preparing a meal.

"That is Jamilla." Yazmina's eyes directed Sunny to a woman who was busy at the sink with her back turned to them. "She came to us after her husband's family accused her of adultery," Yaz explained in a whisper, even though she was speaking in English. "They locked her in the basement and beat her terribly. Then her husband tried to kill her. Fortunately she was able to escape."

The woman turned to reach for a dishtowel, and Sunny had to try not to wince at the sight of the mottled, burned skin covering half of her face.

"And this is Habiba." A slight woman in a green head scarf and hennaed hands stood at the counter, chopping zucchini with a knife Sunny recognized from the old coffee shop. "*E Sunny ast.*" This is Sunny. The woman nodded and returned to her work. "Habiba was drugged by her mother-in-law and forced to have sex with men other than her husband, who was living somewhere else. She has been here for one year now."

Yazmina next led Sunny into a bedroom, where a woman was sitting on the bottom half of a bunk bed braiding the hair of a little girl, who couldn't have been more than five years old. Sunny dug into her bag for a granola bar she'd been carrying around since the flight.

"*Tashakur,*" the girl said, taking it with a smile that lit up the room.

"*Salaam, khob asten?*" Sunny said to her mother, whose eyes were fixed on Sunny's scarf, a blue flowery one she'd bought in Dubai. Channeling the generous spirit of the Afghans themselves, Sunny unwrapped it from her neck and offered it to the woman.

"*Nakhair, tashakur.*" No thank you, I cannot.

"*Luftan.*" Please, Sunny urged.

The woman again shook her head.

"Tell her I insist, Yaz."

Yazmina smiled and rattled off something in Dari. The woman giggled and took the scarf. "*Tashakur.*"

Sunny was frustrated at her inability to communicate with the women. Her Dari, though coming back a little more every day, sucked. She didn't yet trust herself enough to carry on a proper conversation. Who knows what trouble might come from the wrong words spilling from her mouth? Most of what she remembered were the curse words Hala had taught her.

"They seem happy," she said to Yazmina as they exited the room.

"It is heaven compared to what they left behind. But it can also be boring."

The other bedroom was dark, the curtains drawn shut. "*Salaam*, Fawiza."

Sunny could barely make out the curled-up figure on the top bunk leaning against the wall. Yazmina pulled back the fabric from the window. The girl blinked at the sunlight. She looked even younger than Yazmina had described on the day she and Ahmet had picked her up on the outskirts of Kabul. What little hair she had on her head was like peach fuzz, and her limbs were like toothpicks.

Fawiza pulled a blanket tightly around herself. The girl's helplessness at her situation was something Sunny had seen before. When she had first come across Yazmina at the Women's Ministry a dozen years ago she could sense her trauma. When

71

she'd overheard the story of how Yaz, a young widow, had escaped the men who had taken her from her uncle's house in payment for a debt owed, how she was beaten and discarded when they found out she was pregnant and therefore worthless to them, how she was alone in Kabul, had nowhere to go, Sunny knew she had to do something. She would never forget Yazmina's eyes as they had looked at her even then—proud and defiant. This girl's eyes seemed dead, empty of emotion. It broke Sunny's heart.

"Feba says she has barely eaten. And she must have been going hungry for some time already. She's skin and bones under that dress."

"She looks like she's in shock or something."

"I don't know what to do. We do not usually take them this young. She belongs in a family."

"I thought you had a psychologist on staff. What does she say?"

"She has gone. She took her family to Turkey to get away from here. And even if we were able to help this girl in that way, then what? She is too young to be on her own, and too fragile to be placed with a family. I fear she might do herself harm in her state of mind. I'm honestly not sure what to do."

Sunny went to the window and looked out at the courtyard, where the three jogging women were now hanging laundry. Yaz came and stood next to her. Sunny could practically feel the anxiety oozing from her friend's pores. "There is a solution, you know."

Yazmina slowly nodded.

"So are you thinking what I'm thinking?"

72

Yazmina hesitated before answering. "I might be. What are you thinking?"

"Well, that we need to take her back to the coffee shop with us. At least for a while. She's obviously in no shape to be here, on her own."

Again Yazmina slowly nodded. Then she turned to her friend with a smile. "You have the mind of a genius, Sunny jan. And the heart of a mother."

IO

The breeze blowing in from the mountains was a welcome relief to Kat as she climbed the steep stairs leading into her old neighborhood of Karte Sakhi in western Kabul. From afar, the smattering of houses painted in aqua blue and hot pink looked like confetti sprinkles amid the other, mud-colored facades set against the brown hillsides; but up close the houses felt more formidable, as if they might topple down, one on top of another like a stack of dominoes, and land in a heap below the cluster of towers that gave Asamayi Hill its new name: Television Hill.

It was warm and, despite the wind, Kat was sweating bullets under her head scarf. She was tempted to yank it off but didn't want to attract any unwanted attention. Besides, she'd have to put it back on before nearing the house, before seeing her father. And the heat wasn't the only cause of her discomfort. Kat was petrified. What would she even say to him? In her mind he was still a monster, yet she was determined to accomplish what she'd set out to do this day.

She'd hoped to easily recognize the home she'd lived in until she was nine, but the streets were confusing, the houses a jumble. There was hardly anyone around, only a few clusters of people passing from the opposite direction. She realized she was lost. What had made her think this was a good idea? Kat wondered. This whole thing was a big waste of time. She turned around and began to retrace her steps.

She was halfway down the hill when she heard the chatter of little voices approaching from behind. A man cleared his throat. "*Ajala konen shahzada'ha.*" Hurry, Daddy's princes.

Kat stopped dead in her tracks at the unmistakable sound of his voice.

Two boys, one maybe seven, the other about five, scrambled to keep up with their father's, *her* father's quick pace. As they passed, the familiar scent of Pine cigarettes filled her nostrils. Kat, heart pounding, remained frozen as she saw him grab the smaller boy's hands and swing him into the air. The child squealed with delight.

Then it sunk in. Her father had a whole new family. He'd simply moved on with his life as if nothing had ever happened; left the past—and his daughter—behind without a thought. And he had finally gotten the sons he'd always wanted.

Kat hurried to follow them as they walked down the hill, pulling the scarf tighter around her head. She watched her father from behind as the kids hopped and skipped in the safety of his steadying hands, hands that she remembered as strong and calloused, and sometimes quick to strike. When they reached an old playground, Kat was certain she'd been there before. Had he taken her there? The old metal Ferris wheel, the painted cars that spun round and round—it all felt so familiar. As Kat watched her father pushing the children on the rickety swings, little snippets of things she hadn't thought about in years started coming back to her. How she'd try to run into his arms when he returned from the mosque in his crisp, white *shalwaar kameez*, only to be placated with an absent-minded pat on the head; or when he'd begrudgingly take her for ice cream near Shahr-e Naw Park, barely speaking a word as they strolled beneath the shady trees.

The boys jumped off the swings and began chasing each other around the playground. Her father looked relaxed, his eyes closed, his head tilted to the sun. He hadn't changed much, bore no traces of the trauma that *she'd* worn since that day long ago. Her face half hidden by the scarf, Kat took out her phone and snapped some photos, tucking it away hastily when he called for the kids and exited the park. She felt like a stalker.

Now he was headed toward the mosque, which shined like a beacon in the daylight under its bright aqua domes. She stopped behind a pillar as the children slipped from his grip to run across the tiled terrace. Her father took the opportunity to lower himself to a squat for a smoke. She was tempted to approach him, but what was she supposed to do? Just walk up to him as if it were some weird coincidence that they happened to be in the same place at the same time, and then see where it went from there? How would that even go? *Hi, it's Kat. Katayon. Your daughter. Remember me? How's it going? Long time no see.*

Before she could even come close to figuring out what to say she saw him stand and begin walking her way, the cigarette dangling from his lips. Kat panicked. There was nowhere to turn. If she dared to tuck herself further behind the column it would seem suspicious and surely draw his attention. It would be the same if she darted away. It was too late, anyway. Suddenly he was right there, within eight feet of her, his eyes looking straight into hers.

As he lifted his arms into the air she heard the word *padar*, father, slipping from her mouth in a whisper. Kat steeled herself for the encounter that she had both dreaded and, somewhere deep down inside, longed for for so many years. Then she heard two claps. From behind her the children came running at his beckoning, the littlest boy leaping into his arms to accept the embrace that should have been Kat's. He turned and, with his children, walked away. Her father had looked right at her and not even known her, his own flesh and blood. Not one hint of recognition, there so close to her side.

Later that evening, alone on the coffee-shop rooftop, Kat was struggling to sort through her emotions. She'd never expected the old hurt to come roaring back with such ferocity, never in a million years expected to feel so vulnerable in her father's presence. She'd gone with a fire in her belly, and left feeling as if she'd been kicked in the gut. It was as though being in Kabul was playing tricks with her mind, forcing her to feel things she'd thought were buried deep in the past.

She scrolled through the photos on her phone as the last call to prayer began to ring out from the minarets around the city. The sound of the muezzins' timeless echoing sent a chill down her spine. Then she gazed up at the smattering of stars beginning to poke through the night sky and made a decision. She was finished. Done. She didn't need a confrontation with her father. She'd seen enough. She would leave Kabul and close that chapter in her life, close that whole damn book, once and for all.

11

Halajan closed her notebook and eased herself back into the chair, her face still warm from the anxiety that came from sharing her poetry out loud. The other women were chattering their praise, encouraging Halajan to write more, share more, say more. She couldn't help but smile. This poem had been particularly crass—at least in her opinion— skewering both the Taliban and those who refused to stand up to them in one stroke of the pen. She had been relieved to hear them laughing.

Nooria was up next, reading from her phone a piece she was planning on presenting at their first public reading, scheduled for the week after next at that café in the Pole-e-surkh district. Halajan was not yet sure if she'd participate. On one hand, the thought of touching strangers with her words was exhilarating. On the other, it terrified her. It was hard enough to bare her

79

creations among her fellow poets, and she'd come to know these young women and trusted their opinions. After all, they were putting themselves on the line as well. But strangers? That was a whole different ball game, as Kat would say. And then there was the matter of holding the reading in public. Everyone would be inviting their friends and their families. How could Halajan do that, when it was only Layla, and now Sunny, who knew of her secret hobby? As open-minded as her son had become, Ahmet would turn crazy at the sight of his mother speaking in public the type of words that could put her in grave danger should the wrong ears be listening. And the rest of them? Though they probably wouldn't object, the thought of putting her innermost feelings on display in front of those so close to her would be like appearing naked before them. There was no way she could do this with her family present.

Whether she would decide to perform or not, Halajan would never abandon the group. Writing had become a welcome and much needed outlet for all the frustration and rage she'd carried over the years, after having lived a life turned backward and forward and backward again by the whims of idiotic little men who were seduced by a sniff of power. Being able to read, spell, and write had opened up a whole new world for her. When she thought of all that time wasted, the six years of unread letters the widower Rashif had written to her without knowing of her illiteracy, she wanted to cry. Six years of Halajan secretly pocketing into the folds of her *chaderi* the vellum pages covered with Rashif's beautiful penmanship, each one hand-delivered with his loving smile. Six years of hiding their mutual attraction from the disapproving eyes of her son, so stuck in the old ways back then that he would have never understood. Six years of lost time, time that perhaps could have been spent together.

Water under the bridge, as Sunny liked to say. Halajan remembered, with lingering shame, the day Rashif finally caught on that she couldn't read. He had given her a gift—a collection of poems written by her favorite poet, Rumi. That afternoon, Rashif had asked Halajan to read one of Rumi's poems to him. She'd flipped through the book, chosen a page at random, and recited her best-loved poem by heart. Unfortunately, Rashif had noticed that the poem she had chosen was located on a different page. It was after that that Yazmina had begun to teach her to read.

To Halajan, the ordeal she had gone through, hiding the fact that she could not read and write for so long, made being able to do so now that much sweeter. Each word read was a key to unlocking the mysteries of the universe, and each one written a piece of ammunition in the battle against ignorance and oppression. Finding the poetry group had been like coming across a long-lost tribe of women the same as her. Sure, they were all a lot younger, but every one of them embraced the power of words, unafraid to let their opinions be heard.

Until now. Halajan had become used to meeting up in private, in a different location each week. She liked the feel of it—clandestine. Or at least that's how she perceived it. She knew there were other groups who met, sometimes men and women together, often gathering at the cafés to share their work with each other. Halajan preferred the camaraderie of women, and the privacy that came with meeting in their homes.

But what good were her words if only a handful would hear them? What if Rumi had thought that way? And a public venue could be the very place where she just might inspire a random person in a way that could change the world. Who knows? She thought of the days when Sunny used to bring in important speakers to the old coffeehouse, like that famous woman doctor from India, or that member of parliament who spoke out against injustices. The place would be filled to the rafters, buzzing with excitement, ripe with ideas and opinions and questions. She'd never forget the amazing feeling that came from a roomful of people whose brains had been set on fire. Now she was to be the one in the limelight. Despite her fears, Halajan felt a slight thrill at the thought. Perhaps she *would* invite Rashif. And perhaps, as part of her reading selections for that evening, she would include a little love poem, written just for him.

12

ayla arrived at the apartment building arm in arm with Needa. "*Salaam,*" her friend said to the gatekeeper. He simply nodded, barely looking at them, and allowed them to pass. Needa squeezed Layla's wrist as they hurried inside.

Layla checked her image on her phone's screen as the elevator rose to the third floor. She was glad she'd chosen the flowy green blouse to wear over her jeans; it brought out the color in her eyes. She pushed back her scarf to allow her hair—which she'd stroked a hundred times with her brush before leaving the house—to shine.

"Fixing yourself up for someone special?" Needa teased.

Layla knew she was blushing. She had not yet spoken to anyone about her attraction to Haseeb. Was it that obvious? She chose to ignore her friend's remark and tossed the phone back into her purse.

Strains of Sharafat Parwani's hit song "Lala" met her ears the minute the elevator opened, the drums thumping from behind a closed door. Layla's stomach did a little flop. She didn't know the guy who lived in this apartment all that well, but since he was a friend of Haseeb's from the university she'd assumed the gathering would be one she'd be comfortable attending. It was to be a small group, she'd been told, most of them people she had some acquaintance with from school, or from the café. But now she was beginning to wonder. In their messages Haseeb had sounded so pumped up about the occasion. She'd heard about those other types of parties—big, crowded ones where boys would bring the sort of girls they would never in a million years respect, where they lost themselves in marijuana and hashish, hookahs and hookups. Girls like Layla and Needa wouldn't dare go to a party like that. To risk their reputations, and that of their families, would in no way be worth it. Besides, it didn't really sound like much fun, at least to her. What she'd been hoping for, and looking forward to, was an opportunity to be in a private space with young men and women, to talk, to relax, to just hang out and be herself. And, yes, to be near Haseeb.

When the door to the apartment opened Layla breathed a sigh of relief. The music had been turned down, and over the host's shoulder she could see a room with perhaps fifteen or twenty people inside, sitting and standing around chatting, sipping from cups, eating off paper plates. The smokers were out on the balcony. What she didn't see, however, was Haseeb.

"He's not here yet?" her friend asked.

"Who?" Layla slipped off her shoes and added them to the pile near the door.

"You are hopeless, my friend." Needa took Layla's hand and led her into the room.

The talk that afternoon seemed to be mostly about the upcoming pullout of the US troops, now just over three weeks away. The discussion was a lively one. *Berim ya bashim?* Should we stay or should we go? That seemed to be the big question. Some of them knew people who had already left, friends with money and passports and the ability to get visas. Turkey and Dubai seemed to be popular destinations. A few of her friends were wrestling with the thought of leaving their families behind, even if it was only temporary. It was a tough decision, choosing to go ahead to pave the way, or to at least find work to support their families whatever the situation turned out to be. Yet others, like Layla, thought they were overreacting. No way would the Taliban be able to enter the capital. The Afghan army's best troops were protecting the city and, besides, the foreign forces would have never put in so much hard work just to toss it all away. Something would be done.

"But really," Layla interjected, "it's people like us, people of our generation, who will do the fighting. They will never be able to silence our voices."

"Yet the Taliban . . . we've all heard how they treat women," someone said. "What will happen to our voices if we're shut up inside our homes, if we're no longer allowed to work, or go to school?"

Layla shook her head. "Not going to happen. Even if they do come into our city, how can they silence every one of us? What, they're going to win a fight against Instagram, Twitter, the whole Internet? That is our megaphone. My grandmother," she said, actually referring to her sister's mother-in-law, Halajan, "used to tell me that the power of a girl with a book is the best weapon for progress. Why do you think the Taliban never liked girls going to school? Well, I have news for them. Now we have even better weapons. We are the ones who hold the power, and can outsmart those assholes with our eyes closed."

The talk then turned to the women's rally, scheduled to occur in two weeks' time. Layla was deep into sharing the plans for that day when she felt a presence behind her.

"What have I missed?" It was Haseeb, looking incredibly handsome in tapered gray slacks and a tight white shirt, open at the neck.

Layla peeled off from the group to greet him, conscious of Needa's smile. "I thought you might not be coming," she said.

Haseeb's gaze was pointed over her head, his eyes shifting around the room. "Why would I not come?" he asked without looking down.

"Well, I am glad that you did." Layla smiled.

Haseeb didn't answer, just stood there shifting from leg to leg.

"Are you not happy to see me?" she asked in almost a whisper.

"No. I mean yes! Of course I am."

Still, Haseeb seemed distracted, even a little sad. This was not the Haseeb who had been texting her only hours before.

"Are you okay?" she finally asked. "Are you not comfortable here? It was you who said we'd be among friends."

"I'm good," he insisted with a weak smile. "Honest. Come on. Let's go get something to drink."

Layla followed him into the kitchen, where they stood behind the open counter that separated them from the rest of the party. Just being so near him was making her dizzy. Then she noticed the platters of chicken wings and pizza beside her and remembered that all she had eaten that day was a bowl of Frosted Flakes—a gift from Sunny from the States—and a can of Mountain Dew. She pulled up a stool and sat, her long legs dangling beneath her.

Haseeb poured them each a cup of Coke and helped himself to some food. "Hungry?" he asked.

Layla picked at a slice of pizza and watched the party as it unfolded around them. She was still a little nervous about being in the open with Haseeb, and his mood was making her feel even more uncomfortable than she already was. It was true, they were surrounded by friends, people they should be able to trust. But you never knew. Being privy to a girl's relationship was knowledge that could be used as leverage, as a weapon against her or her family in the case of a disagreement, money owed, or all sorts of ugly situations.

If the two of them were engaged, it would be a different story. But Layla was in no hurry for that, and perhaps never would be. And yet. There was something about the man beside her that made her want to forget every rule she'd ever been taught, that made her want to run her fingers through that tangle of hair, feel those strong arms holding her close, taste the sweetness of his soft lips against hers. Never had she felt this way about any guy. She knew the difference between a crush and whatever it was she was feeling now. Her first crush had been while she was staying with Sunny in the States. It was Kat's boyfriend, Sky, who had briefly captured her affection. He, however, apparently thought of her more as a little sister, not someone whose attention should be taken seriously. Layla had been devastated, and her relationship with Kat had been turned upside down. There had been a few other attractions after that. But nothing like this.

She brought the cold cup of soda against her forehead, as if it might freeze away the thoughts she feared she was wearing all over her face. How she wished she didn't have to bury her feelings so deep inside. But to become engaged, then married? Having lived much of her life without a father, a brother, an uncle, the thought of being somebody's property terrified Layla. Perhaps her sister's husband, Ahmet, believed he could control her but, she thought as she imagined his reaction to learning she was at a party, he obviously could not.

Her gaze turned to Mohammad and Nasima, one of the few married couples in their circle of friends. They appeared so comfortable with each other, even in public. Layla was envious. Mohammad was clearly loving to Nasima, and he seemed to continue to respect her independence even after marriage, just as she knew Haseeb would. But theirs wasn't everybody's story. Layla was smart enough to know that regardless of how open Haseeb might be to an equal marriage where they both had their freedoms, his family might not be. She didn't know them, they had never met. How likely would they be to accept Layla—a woman unknown to them, from a family they were not familiar with—as a bride for their son? And if they did accept her, what if they then put pressure on Layla to have Haseeb's babies, stay home, and care for her new family, do everything a dutiful wife was supposed to do? In that situation she'd be forced to walk away from him, no matter how much she loved him or how handsome he was. She would never give up her freedom, not even for Haseeb.

Of course, she and Haseeb had never spoken of marriage. Layla closed her eyes and took a deep breath, aware of how ridiculous she was being. She returned her attention to the man beside her, and struck up a conversation about their classes, the upcoming rally, the weather—anything that kept them from looking or sounding like a couple in love.

When Needa came to join them Haseeb excused himself and crossed the room to speak with a guy Layla recognized as his cousin. She saw the cousin whisper something into Haseeb's ear and could have sworn the guy was looking right at her as he said it. Haseeb frowned a little and shook his head. The cousin shrugged his shoulders. Layla couldn't help but wonder what was going on. Maybe it had nothing to do with her. And maybe it did. All she knew was that this whole love thing was making her crazy.

Someone cranked up the music. Someone else yelled out, *They will never silence our music! They will never silence us!* Layla shook off her worries and leaned her body against Needa's, and together they began to sway with the beat. She caught Haseeb smiling at her from across the apartment. Layla leaped from the stool, phone in hand. With the music driving her, she pointed the camera lens down and weaved her way through the room, ending her video with the assembly of shoes by the door—men's sneakers and slip-ons, women's sandals and heels, all jumbled together in one huge pile.

#futurekabul #freedomforever #Kabulnights #peacefulAfghanistan
Thank goodness Ahmet never went on Instagram.

13

"I tell you, Candace. Yazmina has done an amazing job with the shelter. I wish you could see it. You'd be so proud."

The sun had already set before Sunny and Yazmina returned to the coffee shop. Sunny couldn't wait to get back and settle in on the rooftop to call her old friend in the States. She missed Candace. Though when they first met, Sunny had reacted to Candace like nails on a chalkboard, now she was her favorite partner in crime. The two of them had been through so much together—the violent loss of their friend Isabel at the hands of a suicide bomber, Jack's fatal skiing accident, the hatching of a crazy plot to double-cross a creep who had been trying to defraud Sunny of Jack's estate. Candace had been at the coffee shop for Ahmet and Yazmina's wedding, had supported Sunny in her efforts to save the business when they needed more income to improve security measures, had dived right in to make the dream of the shelters a reality. Sunny and Candace had, together, gone from two young, invincible hotshots to a couple of single, middle-aged women who should probably be thinking about a retirement plan and heading to the pickleball court. As if that were ever going to happen.

"And you know, being there at the shelter? It was the first time I've seen Yaz truly happy since I arrived. It was as if she were born to do this."

"And that's also why she's so unhappy, I gather."

"I can understand how worried she is—more about those women than she is about her own family. Where on earth are these women going to go when all hell breaks loose? They'll be sitting targets for the Taliban."

"Let me give it some thought. Maybe there's something we can do about that."

"God, I sure hope so. Without a solution for them, Yaz will never even consider leaving. And on top of that, we have a newcomer at the coffee shop."

"Who? What are you talking about?"

"She's just a kid. Maybe fourteen or so. She made her way to Kabul all by herself. Thank God someone connected her with Yaz and the shelter. Something awful must have happened to her, but we're not sure what. I've never seen a child so withdrawn. The girl seems to have absolutely no will to live. It's horrible, Candace. Yaz—well, actually both of us—decided today that she'd be better off here, in a home with a family."

"Wow. I get it, Sunny. But *another* thing for Yaz to stress about? That poor woman is going to break."

Sunny turned her face up to the sky, the stars above like a blanket of fireflies. "I wish you were here, Candace."

"Yeah, I wish I was there too. But you know how impossible that would be."

Sunny knew all too well what would happen if Candace dared step foot in Afghanistan again. It was because of Wakil, the handsome, rich, and younger man Candace had met while she and Sunny were living in Kabul. He'd charmed Candace for the connections she had to big money, looking for funding for his "school." Candace had had too many stars in her eyes to recognize the truth—that he was a Taliban recruiter grooming young boys to join the cause. She'd discovered all this in the most tragic way imaginable, one that had ended up costing their dear friend Isabel her life. When Wakil found out that Candace was the one who had tipped off the police about his activities, he vowed to seek revenge. Which he did, after he bribed his way out of prison. At that time Candace was popping in and out of Kabul frequently, helping Yazmina and Ahmet get the shelter rolling. The man had eyes everywhere, and one day there was a terrifying attempt to kidnap her. If there were a next time, he'd be sure to succeed.

"So how is everyone else faring?" Candace asked. "Layla, the kids?"

Sunny laughed. "The kids are great. Lively, curious. Oh, to be young and oblivious. But, Candace, you would not believe Layla. That girl has become a force to be reckoned with, with quite a following. She's like the Kim Kardashian of the women's movement over here. And she's organizing a big rally for a couple of weeks from now."

"Wow. That's awesome."

"And Kat thinks she might have a boyfriend." Kat had shared her suspicions with Sunny. They'd agreed to keep it among themselves.

"Uh-oh."

"Uh-oh is right."

"Does anyone else know? Yaz? Ahmet?"

"Only Kat, and it's just speculation."

"That's good. But how long is Layla going to be able to keep that up?"

"Right? Those two would go batshit crazy if they thought she was seeing someone they didn't know."

"And even if they did know him, they wouldn't want her dating. They'd want her married. That is if they even approved of the guy, which they probably wouldn't, knowing the two of them were sneaking around behind their backs."

"The whole thing is a recipe for disaster," agreed Sunny. "Ah, young love. I remember it well. Those were the days, right?"

"Not really. Give me a good book, a blanket, and a glass of Merlot any night and I'm a happy camper."

Sunny laughed. "I know what you mean. Why do men insist on complicating our lives?"

"Are you talking from recent experience?"

"No. Yes. Maybe."

"Personally, I like Brian," said Candace.

"I like him too. That's not the question. I like a lot of people. I just don't need to spend my whole life with them."

"I hate to be the one to tell you, but your whole life isn't as long as it used to be."

"Tell me about it. Just being here is a good reminder of how things can end in a flash."

"Literally."

"Oh, Candace. I wish I could magically swoop everybody up and take them home with me."

"But even if you could, that's not what they want, right?"

"No."

"Well, fairy godmother, then I suggest you just dig in and do what you can to help while you're there. And, please, try to enjoy yourself a little, would you?"

14

Friday, August 6, 2021

"Tell her to try these. They look as though they might fit."

Kat took the pair of Nikes from Sunny and interpreted. The woman, who was one of the displaced people in the makeshift camp at Shahr-e Naw Park, had shared her story with them a couple of days before. "We left in our slippers," she'd said. "When the rockets started falling, we had no time to get our shoes." Her husband had been hunted down and killed, shot simply for being the brother of a member of the town's police force.

There seemed to be even more people crowded into the park than when Sunny had arrived in Kabul a week and a half earlier. The place looked like a crazy sort of quilt, with cloths of every color of the rainbow strung between the trees in an attempt to provide shelter from the scorching summer sun. Crying babies, ringing cellphones, women calling for their children, people huddled around listening to news reports—the chaos was inescapable. Sunny and Kat had just arrived, after packing up whatever supplies they could carry from the coffee shop in two wheelie bags—food, water, clothing Najama and Aarezo had outgrown, blankets from Halajan's cupboards to spread on the hard ground. Sunny was down to the last pair of shoes she'd packed for this trip, the old brown suede Birkenstocks that Kat always liked to make fun of, until Sunny had pointed out that they'd become quite trendy again with kids less than half her age. Kat had also pared down her wardrobe to a few T-shirts and a couple of pairs of pants, donating the rest to those in the park who needed it. *Less to carry home*, she'd said with a smile. It was apparent that no official help was coming for these people. And the stream of refugees pouring in daily seemed endless.

After just five minutes in the park word had gotten out. Sunny and Kat found themselves surrounded by a sea of desperate people, swarming to get whatever was on offer. Even amid the chaos, Kat managed to get some of their stories. Most were from the northern provinces. Some had come by car or bus, others—from nearer by—on foot. The majority were women, the men in their families either dead at the hands of the insurgents or remaining behind to bury others who were. Some had been sent to Kabul by fearful husbands and fathers, who had stayed behind to protect their homes. All had the same haunted look on their faces, and the nervous energy that came with not having a clue about what to expect next. They heard plenty of stories of atrocities happening in the overrun provinces—women being hit for not wearing the proper head covering, men beaten with rubber hoses for appearing to support their government, homes completely destroyed by mortar, or set on fire. None of the stories bode well for the future of the country. And if the Taliban did end up in Kabul? "My family and I will continue to run," one woman had told them.

Though their bags emptied in a nanosecond, the surge of people looking for help continued. Sunny and Kat had to push their way through the crowd to get out. "*Bas ast dga!*" No more! Kat held out an empty hand.

Sunny felt light-headed from the midday heat. "I need to sit for a sec," she said to Kat as she peeled the shirt away from her damp body. Kat grabbed her hand and pulled her toward an exit to the street, where a seedy group of local men and boys were shamelessly eyeing the women inside the park, as if they were on display. They continued down the sidewalk adjacent to the park until they found a quiet, shady spot away from the crowd. "Oh man, I don't know how they do it, out here day after day like this," Sunny said as she rested atop her empty suitcase.

"Seriously," Kat agreed. "But what's their choice, when you think about it?"

"True. Sadly. I wish I knew what the answer was. Or at least I wish *someone* knew."

"Right?" Kat wiped the sweat from her brow with the edge of her T-shirt and boosted herself up to a seat on the wall. "Aren't you going to answer that?" She pointed to Sunny's pocket, which was buzzing.

Sunny shrugged. "It's probably just Brian."

"Ouch. *Just* Brian?"

Sunny laughed. "I didn't mean it that way."

"How *did* you mean it?"

"I don't know. I guess that it's kind of hard sometimes, being so involved in something that the other person isn't a part of. How do you even begin to describe all this?" She gestured toward the surreal scene behind them.

"Hmm. Well, all I know is that if I had a guy hot for me like Brian is for you, I'd take his calls."

"You do have a guy hot for you. C.J.? Remember?" Sunny couldn't wait for C.J. to surprise Kat with the proposal only he and Sunny were privy to. She constantly found herself biting her tongue to keep her big mouth from giving everything away. Secrets never were her strong suit.

Kat laughed. "Of course I remember. All I'm saying is that you really should give Brian a chance. He's smart, he's good-looking, he's funny, he's age-appropriate, what more do you want?"

Again Sunny laughed. "I agree, he's a great guy. But it's hard to think about being with someone who's never experienced anything like this, except in books. Afghanistan is such a huge part of my life, a huge part of who I am."

"It's not like Brian has never gone anywhere, you know."

"But it's different. For instance, a man like Jack—"

"A man like Jack is the kind who goes flying off a mountainside at a zillion miles per hour and ends up leaving you a widow."

Sunny didn't answer. In a way, she knew Kat was right. She had grown fonder and fonder of Brian over time. But in Kabul

Jack's presence felt so near, the memories so fresh. Everything she saw reminded her of him. She couldn't even pass the little closet in the coffeehouse where they'd shared their first kiss without tears springing to her eyes.

"And you?" she said to Kat. "Are you counting down the days until you see C.J. again?"

Kat sighed. "I am. You know, as much as I've loved being here, I'm kind of done."

Sunny raised her eyebrows. "But not quite, right?"

"What do you mean?"

"Your father? I thought you were going to go see him."

Kat was silent.

"Are you still planning on it? There's not much time left."

"I already did," Kat said in almost a whisper.

Sunny's head whipped around. "What? Alone? When? What happened? What'd he say? What'd you say? I *cannot* believe you did not tell me this!"

"He didn't say anything."

"Wait. You mean you didn't speak to him?"

Kat shook her head.

"Why not?"

"He looked right at me, Sunny. He didn't even know his own daughter."

"Well, you're ten years older now. You're a grown woman. You've changed your hair a gazillion times since he last saw you. You dress differently."

Kat shook her head. "Don't make excuses for him, Sunny. A man should recognize his own flesh and blood."

99

It broke Sunny's heart to see how visibly hurt the girl was by the encounter. "Oh, I don't know," she said. "Would he ever in a million years expect to see you here in Kabul? You know what it's like when you see people out of context. It's hard to make the connection."

"I'm his *daughter*, Sunny."

"Maybe you should give it another shot?"

"Uh-uh. Not gonna happen. The guy has a whole new family now. Two kids. Boys. I saw them with my own eyes. And obviously there's a new wife at home. It was as if my mom and I never existed, as if what happened had never occurred."

"Come on, Kat. You can't know what goes on in his head. Maybe he thinks about you a lot. Maybe he misses you and would give anything to see you again."

"Please. He never wanted a daughter in the first place. And really, Sunny? The man murdered his own wife, or at the very least made her so fucking miserable that she did it herself. And then he just walked away and wiped his hands of it, like we were a bad dream he'd rather forget."

"I'm not saying you should forgive him for anything. But you did say that you wanted to talk to him. It could help you move on." Even saying those words, Sunny knew they didn't quite ring true. How does one ever completely move on from something like what Kat went through?

"I can move on all by myself. Ten days, and I will never have to worry about seeing that man's face ever again."

Sunny tilted her head to savor a faint breeze that was rustling the leaves of the trees above. Ten days, she thought.

Ten days left to soak in all that she could of Kabul. Ten days left to spend with her dear friends, face-to-face. Ten days left in her beloved coffee shop, a place she feared she may never set foot in again.

15

A surprise was waiting for Sunny at the coffee shop when she and Kat arrived back from the park. Bashir Hadi had returned home from India and was there in the kitchen, not looking a day older than the last time she'd seen him, eight years earlier.

"Bashir! You're back!" she shouted as she leaned in for a hug.

"And now the whole neighborhood knows." Halajan laughed.

"I could not live with myself if I didn't see you while you were here in Kabul," he said with a smile as wide as the Mississippi River.

Officially her barista at the coffee shop, Bashir Hadi was much more than that. This lovely man had saved Sunny's butt more times than she could count. He'd kept the coffee shop up and running through burst pipes, power outages, shattered windows— you name it, he fixed it. It had been his urging that had pushed

Sunny to build a new blast wall to keep their customers coming. And when those customers seemed to dwindle down to nothing, it was his idea to find new ways to bring them back. But it was the day—after Sunny was long gone from Kabul—when a lone gunman invaded the coffee shop with a barrage of bullets from his assault rifle that Bashir Hadi had become a true hero. Had he not taken action, many more lives would have been lost.

"You came back just for me?" Sunny couldn't stop smiling.

"Yes, you, Miss Sunny. And also my shop. My cousins have been looking after it while I've been in Delhi. It is time I return to my duties."

"And your wife? Is she back as well?"

Bashir Hadi shook his head. "Sharifa is to return in two weeks, *inshallah*. Her knee needs more time to heal before she travels." He filled in Sunny on his two children, both at university in Germany, in the same city as Halajan's daughter, Aisha. The younger one, who Sunny remembered as having struggled with reading, was studying to become a doctor. "And your family?" he asked, as was the custom. She watched his face redden as he remembered Sunny didn't really have any family anymore, now that Jack was gone. Those here in the coffee shop were her family. "And you," he continued. "Have you been staying out of trouble since you've been here in Kabul?"

For Sunny, having Bashir Hadi around during her time running the coffee shop was like having her mother around, only he was more attentive and *way* more protective. Sunny could never leave the café alone without having to endure a lecture first. *You should not be driving, and you should not be alone. But since you insist, be sure to lock your doors. By all means, do not drive with the top down. Keep your windows up. Avoid the road-blocks. Do not stop unless you have to. Don't take the side roads, or the alleys. And be sure to call me when you get there.* And if she chose to walk? That was even worse. *You are courting kidnappers. You are at the risk of being shot. Keep your head down, and do not speak unless spoken to. And never, ever, take the same route twice.* It used to drive Sunny nuts.

"Don't worry," she said to him now. "These guys haven't left me alone enough to get into any trouble."

Hala cackled. "If you want trouble, Sunny jan, I'm sure I can find some for you."

Bashir Hadi crossed the room and poured Sunny a perfect little cup of espresso from the machine that had been his pride and joy. Sunny noticed the slight limp that had plagued him ever since the day of his heroic act.

"You don't have to wait on me," she objected.

"It is my honor, Miss Sunny."

She smiled coyly. "You didn't happen to bring any of your date bars, did you?"

Bashir Hadi reached behind the counter and revealed a bag. "I stopped by the shop before I came here. Would you like one?"

"You are a saint, Bashir." Sunny bit down on one of the luscious, chewy treats she hadn't tasted in years. "Better than ever," she said with a thumbs up. "When did you say Sharifa is scheduled to return?"

"In two weeks. That is, if she is well enough. If not, I will go be with her until she is."

Sunny did the math. Sharifa would make it back before the foreign troops were out, but then what? What kind of a future would those two be facing in this country? Bashir Hadi and his wife were both Hazara, the Shiite minority continually targeted by the Taliban. The stories were atrocious, tales of suicide bombings and armed attacks. But Sunny kept her mouth shut, at least for the moment. Bashir Hadi was a strong man, proud of his Mongolian heritage. She'd seen him more than once deftly deal with the insults and ignorance lobbed his way. Still, keeping quiet didn't mean she wasn't going to worry. Bashir Hadi's future was now added to Sunny's list of things to keep her up all night.

16

"Well if you ask me, it's a waste of time. I'm not going anywhere, at least not now."

Layla and Halajan were in the back courtyard discussing Sunny's request that morning for their passports. Halajan had found the girl there sitting cross-legged on the ground, looking a little sad, lost in thought in the shade of the pomegranate tree.

"Ach, what is the difference? Sunny jan said all she is doing is making some copies so that she and Candace can file the visa referrals. That doesn't mean we are being made to leave."

"But I don't want anybody to get the wrong idea. You know how bossy Sunny can be," Layla said from her seat on the ground.

"And the two of us, we can be bossy right back." Halajan cackled. "Besides, what if you change your mind?"

"I won't."

"Don't be so sure, *qandom*, little one. For me, it is not a question. I'm old. And I know exactly what I'd be facing, should the worst happen."

"Well I do too."

Halajan shook her head. "No, I'm afraid you don't."

"Things have changed, Hala. There is no way a bunch of uneducated thugs from the middle of nowhere will be able to control everybody, no matter how bad things get. They will never be able to silence our voices." Layla held up her phone.

"And you think that phone is going to stop a bullet?" Halajan pulled out a fresh pack of cigarettes and tapped it against her palm.

Layla scowled at the old woman. "Don't you know those things can kill you?"

Halajan shrugged as she opened the pack. "I'll be dead soon enough, and I plan to do exactly what I want until then." She lit up and exhaled slowly into the air. "But you, you have a long life ahead, and you will need to be smart with your decisions."

"You don't think I'm being smart?"

"I am just saying you need to be aware. There is no way your generation can understand how things can get with the wrong people in power. You don't remember what it was like. You were just a seed in your mother's belly when the Taliban took control the last time, and younger than even Aarezo by the time they were driven out. Me, I know." She flicked a tiny rod of ash onto the pebbled surface at her feet.

"The last time they came into Kabul we had no idea how bad things would get. In fact, many people welcomed the

Taliban, thinking that they might be the ones to bring order to the country, to stop all the fighting that had been going on for so long. And then, before we knew it, it was as though we had awakened into a nightmare. It is hard to think about, but try to imagine. Women were forbidden to work and were forced to wear burqas when they left their homes. And that they could not even do without a male relative. Girls were not allowed to go to school. Men were beaten for cutting their beards, or if they didn't pray five times a day. There were public executions, stonings at the soccer stadium. Music and movies and videos were banned. And television. And back then we had no phones like yours, or computers. Imagine not knowing anything about what was happening around you, other than what you heard from gossip." She paused for a drag from her cigarette. "And you don't think that could happen again? Well, we didn't either."

Again Layla held up her phone. "But this is exactly why it won't happen again."

"You don't think they have the power to silence that as well?"

Layla didn't answer.

"And those rights you are fighting so hard for? We *had* those rights as women. We had rights long before I was even born. Did you know that women in Afghanistan were allowed to vote even before the women in America? And *purdah*—the separation of men and women—it was outlawed when I was a girl. And after that, there was a new constitution, giving women many opportunities. And did you know, that when I was not much older than you, I—"

"—used to wear miniskirts. I know."

Halajan rolled her eyes. "All I am saying is that many of the freedoms we had gained were taken away, starting with the time of the battles between the Russians and the mujahideen, and then they were totally blown to bits by the Taliban. They may be idiots, but they're brutal idiots, idiots with no heart." She finished her cigarette and crushed the butt under her shoe. "So if you are not worried about the Taliban, what is it that you are worried about?"

"Me? I am not worried about anything."

"Then why are you sitting here doing nothing in the middle of the day, looking as though you have lost your best friend?"

Layla bowed her head. "Because I think I might have," she said in a voice so low that Halajan could barely hear her.

"Did you and Katayon have a fight?"

"What? No, not Kat."

"So who are we talking about then? What is the name of the girl who is making you feel this way?"

Layla spoke into the hot summer air. "It is a guy. And his name is Haseeb."

Halajan felt her breath catch a little in her throat. "Well, you know what the poet Rumi says. *The deeper the grief, the more radiant the love.*"

"I don't think your Rumi can help, not with the way I am feeling."

"This Haseeb, tell me about him."

Layla's face seemed to go from darkness to light in a flash. "Oh, Halajan. He is the most handsome man I have ever seen. He is tall, with dark hair, and a strong face. And so intelligent. He is studying to be a lawyer! And he is kind." Layla paused. "Or at least he used to be."

"So what happened?"

"That is just it! I don't know. The last time I saw him was Thursday, when we were at a party—I mean a gathering—together. He was acting a little strange, sort of aloof. I tried to tell myself that it was nothing, but since then he has become slow to answer my texts. I asked him if anything was wrong, and he denied it. But today he has not answered me at all. I don't know what to think."

"*Saber azizam.* Patience, dear. These are strange times we are living in. Perhaps he is simply distracted." Halajan took another cigarette from the pack. "Have you told anyone else about this friendship?"

Layla shook her head. Halajan understood. As bold as Layla was with the rest of her life, this was the one line she would never cross. Halajan had been the same way.

"I know everyone would love him," Layla said, "were they to meet. But I cannot think of any way to make that happen without causing anger, especially from Ahmet."

Halajan ran her fingers through her short hair. "My son is an obstacle that can be overcome. Even at the age I was when Rashif and I reunited—already an old widow—I would have never dared to choose a husband for myself. I knew that without the proper introductions, without the agreement of the male head of the family—who was my own son—nothing would ever happen. A relationship like ours could bring humiliation, or worse, to our family. I tried to keep what we had between us a secret. And, yes, when Ahmet found out, he was furious. He wished for harm to come to Rashif for what we were doing—simply exchanging letters and a few quick words face-to-face when we had the chance. But something inside Ahmet changed when he realized what a good man my Rashif was. He somehow allowed himself to bend the rules he'd wrapped himself so tightly in." She flicked on the flame of her lighter. "So, you never know what might happen. But be careful, *dukhterem*, my child. As open as your family seems, there are some things that have not changed."

Next door the neighbor was calling for her daughter to gather the laundry from the line. Halajan checked the sky for clouds, but found none.

Layla pointed with her chin to the tote bag at Halajan's feet. "So how is your poetry going?"

"It's all right. Some days it feels as though my pen is alive. Others, it is like my mind is stuck in the mud of the Kabul River."

"I think that's what it's like, being an artist."

Halajan smiled at the thought of herself as an artist. "Perhaps. But I need to come up with some more ideas before next Saturday."

"Why? What is Saturday?"

"There is to be a reading. In public. At the café in Pole-e-surkh."

"Seriously? That is wonderful, Hala. I wish I could come, but I have a big event that day too. We are holding a rally, hopefully the biggest one yet. And I am to speak." Suddenly her head whipped around, her eyes resting on the door behind them. "But don't tell Ahmet," she pleaded in almost a whisper. "Or my sister, for that matter. I know she'd be proud, but I think she's been listening to Ahmet and his worrying."

"Of course." Halajan shook her head. "You must do what is right. You've been working hard for this. It's important to you."

"It is." Layla brushed at some dust on her jeans. "But I wish you had *someone* there at the reading to support you."

Halajan turned her face to the sky. "I was thinking of inviting Rashif."

"You should do that. He would be so proud of you, Hala."

"I am writing a poem, just for him."

Layla stood, and when she did Halajan noticed the tears in her eyes. The old woman wrapped her wrinkled arms around the young one and held her there, under the pomegranate tree, thinking about all she had seen in this country during her years on earth, and all that Layla had yet to encounter.

17

Aarezo and Najama were bent over their drawings, giggling at some shared joke only the two of them were privy to. *Ro Dar Ro*—what the Americans called *Family Feud*—was playing in the background on the same old television set Sunny had introduced to the coffee shop back when Ahmet was working as its guard. Now here he was, still in the same place, but instead of being inundated with customers who had to be convinced to leave their guns at the door, he was buried in paperwork. He stood and stretched, his eyes falling on Fawiza, the runaway girl Yazmina had recently brought into their home. She was sitting by herself at a table in the corner, absent-mindedly folding laundry as she watched Najama and Aarezo with an unreadable expression on her face. When he turned, he noticed that Yazmina had been watching the girl as well.

"It has been three days already," he said in a quiet voice.

"Yes, I know. Three days where she has not spoken, where she has barely eaten."

"And you still have no idea of her story?"

Yazmina shook her head and leaned in to whisper. "Only what I learned from the couple that sought help for her. Like I told you, she was alone on a bus, dressed as a boy. They got on the bus after she did, and she would not tell them where she was from. She knows nobody in Kabul. That was all anyone could get out of her."

"How do we know she hasn't committed a crime?"

"Ahmet! She is only a child."

"What if she disobeyed and simply ran away from her parents?"

"She would not run away to Kabul for no reason. She is obviously fleeing something bad."

The girl had taken a pause in her chore. Aarezo stood and offered her a crayon, but Fawiza simply lowered her head in response.

"Personally," Yazmina added, "I am worried that she will do harm to herself."

"And personally, *I* am worried that someone will come to our door looking for her and we will all be put in danger. I thought we had an agreement—no women from the shelters in our house."

"Listen to yourself, Ahmet! It wasn't that long ago I remember you saying that helping one girl is like helping one hundred. Are you suggesting we turn our backs on her?"

"All I am saying is that this is why we have shelters, to help girls like her. We should take her back there where she will be safe, so we can all be safe." The last thing Ahmet wanted was to have yet one more reason for their life to draw unwanted attention. There had already been enough trouble in the past, and now, with the country on edge, who knew what might happen? It was like trying to keep a lid on a box of frogs. What they were doing in their work—trying to give women a way out of a bad situation—was enough to make them a target. But on top of that, their association with Americans and other foreigners could make them suspect in the eyes of both the fundamentalists and the Taliban.

And then there was Layla, so public with her politics. And his mother with her big mouth, who would speak her mind to anybody, no matter how threatening they might be. Ahmet had seen what was starting to happen in the rest of the country. In the districts, the police and armies were caving in, handing over their arms to the Taliban. Just yesterday, the Taliban seized Zaranj, the first provincial capital to fall. And it fell without a fight.

He'd heard from acquaintances about people attempting to leave the country. Those who had worked with the foreign military—translators and such—were waiting for their Special Immigrant Visa applications to be approved, which apparently was a very difficult and very slow process. Not many were getting out. But Ahmet and his family were not even eligible for that special visa. They hadn't helped the military or been contracted by the US government—they'd worked in a coffeehouse. The fact that they'd turned the coffeehouse into an American-based NGO might qualify them for the new P-2 visa that Sunny was trying for on their behalf, but nobody was certain. At times, listening to others talk, Ahmet had thought about leaving, thinking it might be best for his family. But he had never mentioned these thoughts out loud, not even to Sunny. Why should he? He understood Yazmina's reluctance, and was positive his mother would never be willing to give up and leave the city of her birth. Ahmet himself was far from sure that he would ever want to live anywhere else.

"*Khudawanda rahm ko!*" God have mercy on us!

Ahmet turned to see Yazmina's eyes glued to her computer screen.

"What?" He pulled his chair closer to see what she was looking at.

"Sheberghan is falling." As Yazmina clicked, up popped videos of lawless mobs looting government offices, stealing everything in sight. Captured military Humvees and pickup trucks sped through the streets flying the white flags of the Taliban, while some locals seemed to be cheering them on. In Sheberghan? The home of the infamous warlord Marshal Abdul Rashid Dostum? His followers had been supposedly leading the fight against the insurgents. To Ahmet, this made no sense.

"It says online that the Taliban has released hundreds of prisoners into the city," Yazmina said. "This cannot be happening. Can you imagine?"

"Of course I can imagine. Ours has become a country led by cowards."

Yazmina changed the television channel to the evening news and shooed Fawiza and the girls out to play in the front patio. There were no updates from Sheberghan. The local stations had been shut down. Instead they were airing video from Kabul earlier in the week, when the Taliban had bombed the house of the defense minister, and a story about the killing of President Ghani's former spokesman the day before. There were images from the provinces of buildings on fire, refugees fleeing on foot, and soldiers swearing to die for their country.

"As if we should believe that," Ahmet scoffed.

"And when did you become so cynical?" Yazmina asked.

"I am not cynical. Just realistic. I don't know. Perhaps there is no use in fighting."

Yazmina turned to him, her green eyes wide. "What are you saying? That everything we have gained should just be flushed down the toilet? That we should simply sit back and let the Taliban have whatever they want? *You* think that? The person who fought so hard against corruption, the man who took up the cause of women in jeopardy? How can you sound defeated? How can you not continue to stand up for what you think is right?"

"I am still standing up for what I think is right. But at what cost, Yazmina? I look at the faces of these women, those children, and I can't help but think of you and Najama and Aarezo. I hear people talking about what happens when the Taliban enters—young girls and widows being forced to marry the fighters, women risking their lives simply by being alone on the streets. I would sooner die than allow anything to happen to any of you." Ahmet shook his head as he spoke. "I do believe in fighting for my beliefs. But I will *always* put my family first."

They sat without speaking for a moment as the talking heads on the TV debated the consequences of the Americans' departure and argued over the slim possibility of the troops remaining in Afghanistan to continue and fight.

Yazmina reached across the table and wrapped his hand in her long, slender fingers. They were warm and comforting against his skin. "You are a good man, Ahmet. Do not let all this chatter sway you from the person you have become. We have lived with the sharks circling for twenty years now, yet still we stand strong. It will be fine. *We* will be fine."

From across the room Yazmina's phone began to ring. She peeled her hand from his and stood to answer. Ahmet watched as his wife's face paled. *Yes. No. Try to stay calm*, she was saying.

"It is the shelter in Kunduz," she explained to Ahmet with the phone held against her chest, her eyes wide. "It looks as though that city might be next."

18

Sunday, August 8, 2021

Yazmina was worried sick. Ahmet had left Kabul in the old Mercedes late the afternoon before, heading north to Kunduz to calm the panicked director of the shelter there and to assess for himself what was happening. He'd called halfway into the seven-hour drive, but Yazmina hadn't heard from him since.

She could understand the director's alarm, the enemy's approach was so aggressive, so rapid, so near. There had been air strikes and street fighting every night from dusk until dawn. The last time the Taliban occupied Kunduz, back in 2015, they were relentless in their treatment of women, and in particular targeted those organizations set up to protect and support women. Those places were burned and looted, the people

119

running them harassed and threatened with death. Aware of the need, she and Ahmet—with the help of Candace—had opened up the small shelter there shortly after the Taliban had been pushed out. The question now was just how bad things might get in Kunduz this time around should the Taliban succeed in gaining control. She sat at her desk staring at her phone, willing it to ring, holding firm to the hope that he would reach there without incident, *inshallah*, and would figure out the best way to keep everyone safe in the event that insurgents were able to take the city.

"Any word?"

Yazmina looked up from the silent phone to see Sunny standing in the doorway. "No. Nothing yet."

"It's getting pretty hairy, Yaz. Brian just texted me that the US embassy here is advising all Americans to get out of Afghanistan immediately."

Yazmina's heart took a tumble. "So you must leave us?"

Sunny shook her head. "My ticket's for the sixteenth, less than a week away."

"But they are saying to go now. You should listen to them, Sunny jan."

"I'll be fine. It's only a few days."

"But—"

"What, I'm gonna leave you now, while you're a nervous wreck waiting for Ahmet to return? And what if he ends up coming home toting a carful of women who now have no place to stay? You'll need me here to help, right?"

"*Khuda na kuna!* God forbid. Our Kabul shelter is already too full." Yazmina put down the phone and rubbed her face with her hands. "But I am serious, Sunny jan. You should think about changing your tickets. I could never forgive myself if something happened to you here."

Sunny raised an eyebrow. "So you *do* think the battle will make its way to Kabul?"

"I didn't say that. But maybe the American government knows something we don't."

"Well I hate to say it, Yaz, but I think they know a lot of things that we don't. I hear plenty from C.J. The kid seems to be as plugged in as his father was. The chatter is that the powers that be may have underestimated the timeline for what will happen after the troop pullout. But what you have to face up to is that what's going to happen is inevitable. It's not an 'if', it's a 'when'."

"But they can't—"

"And no matter what," Sunny continued, "you really need to start preparing the family to leave."

"But Sunny, we—"

"Have you two seen what's going on?" Layla burst into the room with an iPad clutched to her chest. "It's Kunduz." She held out the screen. Sunny and Yazmina watched as Layla scrolled through images of shattered storefronts, the sky filled with smoke.

"What is happening?" Yazmina's voice was almost a whisper.

Layla stopped at a video and pressed 'play'. A reporter from Al Jazeera was describing Taliban in the Kunduz police compound, in the intelligence compound, in the government compound. Her report ended with a shot of the Taliban's white flag flying high atop a pole in the city's main square.

121

Yazmina grabbed her phone and stabbed frantically at the screen. "There is still no answer. What if something has happened to him? What if he got caught up in the fighting? What if the Taliban found him helping at the shelter? They will kill him!"

Just then Halajan's voice rang out from the courtyard. "Yazmina?"

Yazmina turned to the others with a finger to her lips. "Do not say a word to her about this."

"Yazmina!" the old woman called again. "Come quickly!"

It was Kat who had found the girl first. Her arms piled high with clean laundry, she knew something was wrong the minute she turned the handle of the door to the room Najama and Aarezo had been sharing with Fawiza. The door was stuck, as if something had been deliberately jammed up against it. She let the bundle drop. Then came the smell, the odor of gasoline that brought Kat straight back to the most horrible day of her life.

For a second she felt paralyzed by the anguish that came from the memory of not being able to save her mother; the terror felt as real as it had ten years before. But the sound of prayer coming from behind the door snapped Kat back to the present. She shoved her shoulder hard against the wood until the door inched open enough to squeeze through. And there was Fawiza, sitting on a *toshak* with Halajan's purple lighter squeezed firmly in her hand.

"Put it down, Fawiza." Kat nodded at the lighter and took a cautious step forward. She had to stop herself from flying at the girl.

Fawiza didn't move. Her eyes were pointed at Kat yet appeared to be looking straight through her.

Kat took another step and held out her hand. "Please."

Fawiza dropped her fist into her lap.

Kat sat down on the floor beside her and peeled Fawiza's fingers from the lighter, one by one. Then she folded the girl in her arms and held her tight, feeling the pain passing between them like an electrical charge. "It will be all right, *qandom*," she whispered over and over as their tears began to flow.

That was how Halajan found them.

"What's up? What now?" Sunny had followed Yazmina out to the courtyard, with Layla not far behind.

"It's the girl, Fawiza. She has tried to kill herself," Halajan said.

"Holy shit," Sunny said, taking in the can of gas and the kitchen rags Halajan held in her hands. "Is she okay?"

"Of course she's not okay. How desperate does one have to be to want to leave this earth so young? There is so much to live for. I told her that."

"Holy shit," Sunny repeated.

"You said that already. Thank goodness Najama and Aarezo are out with Rashif. This is not something for their eyes to see."

"What are we going to do?"

Halajan shrugged. "What is there to do? When a person loses their will to live—"

"But we have to do *something*."

"Do not tell my son. He is already worried enough about her presence in our home."

Yazmina looked up from her silent phone, her face pale and drawn.

"Are you okay, *dokhtar*? The girl is safe for now. It will be all right. She has not harmed herself."

Yazmina nodded once, and again turned her attention back to her phone.

"Do you think she'll try again?" Sunny asked.

"Who knows?" Halajan placed the fuel can on the patio table and tightened its lid.

Sunny shook her head. "You know, Hala, sometimes I think I don't understand a thing. What kind of a world is it that we live in where a child can believe death is her best option? And it's not just here that I'm talking about. It happens in too many places, for too many reasons. It just makes no sense."

"Since when has the world made sense? Do you really believe it's going to start happening now? Look around you, Sunny jan."

Sunny closed her eyes and sighed. "I guess you're right, Hala. I don't know *what* I believe anymore."

"Me, I believe in myself. And I believe in love. *Love is the bridge between you and everything.*"

"Rumi?"

Halajan nodded as she fished in her pocket for a cigarette.

Sunny thought about what her friend had said. She did believe in love. But sometimes she had to wonder, thinking of that poor little girl upstairs, if love could ever be enough.

*

Fawiza sat alone in Kat's room upstairs from the coffeehouse—where she would now be sleeping—and picked at some cookies and dried fruit Kat had brought up to her, insisting she eat. She had come so close that afternoon. Her final prayers—asking for Allah to forever watch over her sisters—had been said. She'd folded the blanket and placed it neatly atop the *toshak*. The rags from the kitchen had been moistened with the petrol she'd found near where they keep the car. The plastic lighter she'd secretly taken from the old woman had been resting in her hand. And then the door opened, and Kat seemed to float across the room like a blue-haired ghost. At first she felt angry to have been interrupted. But being held so close, feeling the warmth of another's body against her skin, made Fawiza think of cuddling up with her sisters on a cold winter night. And for one quick moment, that made her smile.

Then the old woman showed up, going on and on about how Fawiza had so much to live for. So much to live for? What did this woman know? What *could* this woman know, living in a house like this, her family fed well every day, her grand-daughters able to read and write and dream about a future of their own? How could she imagine what Fawiza was feeling, a loneliness so deep that it had no bottom? What was to live for, when she'd never, ever see her family again? Her only comfort was that they'd never know of this, what she'd tried to do. Her family would never hear of it and would never have to endure the dishonor that would come to their reputation from a daughter who had attempted to take her own life.

*

Sunny stood on the roof, phone in hand. "Oh my God, what a day. You would not believe what's been going on around here."

"Try me."

Hearing Candace's southern lilt was like sipping on a mellow glass of Tennessee whiskey. "Okay," Sunny replied as she dropped into a chair. "First of all, Ahmet is missing."

"Missing? What the hell are you talking about?"

"Not really missing-missing, but he took off for Kunduz yesterday afternoon, and Yaz hasn't been able to reach him since he checked in on his way there."

"Kunduz? Have you seen what's going on there?"

"Of course we have. That's why we're so worried. Yaz and Ahmet got a call from the shelter there right before everything went down. The director was freaking out. Ahmet had to go up there."

"Did you see that they took over the prison and released all the prisoners?"

"Fuck. That I did not see."

"You know what that means? The Taliban will double their forces with their help. And some of those men on the loose will be the very same ones who caused our women to seek shelter in the first place. Those men will not only be going after all those who spoke out against them, but also those who helped them do just that."

"So you're saying it's not just the Taliban who will be after the women. And it's not just the women they'll be after."

"Exactly. How is Yaz holding up?"

"She's a wreck. She's downstairs waiting for him to return as we speak." Sunny stood and began to pace the length of the roof.

"Well, Ahmet is no dummy. You saw how he put his street smarts to work when he was the guard at the coffeehouse. Nothing, nobody could get past those two eyes of his."

"True. But he'll need another pair in the back of his head to keep up with all this shit."

"Let's just try to stay positive, Sunny."

"Oh, I am. But that's not all that's happening around the coffee shop."

Candace chuckled a little.

"What on earth are you finding funny?"

"Nothing. I just can't believe you still call it the coffee shop. I hate to be the one to tell you this, but it hasn't been a coffee shop for eight years already."

"It will always be the coffee shop to me."

"If you insist, Sunny. Anyway, tell me what you were going to say."

"It's about the girl, Fawiza? Have you heard about her from Yaz?"

"I have not."

As she paced, Sunny filled Candace in on Fawiza's story, ending with that day's suicide attempt. "How fucked up is that? A girl of fourteen trying to light herself on fire?"

"It's all she knows, unfortunately. How's a girl like that supposed to have hope, or think there's any alternative, when thousands of Afghan women choose that exact way out of their crappy lives each and every year?"

"Is it really thousands?"

"Sadly, yes. And the number's only going to go up."

Sunny stopped at the edge of the roof and looked out over the city toward the jagged mountain ridge in the distance, dark and silent in the night. "What's it going to take, Candace? What else needs to happen before Yaz and Ahmet get their act together to prepare for leaving?"

"The writing seems to be on the wall, but it also seems like they haven't read it yet. I guess we're just going to have to keep working on them, right?" Sunny could hear her old friend taking a sip of something on the other end of the line. "And what about you, Sunny? I know you're aware of what the embassy is saying. What are *your* plans?"

"Me? I can't leave now. I'm not gonna bail on them. I have a week, a little less, to do whatever I can to help. And if I have to, I'll stay even longer."

"Well, just be careful, please. Think of what Jack would be telling you."

What *would* Jack be telling me? Sunny thought after they ended the call. Jack had always been honking on Sunny to be more cautious around here. It had been him who convinced her to leave Kabul in the first place, that it was time to give Afghanistan back to the Afghans. *We Americans infantilize everyone not like us*, he had said. But what would he say now? Things were not the same as they were back then. She knew he'd do anything possible to help their friends. So shouldn't she be doing just that?

Sunny looked to the sky for an answer, which came in the form of a brilliant, lone star streaking across the darkness.

19

Monday, August 9, 2021

It was long past midnight when Ahmet finally walked through the coffee shop's door, exhausted and alone.

Yazmina had fallen asleep in a chair, her phone still resting in one hand. She jumped at the touch of his fingers on her cheek. "Ahmet! You are here!" She stood and grasped his arms, her eyes moving up and down his body as if she were trying to make sure he was real. "Sit. Let me get you some tea," she insisted. Although she had never been happier to see him, to her Ahmet looked terrible. What had happened during those thirty hours away from home? What had he seen? She was almost afraid to ask.

She didn't have to. As he sipped the soothing chai, Ahmet spilled his story, as though purging himself of the experience. "The drive to Kunduz took much longer than usual. There were so many Taliban checkpoints along the way, and each time I was stopped I had visions of being dragged away from the car. I saw others being questioned, mostly young men. I assumed they were looking for government officials or people who worked with the armed forces. But still, I was nervous. So I used the story that I was on my way to a funeral. And, *Khuda ya shokr*, thanks to God, it worked. All I could think about was you and the children." Ahmet wiped a tear from his eye.

"It was very late when I reached the outskirts of the city, the middle of the night," he told his wife. "I could see the missiles fired by the army falling from the sky. I had no choice but to keep going. In the city, the streets were empty. Why would anybody dare to go out? It was such a strange feeling to be there, alone like that. So many places had already been ruined by the air strikes, others were still on fire." He paused for a sip. "When I got to the shelter, the guardhouse was empty. I tried calling on my phone, but there was no signal. I thought perhaps the towers had been destroyed. I had to scale the wall. Luckily, it was dark out and, like I said, nobody was around. I could see that all the lights were off inside the house, so I banged on the door, and shouted that it was me, Ahmet, and not to worry. No one came. Finally I had to break a window to enter. But nobody seemed to be inside. There was no electricity, so I walked from room to room using the light from my phone, holding my breath, thinking I would come upon something terrible. But the shelter was completely empty. The beds had been made, and in the kitchen there were dishes neatly stacked to dry. It did not look as though there had been a raid, or any sort of a struggle. At that point, I could hear the bombs still falling. I had no choice but to find a spot to rest until morning."

Yazmina pulled her chair closer and placed a hand on her husband's knee.

"It was not yet daybreak when the sounds of explosions and shooting woke me," he continued. "It was close, and loud, and it did not stop. In the flashes of light from the mortars, I could see men with rifles running in the street. They were everywhere. I knew this could not have been the kind of street fighting that had gone on there before. This was a full battle, and it went on for hours. I stayed still, hidden behind the walls of the shelter, until the noise finally stopped. I was getting ready to go outside, to see what had happened, when I heard the crunch of footsteps outside, in the back of the building. My mind went immediately to what was in the house, the paperwork that would be all the Taliban would need to have an excuse to shoot me, finding me there. I raced around checking all the drawers and cupboards, but there was nothing. It was then that I saw the pile of ashes in the oven. Every piece of evidence of what the house had been used for had been destroyed, *hazar bar shokr*." A thousand thanks to God.

"*Hazar bar shokr*," Yazmina echoed.

"When the footsteps stopped, I waited a while and then went outside. The air was full of smoke. But now the streets were filled with people, the Taliban strutting around with their rifles across their chests, and others clearly in a hurry to get out. So I got in the car and left."

"Oh, Ahmet. I'm so glad you are safe."

"Believe me, I am as well." Ahmet placed his empty cup on the table.

"But why didn't you call me? I was so worried."

"I had no coverage in Kunduz. And by the time I was away from there, my phone was dead. All I wanted to do was get home, to get to you. I was frightened, Yazmina. Maybe more than I ever have been. And the shelter, empty. What happened to them? Where did they go?"

"I haven't had word. But perhaps they all left together, to find somewhere safe." Yazmina checked her phone for messages. Nothing. But for security reasons the shelter in Kunduz operated entirely offline, leaving no digital footprints. Perhaps that is why they hadn't heard anything. Her only hope was that the director had simply been as cautious as she'd been taught to be.

"It makes me think of what we would do if it were to happen here." Ahmet's eyes were dark with dread.

"It is not going to happen here. You know that."

"Just allow yourself to think about it for a minute, Yazmina. If the worst was to occur, what would become of us? Even if we were to somehow make sure the women in the shelter here in Kabul were safe, the Taliban would come for us because of all the work we have done. That alone is enough to make us a target. And then there is our association with the Americans, with the foreigners, which we have had from even before we opened the shelters."

"The Taliban will not be able to take Kabul. I have heard you say that yourself."

"But just suppose, Yazmina."

Yazmina stood to make some more tea.

132

"And then there is the problem of Layla," he continued.

"You are calling my sister a problem?" Though she would not admit it, Yazmina knew what Ahmet meant. He was speaking of his growing concern about Layla's visibility, her outspokenness in the women's rights movement. And he didn't even know the extent of it. Yazmina had secretly been following Layla on social media. She knew Layla was helping to organize a big rally on Saturday. She was proud of her sister. But she had also seen the vile comments that others had made in response to Layla's postings—calling her the most obscene names and suggesting that what she really needed was for somebody to satisfy her sexually, though the words they used were far worse than that. It made Yazmina's stomach turn to see such things. And it made her worry for her sister's safety, which she wasn't about to share with Ahmet for fear he'd forbid Layla to continue with her cause. That would surely crush the girl.

But what concerned Yazmina almost more was the way her sister had been acting lately. Something was off with her. Maybe nobody else had noticed, but Yazmina knew her sister like she knew herself. When she was home, Layla had been spending almost all her time alone in her room. And when she did emerge she looked like a ghost, pale and distracted, her thoughts clearly on something beyond what was happening in the home around her. Yazmina had been meaning to ask Kat if she knew what was up, but what with everything else going on in the household, she hadn't really had the time to do so. Yazmina had to wonder if it had anything to do with that boy she'd noticed liking and commenting enthusiastically on every single one of Layla's posts. Was he someone special to her? Perhaps she should have stepped in when she first suspected that he might be more than just an online fan.

"You need to speak with her."

Yazmina jumped at the sound of Ahmet's voice, wondering for a second if she had spoken her thoughts out loud. She, too, was so exhausted she could hardly think straight. "I will," she agreed, knowing that promising to do so would be the only way to keep peace in the household, at least for now.

20

Saturday, August 14, 2021

Sunny slammed on the brakes as a car that seemed to come out of nowhere swerved around them, horn blaring. "Sorry, Yaz. I can't see a thing back there." She pointed to the rearview mirror. The back seat of the Mercedes was jam-packed with groceries, many that had tumbled forward at the sudden stop.

Yazmina took a deep breath. "It's okay. We're okay."

The day before had begun with the news of an American evacuation. Thousands of troops were being sent immediately to get American diplomats, civilians, and Afghans who had helped the United States during the war out of Kabul. And then came the news that both Kandahar and Herat—the country's second and third largest cities—had fallen into Taliban hands the night before. There were rumors that the US military would shut down commercial flights from Kabul in a few days. Again Yazmina had urged Sunny to try to change her flight. Sunny had reluctantly agreed to check the possibilities, but there were none. Everything was booked.

So here Yazmina's friend was, right by her side. Their trip earlier in the day to Minimum, the new wholesale store, had truly been harrowing. The entire city seemed to be thinking just as they were, concerned about the possibility of dwindling supplies and skyrocketing prices in the aftermath of the US troops' departure, now just a couple of weeks away. The store was mobbed, the shelves emptying fast. Everyone was in a panic. It seemed as if the chaos they all anticipated had already begun. Sunny and Yaz had grabbed everything they could to stock the kitchen in the shelter—hopefully for as long as needed.

"I turn here, right?"

Yazmina nodded and pointed to the left. Sunny slowed as they approached the green gate.

"*Humshera! Humshera!*" Sister! Sister!

Yazmina turned to see a familiar old man in a rumpled suit that had kept its size while its owner had shrunk with age. He scurried toward them in his plastic slippers.

"*Bash k e kaka da e waqt che mega,*" Yazmina muttered. *Now what does this nosy old guy want?* It wasn't ten seconds later that the man was in her face. "*Sham bahkair mudeer saib.*" Good day, she politely greeted the retired government official with a tight smile. But Jan Agha's attention wasn't on her, it was on Sunny. "This is a friend of our family," Yazmina said, knowing she wouldn't be able to get away without an introduction.

The man nodded slowly, as if mulling over the information. Yazmina waited for him to move on so that she could call for the guard to open the gate without prying eyes on them. Jan Agha and his family had lived next door to the shelter for the last six months, and she and Ahmet had so far been successful in keeping what went on over the other side of his wall a secret. Now she could see him checking out the piles of supplies through the open top of the car.

"That is a lot of food for two people," he said, eyeing the sacks of rice, flour, and beans piled in the back. Jan Agha had been told that Yazmina's in-laws owned the house. The laughing he often heard coming from the courtyard? *Cousins who stay there sometimes, helping out.* And the shouts of children he had heard in the past? *More cousins. The children of the other cousins.* And why hasn't he had the pleasure of meeting these in-laws? *They do not go out much.*

The excuse for the ton of groceries in the Mercedes came easily to Yazmina. "Of course it is a lot of food. You haven't prepared yet?"

"Prepared for what?" the man scoffed.

"Who knows what will happen in a few weeks? Look at the chaos in the rest of our country. And now, with Herat and Kandahar—"

"Of course I have seen what is happening. I have also seen the airport, with so many Afghans looking to run away. And what are they running from, I ask? If our rule becomes a collaboration between the government and the Taliban, what is so bad about that? Everything being done according to Shariah law? That is the religion of Afghanistan."

Yazmina bit her lip to keep from saying what she thought. Yes, a collaboration was what some people were predicting, and yes, Shariah was based on the Koran. But there was the question about how the Taliban would interpret Shariah. Yazmina shuddered at the restrictions that could be enforced, and the protections that could disappear.

"And if the Taliban succeed?" Jan Agha continued. "I, for one, would welcome a government that would crack down more on the journalists who undermine with their criticism and promotion of Western values, and the women who have turned their backs on the rules of Islam."

Yazmina had a sudden urge to punch the man in his face. He and those like him would be fine. It was people like Yazmina and Ahmet, and her sister Layla, who would be in jeopardy, not to mention the women in the shelter. But instead of causing trouble with Jan Agha, Yazmina smiled sweetly and nodded her head until he got tired of hearing his own voice and continued toward his home.

It seemed like hours to Sunny before the man was finally satisfied enough with Yazmina's answers and satisfied as well that he had made whatever point he was trying to make. She wasn't sure what was being said, but she could sense Yazmina's anger and breathed a sigh of relief when he finally took his leave.

Yazmina waited until the neighbor was out of view to have the guard open the gate so they could pull into the courtyard. Inside the house things were quieter than usual. The women hardly spoke a word as they placed the groceries on shelves and in the refrigerator. At one point Feba pulled Yazmina aside, while Sunny remained in the kitchen helping to unload boxes and bags. When Yazmina returned she looked even more grim than she had before.

Sunny came down from her stool. "What's up?"

"They have been watching the television. They are scared for their lives. They are wondering that if things can get so out of control that there is no food on the shelves, what else will happen? Our shelters have always been targets, you know that. A woman that has left her family, who is on her own, you know what they think about that. To them she is a prostitute. And if the Taliban does end up in power? They are worried that the shelter will be closed, and that they will be sent home to the same husbands or fathers or uncles who caused them to turn to us in the first place."

Sunny knew damn well what that might mean. Once back home, some of these women could become victims of "honor" killings—the absurdly named practice of murder in retaliation for dishonoring one's families. And if the shelter remained open, the reprisals from the Taliban could be just as horrendous. "Have you heard from the Kunduz director yet?" It had been five days since Ahmet had returned from the empty shelter there.

"Just this morning. There was a message from a number we did not know, probably a burner phone. But the caller used the code words we had agreed on. They are safe, together at another location, but I don't know where."

"Thank God."

Yazmina nodded. "*Khuda ya shokr*," she echoed. "Now, can you come help me find the things around here that must be destroyed, just in case?"

139

After Sunny and Yaz had gathered everything that might identify the women or confirm what went on in the house, Sunny and Yazmina said their goodbyes to everyone. Sunny could see her friend's eyes filling with tears. Feba walked them to the door. Sunny heard the woman mention Fawiza's name. Yazmina shook her head and answered in Dari.

"What did she say?" Sunny asked after they were in the car.

"She was checking on how the girl was doing, if she was any better being in our house with our family."

Sunny didn't bother asking how Yaz had answered that question. Fawiza was a problem nobody could solve. Not now, with their minds on the shitstorm that would inevitably come their way.

Ahmet had never seen Yazmina so angry. Her green eyes were lit from behind, her fists balled as if ready to strike.

When he'd first arrived at the coffeehouse with his arms full of plastic bags, his wife had seemed curious. "Did you buy something for the children?" she had asked with her head cocked to one side.

"I did not," he answered. "In fact there is something for you, and for Layla and Kat, and for my mother and Sunny as well."

"If you are bearing gifts, then why do you look so serious?"

Ahmet tried to smile. "Because it is a serious matter."

Yazmina took one of the bags from his arms and peered into it. When she pulled out the blue fabric her face fell. "And tell me, what is this for?"

"It is to keep you safe. It is to keep you all safe."

"*Burqas?* You want us to start wearing *burqas?*"

"It is just in case, *azizam*, my love."

"Have you gone mad, Ahmet?"

"Not mad, just cautious."

"Really? Because it looks to me like you have moved backward in time, like you have somehow turned into a different man—perhaps the one who used to hold onto the old ways like a dog with a bone, who tried to run his mother's life as if she were a stupid donkey, who once called me *fahesha*, shameless, for giving birth without a husband by my side, not even bothering to learn that the one I'd had was already buried deep in the earth."

Yazmina's words stung like thorns. Ahmet prided himself in being a champion for what was right. Had he not spent years trying to battle corruption within the ranks of his university? Had he not made a promise to help the women of his country? Was it not *his* idea to turn the coffee shop into a women's shelter? It was true that when he had first met Yazmina he was still stuck in a narrow way of thinking, that he was critical and suspicious of her. But once he had let her into his heart, his eyes had been opened to a whole new world. It was as if she had unlocked something that must have been always inside. But now, to her, he was once again the enemy. "I am just trying to protect what is mine," he said with a sigh.

"What is *yours?* You do not own me, you do not own us!"

"I did not mean it that way!"

"Then how did you mean it?"

"Have you seen the chaos on the streets? People running this way and that, scrambling to get money, to get food, to get out of here. And, yes, everyone is buying burqas. They are *all* worried. Everyone is scared." Ahmet had already heard of things happening to women in other parts of the country—gunmen showing up at their places of work and escorting them home, telling them not to return, girls removed from schools, women in conquered villages being forced into marriage with unwed fighters. "I know you are upset, Yazmina."

"Of course I am upset! You want me to go out in this heat wrapped in a blanket from head to toe? You want me to erase who I am, to make myself invisible?"

"If that's what it takes to keep harm away, then yes."

"Then *you* wear the burqa," she said, throwing the pile of cloth at his chest.

"Who is wearing a burqa?"

Ahmet turned to see his mother and Layla in the doorway, dressed to go out.

"Nobody is wearing a burqa," Yazmina answered. "But Ahmet seems to think that we should." Again her eyes burned right through him.

"Pfft. Don't be ridiculous," Halajan said. "Why would we do that when nobody but you is saying we must?"

"You do not understand. You were not in Kunduz when the Taliban came in. I was. I saw the look in their eyes. I saw people running, scared. There were dead bodies, right on the street. Mazar is sure to be next."

"But they are not here in Kabul, are they?" Layla asked.

"Maybe not now, but they will be. Why do you think the foreigners are rushing to get all their people out? Why do you think so many of our own people are trying so hard to leave? Why can't you just, all of you, for once in your lives, listen to

142

me and do what I say?" Ahmet regretted the words the minute they left his mouth.

Yazmina turned and stomped off to their room upstairs. Layla gathered her belongings and headed toward the door.

"And where are you going?" Ahmet asked.

Layla and Halajan exchanged a look, one that told him they shared something they did not want him to know.

"Please," he begged. "We are surrounded by trouble. Please don't invite any more into our home. Do not go wherever it is you are thinking of going."

"You are worrying too much, *laalaa*, big brother. Some things are too important to be scared for."

"And what is so important that—"

But before he could get an answer, Layla was out the door.

He turned to his mother. "And you? What is so important in your life that you can't listen to my wants?"

"It is not always about you and what you want, Ahmet."

"All I want is for my family to be safe."

"But we have our lives to live. For as long as we can. And you should be doing the same, instead of shopping for burqas." She hoisted her tote bag onto her shoulder.

"So you are going out? Alone? Burqa or no burqa, I forbid you to—" Ahmet stopped mid-sentence and dropped his head into his hands.

"Here I am, *hamsarem*! My wife." Rashif was all dressed up in his white *shalwaar kameez*, as if he were heading to mosque.

Halajan looked him up and down and beamed. He took her arm, and together they walked out the door.

143

21

It was exhilarating, the energy of the crowd, the sight of the Afghan tricolor being waved high in the air, the chants of *Allahu Akbar*, God is great—the slogan widely used by Islamist militants like the Taliban during an attack now reclaimed as a rallying cry in support of peace and solidarity. It was clear to Layla that this rally had taken on more meaning in light of the recent surge through the country. Now there was more than gender equality on everyone's minds. She pictured Ahmet just hours before, holding those burqas. Is that really what people thought they could be facing? Layla had a hard time buying that. She looked at the crowd around her. These women would surely never allow that to happen. Nor would the men who stood by their sides. There were plenty sprinkled in the crowd today, chanting and cheering alongside the women. Yet, at least so far, she had not been able to spot Haseeb.

It had been four days since she had seen him in person. That afternoon, outside the university, he had seemed almost surprised at her presence. His cheeks had reddened as Layla approached, and it had seemed difficult for him to look her in the eyes. Her heart had started to race when she saw him leaning against a column, looking so good in his jeans and sneakers. But her feelings were as mixed up as a sack of marbles. Though she'd been happy to see him, she was also angry, and confused. He'd been so distant since the party. Had she said something, done something, to offend him or make him think poorly of her? She had racked her brain trying to think of what it might have been but could come up with nothing. And when she'd asked him point blank, via text, Haseeb had insisted she had done nothing wrong. He had just been busy, distracted. *Yes*, he assured her. *I still care for you.* But something in his tone had changed. She had reminded him about today and he had said he would try to come. And yet here Layla was, alone in the crowd, wishing for something no amount of protest could deliver.

Halajan stood with her hands resting on the table, there to steady her should her wobbly legs decide to deceive her. Never in her life had she felt so nervous. She had chosen to be the last to read, and as her turn drew closer she found herself half hoping that something would happen to interrupt the event—perhaps a bloodless raid, or even a small fire. But things continued to run smoothly and before she knew it there she was, standing in front of the others, as well as in front of her husband. What was it about his presence that made her feel as though she'd rather be facing a pack of wolves in the forest than be standing in this café with all eyes upon her?

And then she thought about the letters—the ones he had secretly written to her every week for six years. The ones that were now tied up in little bundles, like treasure, stacked neatly in the drawers of the wooden cabinet in her sleeping room. It was through those letters that she had truly learned what kind of a man Rashif was. Though most were filled with the bits and pieces of daily life, between the lines she could hear his heart. His letters spoke more than could be told in a conversation. There is something about the written word that holds a special power, as if committing one's thoughts to paper gave them more meaning, made them count more. She pulled the notebook from her tote bag, cast her eyes around the tables one more time, and began to read.

The first poem seemed to go well, judging by the nodding heads and knowing smiles coming from her audience. She had written about learning to drive. The second and third came easier. And then it was time. She put down her notebook—this one she knew by heart. Halajan took a deep breath. "This is a poem for my husband."

She didn't dare look at Rashif until she had finished. And when she did, the tears running down his cheeks matched the ones on hers.

It was after sunset, and Sunny was back on the coffee shop roof. My happy place, she thought with a little snort. Happy my ass. She had just finished viewing some videos online. The sight of

Talib up north, taking over the palace of Marshal Dostum, the old warlord, turned her stomach. There they were, lounging around on his gold-plated furniture with their rifles still slung across their chests, pretending to have a tea party with his gold china as if they were children playing grown-ups. It was disgusting. And President Biden, rushing to send another thousand more troops, assuring that the withdrawal would not be a hasty rush to the exits, putting the blame on that asshole Trump for the chaos. But, honestly, who would those thousand troops benefit? They were not coming to fight, to protect people like Yazmina and her family once the withdrawal was complete at the end of the month. They were coming to rescue their own. Afghanistan's president, Ghani, wasn't much better. He'd appeared in an address to the nation that day and had said he was "aware of the situation in Afghanistan" which "is in danger of instability." No shit, Sherlock! Where the hell have you been?

It had been a rough day in Kabul. In the afternoon she'd gone with Kat to try to get money from the bank, just in case it became hard later. The lines stretched down the street for almost as far as you could see. The mood was tense, and Sunny worried that the bank might have to close its doors. After an excruciatingly long wait, they withdrew as much as they could and turned to home with their purses full.

The park had been even more jam-packed with refugees than before. From the car Sunny and Kat could see buses and vans being unloaded, more families arriving from the provinces with mattresses and pots and pans, and the belief that the city offered the last chance they had at survival.

But up there in the quiet of the coffee-shop roof, that all seemed so far away. She checked the time. Candace would be awake soon. Sunny would put in a call to her in California, to hear her thoughts on what might be done about the women in the shelter. Without a plan for them, Sunny knew Yazmina would never be able to even think about *her* future. And that was something Sunny was determined to help resolve before her own departure, just two days away. That, and to help Kat change her mind about making another attempt to see her father. Not that she really expected, or even wanted, Kat to have any sort of relationship with the man, but she had come to think that the girl needed some sort of closure. When would she ever get this chance again? Although thrilled that Kat was in for a surprise with C.J.'s proposal, Sunny worried about her ability to truly thrive in a marriage when she had so many unresolved issues. If only Jack were here. He'd know what to do about everything, or at least claim to know. Always the knight in shining armor, that guy.

Then Sunny's thoughts turned to Brian in a way she hadn't expected. How nice would it be, right now, to be sitting with him sipping a glass of Pinot, watching the sunset over Puget Sound? How nice would it be to be thousands of miles from the madness that seemed to be gathering like a tornado, ready to take aim, with nobody able to predict exactly where or when it would strike?

Yazmina couldn't sleep. How could anybody, with everything around them so unsettled? She listened to Ahmet's soft snoring beside her. She was still angry with him, but less so than earlier. He was a good man, that she was sure of. Perhaps all the craziness from the outside world had crept in through his skin like a virus or the venom from a snake. The entire city seemed to be buzzing with opinions and rumors. It was enough to make anyone become unhinged. *We should all be preparing for the worst. There is no cause for alarm. It is not going to be as bad as one thinks. It is going to be worse than we can imagine. Will we be able to get our news, communicate with the world? Will there be fighting in the streets? Will we have martial law? Will there be rioting, looting, kidnappings?* Yazmina didn't know what to think.

Tonight the Taliban had claimed victory in Mazar. Earlier in the week the people of that city had been out in the streets living normal lives, doing their shopping and sipping their tea. Now they were saying the militants were already going door-to-door, beating and lashing people for breaking their rules. Could that happen here? Would that happen here? Maybe Ahmet hadn't been so wrong, after all. Maybe it was only a matter of time. She feared for her daughters. What would their lives look like if they were not allowed to go to school, not allowed to dream of a future with choices? She worried about her mother-in-law, who would be broken in two by having to live like that once again. And she was petrified for Layla. She had known where her sister had gone today, had seen what she'd been planning thanks to Instagram and Facebook—the very things that could land them all in the most terrible kind of trouble, should the worst happen.

Yazmina stood, looking down at the peacefully sleeping man beside her, envious of his ability to escape into a dream. "Rest well tonight, *azizam*," she whispered. "Rest well, while you can."

22

Layla was out of class earlier than expected as her test that morning had been canceled. Everyone had been so distracted in the past few days that the instructor decided it simply wouldn't be worth it. So Layla opted instead to go for coffee. Exiting onto the sidewalk, she switched on her phone and texted Kat, asking her to join her at their favorite café in Shahr-e Naw.

It was still mid-morning, but the streets seemed even more packed than usual. Layla made her way through the crowd, scrolling through her phone as she walked. She'd hoped to see a message from Haseeb, but there was none. Instead what she found was a bunch of social media posts saying that the Taliban had arrived at the outskirts of Kabul. Could it be true?

Layla stopped and looked up from the screen. Sure, there were tons of people scurrying about, their shoulders hunched, their faces grim. The bank she had passed had a line a mile long, as did the pharmacy. But that wasn't any different from what she'd seen yesterday or the day before. The shops and markets were open, the juice vendors were hawking their wares, a garbage collector was hard at work picking litter from the gutters. Layla slipped the phone back into her pocket and continued on her way.

By the time she reached the café the sky was buzzing with helicopters. She ducked inside and spotted Kat, alone at a table in the corner, her face buried in her phone. Layla slipped into the chair across from her friend, who looked up at her with wide, worried eyes.

"What the fuck is happening, Layla? I'm totally freaking."

"It's hard to really say." Layla searched her phone for answers, which were nowhere to be found in any reliable form. "Here," she finally said. "Look at this." She handed the phone to Kat. A Taliban spokesman had posted a statement claiming they would not enter the capital by force.

"So you think that's good news?" Kat asked with a weak smile. She handed the phone back to her friend.

"Who knows? Some people are saying the Americans are going to take over security."

"But how do we know what to believe?" Around them the café was quiet, the barista and the few remaining customers huddled silently over their devices or in hushed conversation with those on the other end. "Shit," Kat said suddenly. "C.J. just messaged that he's heard the American embassy is going to yank the last of their staff out and lower the flag. They're about to send out an alert."

Layla raised her eyebrows. "That can't be good."

"He's so worried about me he hasn't slept for nights." Kat shook her head. "This is all so incredibly fucked up."

"It is." *You are lucky*, is what Layla really wanted to say to her friend. *Lucky to have someone sleepless over you.* "I'm sure you will be happy to see him again," she said instead.

"Yeah, just one more day. And, believe me, it can't come soon enough."

Layla felt a lump form in her throat. She didn't know if it was because of the realization of how much she was going to miss her friend, or the thoughts of Haseeb, or if it was from the tension seeping in from the city around her. Or maybe it was all three. She dabbed at the corner of her eye with her scarf.

"*You're* not freaking out on me too, are you? Maybe we should just go." Kat pushed back her chair and stood.

"I'm fine. Seriously, there's no need to panic."

"Really?" Kat glanced out the window toward the street. "I wouldn't be so sure of that."

Layla gathered her things and followed her friend, who was already out the door. The traffic jam in the street was even worse than before, the sky even louder. People were shouting into their phones, darting between the slowed cars.

Layla stopped a woman clutching a pile of papers to her chest. "*Chi gapa ast?*" What is happening?

"The Taliban have entered Kabul! They are inside the city!" The woman rushed away.

Layla and Kat locked eyes.

"Do you think it's true?" Kat was shaking, as if it had suddenly turned to winter.

"It is hard to say." Layla scrolled frantically through her phone. "How do we know what is rumor and what is real?"

The phone went off in her hand. It was Yazmina. *Get home now!*

Layla assured her they were fine, that they would be there soon.

What are you wearing? Is Kat's skirt long enough? Wait for Ahmet to come escort you. Where are you right now exactly?

No, Layla told her sister. We are not far. There is no reason to worry.

Horns honked, sirens blared. They tugged their scarves tighter around their heads and began to search for a taxi, but even the few that could be seen crawling by in the traffic would not pick them up. The sidewalks were teeming with office workers in a rush toward home, and the shopkeepers were locking their gates. Layla and Kat quickened their pace.

Now it was Kat's phone that rang. Layla could tell it was C.J. on the other end, urging her to get off the streets. She jabbed at her phone to try to reach Haseeb, but got no answer. Layla took Kat's arm and pulled her close as they walked. Her friend's breath was coming loud and fast, as if she were struggling to take in air. Kat could not have any sort of a panic attack. Not now, not here. It would attract way too much unwanted attention.

She squeezed her friend's elbow and guided her over a sewer. "So what's the first thing you are going to do when you get back to the States?" she asked in an attempt to distract Kat until they reached home.

153

Kat let out something between a sigh and a sob. "I don't know, Layla. I just want to get the fuck out of here."

The twenty-minute walk seemed to take hours. Someone on the street said he'd passed a group of prisoners on the loose— the guards from the main prison had fled. They actually saw a police officer ditch his uniform and flee his post. Then as they neared their neighborhood of Qala-e-Fathullah, Layla and Kat saw plumes of smoke rising from the Green Zone.

Kat stopped dead in her tracks. "Is that the *embassy*? Is it on *fire*?"

Layla's answer was drowned out by a pair of Chinook helicopters soaring away through the haze. "The Americans are leaving," she repeated once the sound faded. She tugged her friend toward a crossing. "They're probably burning stuff, to keep it out of the hands of the Taliban." A motorcade of Land-Cruisers, sirens blaring, was trying to force its way through the intersection. "Come on. We're almost there."

It was past noon when Layla and Kat finally reached home. Yazmina smothered her sister in an embrace that lasted forever. One look at Kat told Sunny everything she needed to know about how the girl was doing. She led her to a chair and made her some tea and attempted to convince her that all would be fine, not daring to mention that all commercial flights in and out of Kabul had just been canceled. Candace was already on the case, trying to get them both on an evac list. The tension in the coffee shop was high, with everyone shouting out the latest as news and rumors flew through their phones like wildfire. On top of that there were the calls from C.J., Candace, and Brian, all of them checking in at least once or twice an hour to see how everybody was doing and to share what they'd heard on their end. But whatever predictions and warnings were lobbed their way, the reality was that there was not a thing they could do to prepare for something that seemed to be approaching as rapidly and forcefully as a tsunami.

By early afternoon it became clear that the government had collapsed. By evening rumor had it that, across the city, soldiers and police officers were taking off their uniforms, laying down their weapons and walking off their jobs. Then, at around 6:30, the official news of President Ghani's escape finally broke. The Taliban published a statement.

The Islamic Emirate has ordered its forces to enter the areas of Kabul that have been abandoned by the enemy, in order to prevent thieves and looters from harming the people . . . . Mujahideen are not allowed to enter anyone's home, or harass anyone.

An 8 pm curfew was imposed on the entire city; a white Taliban flag flew over the presidential palace. Later that night, watching Al Jazeera, they silently witnessed the sight of the Taliban entering the palace, strolling through its halls, lounging in its lavish rooms and sitting at Ghani's desk. As the cameras rolled, a victory *Surah*, a prayer from the Koran, was recited by one of the fighters: *Indeed, we have granted you a clear triumph, O Prophet.* Then came the head of the Afghan presidential security guard shaking hands with a Taliban commander. *I say welcome to them, and I congratulate them*, were his exact words—chillingly delivered straight into the lens of the camera.

23

Monday, August 16, 2021

As painful as it was, it was good to have something to keep them all busy. Everyone appeared stunned that morning, exhausted as they rose—one by one—from a sleep that had to have been anything but sound. Around the coffee shop everything looked the same. But there was no denying that outside those doors the world had been turned upside down in a flash.

Sunny had been up first and had prepared breakfast for the rest of them. But no one except for the children was remotely interested in eating. Even Halajan was quiet, sipping her tea in silence as if she'd simply run out of will. Layla kept glancing at her phone with a faraway look in her eyes. Yazmina absent-mindedly tended to her daughters as they ate, smoothing their hair and dabbing at their chins with a cloth. Kat, with Fawiza watching her every move, had the air of a tiger trapped in a cage. By now she'd heard about the commercial flights being suspended. They would not be leaving. Not today. Candace had put in a request with the US embassy for their evacuation, but for now Sunny and Kat were told to stay put.

It was more complicated for the rest of them. Sunny and Candace had been talking and texting all night, trying to figure things out. Candace had been in touch with every contact she had inside and outside the embassy and in the military. But the State Department was in charge, and it seemed as though the right hand didn't know what the left hand was doing. They appeared to have been totally unprepared for a crisis of this magnitude. It was a total shit show. Everyone seemed to have a list going, and Candace got the family added to each and every one of them. But that was no guarantee they'd be evacuated. The new US P-2 visa referrals had been filed, which meant that since the safe-house operation was technically an American NGO, with Candace listed as the boss, the family might qualify to stay in the States. If they could ever get there. Yet so far nobody in the coffee shop had mentioned a word about leaving. Sunny made the decision to keep quiet about it until she had a clearer understanding of what the real possibilities were.

The television flickered in the background with the sound muted so as not to attract the attention of the children, who were busy completing a jigsaw puzzle of Disney princesses and unicorns that Sunny had brought them from home. The images on the screen seemed almost as unreal as the one taking shape on the floor. The day before, thousands of Afghans had mobbed the terminal at Hamid Karzai International, spilling out onto the tarmac in a panic. Some had apparently managed to get out amid the chaos, quickly bundled onto planes in an effort to clear the runways. When word spread—as it always did—even more rushed to the airport.

Sunny cleared the unused dishes from the table. When she returned from the kitchen all eyes were glued to the TV. She took the glasses from the top of her head and placed them on the bridge of her nose, and when the image on the screen came into focus what she saw made her gasp out loud. Crowds of people were surging against the walls surrounding the airport, being pushed and shoved in all directions. Hundreds were flooding the tarmac, desperate to board anything with wings. People were climbing up gangplanks, swarming military planes as they taxied for takeoff, actually clinging to a plane as it left the ground. And then there were people literally falling from the sky.

Halajan moaned. "*Khudawanda rahm ko!*" May God have mercy.

The coffee shop fell silent. Even the children had abandoned their play, confused by the show that had turned their grown-ups into wide-eyed zombies.

By midday Ahmet and Rashif decided to go out, to see if they could get a handle on what was actually happening in the city, to try to gauge the mood.

"Already we are being treated like objects to be locked up and left behind," Halajan grumbled once they were out the door.

Sunny couldn't argue. Just the idea of not being able to go out alone was suffocating. She went to open the window overlooking the courtyard, as if that might bring some relief. She checked her phone, checked the time, which seemed to be moving at half its normal speed. She could almost hear the seconds slowly ticking away, like the solemn beats of a drum or the torturous drip of a faucet.

It was two hours later when Ahmet and Rashif returned with disturbing news.

Though the streets had been quiet, almost eerily so, the Taliban were definitely making their presence known. They could be seen in their turbans and long hair, cruising the streets in motorbikes and Humvees once belonging to Afghan security forces, parading around in pickup trucks flying the stark white Taliban flag from front bumpers, gunmen piled in the back draped in the camouflage and night goggles left behind by the foreign troops, with US-made rifles strapped to them. Ahmet shuddered even in the recounting of what he had witnessed.

But worse was something else they had noticed. There were absolutely no women on the streets. All through the city people had begun tearing down ads showing women without head-scarves; billboards and signs for beauty salons had been painted over in fear of provoking the Taliban's ire. It was as though women were being erased from public spaces. And, Ahmet told them in a hushed tone, the word was that the Taliban would begin searching houses that very night.

"But they said they wouldn't! They said it wasn't allowed!" Yazmina furrowed her brows.

"Ach. The Taliban are a bunch of lying liars," Halajan said, using one of the new phrases she'd picked up from Kat.

"Who knows? But we must act as though it is true. And even

if it's not, there are always the thugs and looters to worry about. With the police and government gone . . ."

Yazmina immediately reached for her phone. "I must tell them to lock all the doors and keep the lights on bright, to make sure the shelter looks like it is a home that is lived in."

Of course she was worried about the women in the shelter, but Sunny's concern was for the family in front of her. "The papers, the documents you took from there, where are they?"

Yazmina pointed to her desk.

"But that is not all," Rashif said. "It's not just the things showing that we run shelters or the evidence that we work with Westerners that must be destroyed. We must hide or get rid of everything that might put us at risk, anything that goes against the Taliban's beliefs, anything they would consider un-Islamic."

"What does that even mean?" The color had drained from Kat's face.

"Halajan will explain. She remembers all too well."

Halajan began counting off the old rules on her fingers. "No music, no television, no nail polish, and, Ahmet—bring me the scissors. We will have to do something to hide your fancy haircut. And you and Rashif, you must stop shaving and trimming your beards, immediately."

"Do you really think they will be the same as before?" Yazmina asked.

"You know what they say." Halajan pushed herself up to stand. "A leopard does not change its spots."

Sunny pointed to Layla's phone.

Layla nodded and mouthed the words, "I know."

"Everything. Facebook, Instagram, WhatsApp, Twitter it all has to go. Wiped clean, right?"

Again Layla nodded.

"Come, children," Rashif said. "Let's go outside and prepare a place for a nice fire and find a special spot to bury our treasures. Let's see who can find the most secret space."

Sunny smiled at his attempt to make a game of it and helped usher the girls out the door. When she returned, everyone but Yazmina had been disbursed by Halajan with specific instructions on what to do. Yazmina was sitting stock still, staring at the screen of her laptop. For a moment Sunny saw the younger Yazmina, the one who had arrived in Kabul so vulnerable, so lost. Back then Sunny had been able to throw her a lifeline, one that Yazmina used with all her might to become a force for good for others like her. And now everything she'd help build, including her beautiful family and her cozy home, was as precarious as a boulder teetering on the edge of a cliff. And there was not a single lifeline in sight.

Sunny placed a hand on her friend's shoulder. "Email everything to Candace," she said softly. "Any contracts with foreigners, anything about US funding. Send it, then dump it. I'll go through the loose papers and take photos of anything important, and then we'll burn it all."

The place had quickly become a beehive of frenetic activity. Layla retreated to her room and began sifting through her belongings. She picked up a framed photo Sunny had given her before she'd left the States to return to Kabul. A teenage version of herself was smiling at the camera, Kat and her old boyfriend, Sky, like bookends at her sides. Behind them the Washington State flag and the Stars and Stripes waved proudly in the wind. The state fair. She would never forget that day, photo or no photo, she thought as she began to tear it into tiny little pieces. Next came her student ID from the university, and a poster for a rally held the year before, the one where she'd first spoken in front of a large gathering. She could still feel the adrenaline that had rushed through her veins at the sounds coming from the crowd. She ripped the paper from the wall. That day would have to live in her memory as well. She turned to the clothes in her cabinet. *No jeans*, Halajan had said. And her favorite sheer, flowy tops, the ones she loved so much? She held up the green one she'd recently worn to the party. Those would have to go as well. She unscrewed the little square cap from the bottle of Chance by Chanel Sunny had brought from duty free, breathing deeply, allowing the sweet aroma to fill her nostrils before crossing over to the bathroom to pour it down the drain.

Then she picked up her phone and typed a message to Haseeb. *Please call me right away.* She pushed send and waited. *There is something I must tell you,* she added after five minutes. Layla needed to set up a secure place to chat, a shared passphrase for them to use because, without that, how else was Haseeb to find her? She tried calling, but there was no answer.

Kat and Fawiza were seated on the carpet of their shared room. Halajan had told them to get rid of anything of Kat's that might raise the Taliban's ire. American citizen or not, Kat would still be an Afghan in their eyes. Unsure of exactly what items would be suspect, she unzipped her makeup bag and dumped the contents onto the carpet. Fawiza picked up a lipstick tube and held it between her fingers, as if it were a cigarette.

"Here, let me show you." Kat uncapped and twisted the tube. "Pretty color, right?"

Fawiza nodded.

Kat gestured for her to move closer and placed a hand under her chin. "Right now," she said to Fawiza as she applied the creamy pink to the girl's lips, "you really can't be wearing this. Neither can I, I don't think. But you should learn how it's done. For when you are more grown up, for when things are different."

"It doesn't matter," the girl said, wiping the color from her mouth.

"What are you talking about? I loved to play with makeup when I was your age, to see what I might look like to others when I got older."

"Not me."

"Why not?"

The girl shrugged.

"You have to believe in yourself, Fawiza. Trust me. I know how you feel."

The girl rolled her eyes. "How could you know how I feel?" She pointed to Kat's suitcases stacked against the wall. "Soon you will be gone, away from here, back with your family. Me, who knows what will happen to me?"

Kat pushed the tubes and compacts and brushes into a little pile and turned to Fawiza. "First of all," she said to the girl who had been following her around like a puppy ever since the day she'd attempted to kill herself, "who knows when I'll get out of here. And, honestly? You don't really know anything about what I'm going back to. But, trust me, I know what it's like to feel alone, to not know what's coming next." Kat swallowed, a lump forming in her throat. "I don't know what will happen to you. Yet I do know that there are a lot of people working hard to make sure you have the chance to live a good life. And I also know that that, in itself, can be enough to get you believing that you are worth something." She leaned in to offer a hug only to feel the girl stiffen in her embrace. "You have to have hope, *qandom*, little one." She sighed. "We all do."

Halajan had almost forgotten the horrors of that morning. She'd become lost in the past, alone in her room rereading Rashif's letters. There they were, strewn around her like petals from a flower, sweet and smelling of love itself. How could anything this innocent be cause for retribution, even from someone as thickheaded as a Talib? Yes, there were some mentions of the insurgents here and there. And yes, there was some criticism. But that was years ago. How could they hold that against Rashif now? Yet even if Halajan took the time to select those letters that might spell danger, there was no way she could actually destroy them. That would be like tearing pages from a book, leaving the story half untold. She gathered the letters and retied them into their little bundles. Then she slipped them back into the old hiding place in the rear of a drawer, the one she'd used so long ago to keep them safe from her son's eyes.

Halajan turned to her notebooks and began to thumb through the volumes of rants disguised as art—opinions that would surely not sit well with any Talib who might be smart enough to understand her poetry. If there even was one that smart. She'd managed to fill two notebooks so far, the third remained half used, its blank pages awaiting inspiration. But the past two days had left her numb, as though all of the anger and outrage had been bled from her, like sap from a tree. Now that the threat had become a reality, it was almost as if, in a way, it were less real than before. And that made no sense, not even to her. Where was her spark now that she needed it most? Halajan moistened a fingertip with her tongue and turned to the next page, hoping that perhaps the fight in her words might rekindle the fight in her soul.

Back in the coffee shop, Rashif was busy sewing flash drives into the hems of their clothes. "Nobody will find a thing, not in between my tiny stitches," he said as he squinted at his work over the top of his glasses.

Ahmet entered the room, wiping his hands on a cloth. "I disconnected the battery and hid it under the pomegranate tree."

Yazmina looked at him quizzically.

"They are taking cars, whatever they want. Do you want to be stranded here? We cannot afford to let that happen."

On the television the horror at the airport continued to play in an endless loop. The children had drifted back inside and were now engrossed in the drama unfolding on the other side of the city. Sunny was just about to block the screen from their view when suddenly the picture went black. She turned to see Ahmet standing with a loose black wire in his hand.

"We have to hide it, disconnect it from the outside. They might be looking for houses with cable connections. They have banned it before."

Halajan lowered herself to the pebbled ground of the front patio, her old knees screaming in protest. She dug with a trowel at the dry soil at the base of the acacia tree, the very spot where Rashif had first kissed her so many years ago. A fitting location, she thought, for the eternal resting place of her most honest and heartfelt thoughts. When she had dug six inches deep, she put down the trowel and solemnly placed her three notebooks, one on top of the other, into their grave. "May hope and peace grow from the seeds of your words. *Inshallah.*"

Sunny and Yazmina appeared in the courtyard with their arms stacked with papers. Layla and Kat joined them. Ahmet had made a pit out of stones, and after a few twigs were doused with gasoline from a can, Hala flicked her purple lighter to ignite the flames that would bury their pasts forever.

"And now," she said as the smoke billowed up and out into the Kabul sky, "it is time for us to think up a good story about what we have been doing for the last twenty years."

24

Tuesday, August 17, 2021

The Taliban did not come that night. But that didn't mean anyone in the coffee shop got any more sleep than they had the night before.

Sunny had been on the phone with Candace for hours. It was Candace who told her what President Biden had said in an address to the nation that afternoon, doubling down on his decision to withdraw the troops. *I cannot and I will not ask our troops to fight on endlessly in another country's civil war* were his words, words that made Sunny's heart sink like a stone.

The real purpose of the call was to discuss plans for evacuation. Candace had managed to get the American embassy to email airport passes for everyone, which meant they'd been acknowledged by the State Department. But the moment those passes had become available, shops all over the city were printing them up and distributing them to anyone who asked, so they didn't hold much weight anymore. Candace had called on everyone she knew to try to get the family on a flight manifest, to backdoor them onto one of the embassy buses that were the best chance for safe passage to the airport. She was also attempting to get them included in one of the many rogue efforts at evacuation that were being set up by all sorts of everyday people around the world.

"I assume everyone is packed?" Candace asked.

"Not exactly," Sunny had answered.

"What's the problem? You know they all have to be ready to turn on a dime. We don't have any idea when their call will come. They'll only get that one chance to get to the airport, and that will be it. Done."

"Well, here's the thing . . . We haven't really talked about it yet. At least not seriously."

There was silence on the other end. "You have got to be shitting me."

"It's a fucking *nightmare*, Candace. Everyone is in shock, it all happened so fast. Imagine, one day you're living your life, going about your business, thinking about what you need to get done tomorrow, next week—and then boom! You're being told that everything you've hoped for and believed in for the past twenty years is false. You're being told that everyone has given up on your country, and that you should too. You're supposed to just hang it all up, lock the door behind you and say goodbye. Could *you* deal with all that in just a couple of days' time?"

"Honestly, I don't know what I'd do in their shoes. But I do know that there is no choice in the matter. Once the Taliban figure out their ties to an American NGO, and one that shelters women at that, they're going to be facing a boatload of trouble. And that's sugarcoating the situation, if you know what I mean."

Sunny knew exactly what she meant. "And don't forget about the whole Layla drama. She's gotta be a fucking magnet for their attention. I'm trying not to freak out, but I'm totally freaking out." She checked to make sure her door was closed. She'd been doing her best to hide her emotions from the others, but they were unmistakably there, bubbling right below the surface. She feared for *all* their lives at the hands of the Taliban, as well as the looters and thugs who'd been let loose on the city. Yet she knew that, as an American, she would be able to get out, go home. And that made her feel even worse, knowing the rest of them were sure to face a more difficult time and, even in the best of circumstances, a totally unknown future. She was sick at the thought of going, leaving the family behind, not being there to help. But she was also petrified of staying, because her very presence in the coffee shop could bring them trouble. No matter what, Sunny was terrified for the future of this family that she loved more than life itself, and terrified for the future of this beautiful country that she had once been lucky enough to call home.

"It's up to you, Sunny," Candace said. "They need to be prepared. There are lots of moving parts with this, and we cannot afford to fuck it up."

When Sunny came downstairs in the morning she found the coffeehouse carpet rolled up, and Ahmet examining the hatch that covered the *roba khana*, what Hala had called the "foxhole" where they had once stored surplus food for the coffee shop. She was almost relieved to see him so occupied, as she was dreading the conversation she knew had to happen. "What are you doing?" she asked.

"Preparing a hiding place." He sifted through the tools in his box.

"For your stuff? I thought we took care of most of that yesterday."

"No." Ahmet shook his head. "For the girls."

Sunny suddenly had to sit. Of course he'd be doing that, she thought. They'd all heard horrendous stories about what had happened to young women and girls as the Taliban had made their sweep through the provinces. Many were taken, often right in front of their families' eyes, to be forced into marriage with their captors. It was often hard to discern what stories were true, but, regardless, everyone was fearing for their daughters. She covered her ears as Ahmet began to work.

Yazmina came from the kitchen with two cups of tea, one of which she placed in front of Sunny. Her eyes were swollen, whether from lack of sleep or from crying, Sunny couldn't tell. "Thanks, Yaz," she said after taking her first sip. "Please, sit with me a while."

The screaming of Ahmet's drill bounced off the coffeehouse walls. When he finally stopped, the silence weighed heavy.

Sunny shifted in her seat. "Yaz?" she finally said. "We need to talk."

Yazmina looked up from her tea.

"You're going to have to leave. All of you. It's not safe here." Sunny's eyes darted to Ahmet's hole in the floor.

"I know," Yaz replied in almost a whisper.

"And it has to be soon. Once the foreign troops are gone, there may be no chance."

They watched as Ahmet picked up a screwdriver and fastened a lock onto the inside of the hatch.

"I've been talking with Candace. She's trying to get you all on a list. The next step will hopefully be that you'll get a call, and you'll be bused to the airport. But we don't know exactly when. So you have to be ready."

Yazmina didn't respond.

"Yaz? Did you hear me?

"I can't leave them, Sunny jan."

"Candace is working on getting the whole family out."

Yazmina shook her head. "It's the women in the shelter. And Fawiza. Who will fight for them if I leave? I couldn't live with myself if—"

"Candace has it handled. Trust me."

"But they are still there, in the shelter."

"It's not easy, Yaz." Sunny paused for a sip of tea. "It's like that puzzle over there." She pointed to the half-assembled princesses still resting on the floor. "Not until every piece is in place will we know the whole picture. Candace's plan is to get all of them, including Fawiza, transferred to another, larger organization, one that has a better capability to arrange their evacuation. And according to Candace those women have a decent chance of getting out even before you do. They're super high risk. They're a priority."

"But how can we know they'll be safe?"

"We can't. We can't know anything for sure. But that doesn't mean we should sit around and wait for things to fall apart even more than they already have. Am I right, Ahmet?" Sunny asked as he stood and wiped his hands.

Ahmet lowered his eyelids. "It is true, Yazmina. How can we live like this, so scared for our children's lives that we need to hide them? How will you and my mother survive being locked up in this place, only able to go outside buried in cloth, and dependent on me or Rashif to accompany you? What happens if Layla is no longer able to go to university, no longer able to speak her mind at all? And our girls, if they are not allowed to go to school? What kind of a life is that for our family?"

Sunny nodded as Ahmet spoke, grateful for his support.

"But where are we to go?" Yazmina asked.

"From what I understand, getting on a plane, any plane, is the first step. From there, it's hard to say where you'll be taken. Maybe initially to Abu Dhabi, maybe somewhere else."

"Who is going to Abu Dhabi?" They all turned to see Halajan standing in the doorway, a cup of steaming tea in her hands.

Ahmet took her arm and led her to a chair.

"What? Am I all of a sudden too feeble to sit on my own?" She brushed away his hand as he took a seat beside her.

"Not at all, *maadar*. It is just that we have been talking. Yazmina and me. And also Sunny and Candace."

"And?"

"And everyone agrees that we must leave the country."

"I am not everyone."

"And it must be soon, or we may have no choice."

"Well, I have made my choice, and my choice is to stay right here."

"But *maadar*—"

"Don't even bother, Ahmet. There is nothing you can say that will make me run like a rabbit chased by a fox. Like I have told you, I have lived through this before, and I will live through it again. Abu Dhabi. Ha! I have no interest in going to Abu Dhabi."

"But that would be only temporary, Hala." Sunny scooted her chair closer to the old woman. "From there, the goal would be to get you to the States. To Candace. To me."

"Ach. And what would I do in America? Sit around all day on a beach and drink Coca-Cola with my Hollywood friends? No thank you. I prefer to stay right here." She slapped her hands onto the table so hard that the tea sloshed over the rim of her cup.

"This is not the time to debate," Ahmet said. "You are too old to be on your own."

"And who are you to tell me what to do? I thought the Ahmet who used to strut around telling others how to live their lives had left this place a long time ago. Is he back?"

"Please, *maadar*."

"You tell me I'm too old? Well, maybe I am too old. Too old to go flying through the sky to a place thousands of miles away, a place that puts their old people away to rot in prisons they dare to call rest homes. You go, Ahmet. *Ma mordema begana na mekonm.*" I do not want to die in a strange land.

"What if something happens to you? Who will be here to help?"

"Rashif will be here with me."

"He is an old man."

"We can take care of ourselves."

"You *can't* take care of yourselves. Not with the way things are becoming." Ahmet angrily pushed away from the table and began to roll the carpet back into place.

"I'll be here. I will take care of them."

They all turned to see Layla, who was eyeing Ahmet's handi-work with a look of utter disgust on her face.

"We are not running," she said, shaking her head. "We are not going anywhere."

25

They'd just finished cleaning up from the evening meal when they heard shouting coming from the street outside the coffeehouse gate. Everyone froze.

"I will go see," Ahmet said as he slipped on a pair of shoes by the door.

"Be careful," said Yazmina. "Wait, take this." She draped one of Rashif's old tape measures around Ahmet's neck. "And don't forget the story we have made for ourselves."

"Let me come with you." Rashif struggled to rise from his seat.

"No, please. I am fine. I will be right back." Ahmet saw that the old man was pretending not to hear. "You need to stay with the women," he added. "To make sure they are safe."

Ahmet crossed the pebbled courtyard alone. "Who is there?" he shouted through the gate.

"*Mujahideen Emarat Isalami astim!*" We are fighters of Islamic Emirate.

Ahmet paused. There was no way, at that moment, to know for sure if it was truly the Taliban or not at his gate, but nevertheless he knew he needed to take the threat seriously. He grabbed the crossbar to keep his legs from crumbling beneath him and summoned his most polite voice. "*Salaam alaikum. Insha khairati ast?*" Greetings, is everything okay?

"We are here to do a home search," came the answer.

"You must have the wrong house," he responded. "It is just me and my wife and daughters here."

"Open the gate," barked one of the men. "We have heard there are government vehicles parked behind your house. We must do a search."

"There are no government vehicles here, I promise you. I have no connection with any government. Please, just let us be."

"Open the gate!" the man repeated.

Ahmet looked to the house and back again, then turned the key and pushed the gate open a crack. There were three of them, one tall and lean, the other two with muscles that strained at the shoulders of their tunics, all of them sporting long hair, beards, and guns.

"You talk too much," the tall one said, looking down at Ahmet as if he were an insect. He turned to his men. "Go ahead with the search."

With his heart pounding as hard as a hammer against steel, Ahmet made a show of peering behind them. "Please, but I do not see any women officers with you." The one who appeared to be the leader turned to the others in confusion. "Surely I cannot have my wife and little daughters be seen by strange men in our home." Ahmet wiped the sweat from his brow. "Give me a minute to gather them in one room, and then you can do your search."

"Go. But be quick about it. We will be waiting," the man added, pointing to his gun.

Ahmet dashed back across the courtyard, where everyone was standing by the door. "Quick! You must hide," he managed to say between breaths. "Kat, Fawiza, Layla, Najana. Go now. Yazmina, take Aarezo and *maadar* to the roof and stay there."

"I have no reason to hide," Halajan insisted as she turned away from her son. "Those gangsters do not scare me."

"Not a *word* from you, Mother," Ahmet hissed in a voice he'd never remembered using before. "Just go. Hurry. And take Sunny, too." He slammed the door and slowly made his way back to the gate.

The three men pushed past him with their rifles slung across their chests.

Rashif greeted the men politely at the door. "*Khush amadin.*"

"And who is this old man?" the tall one asked while the others barreled into the room without bothering to remove their shoes.

"That is my father." Ahmet tried to hide the quiver in his voice. "He is a retired tailor."

The leader looked Rashif over, as if he could detect a lie hidden somewhere on his person. For his part, Rashif had his eyes glued on the other men tromping disrespectfully across the coffeehouse rugs. "And who else lives here?" the man asked.

Rashif started to answer.

"I told you," Ahmet quickly interrupted. "Only my wife and two little daughters. We are a small family."

The man's eyes darted to a pile of shoes by the door. "Those are a lot of shoes for a small family."

The henchmen were circling the coffeehouse, picking up drawings left by the girls, sifting through shelves, peering behind pillows. The one who was the leader took a step toward Ahmet, coming so close that he could feel his breath. "And you, what do you do to support this family, to keep this home?"

Ahmet swallowed. "Me? I am also a simple tailor, like my father before me."

"He is a fine tailor, even better than me," Rashif added with an eager nod.

The man looked around at the tables once used as desks, now covered with dusty bolts of fabric and yellowed pieces of old patterns. He then joined the others in a search of the room. They were looking at everything, examining spools of thread and thimbles and jars of straight pins as if they held state secrets. Suddenly Ahmet spotted Layla's phone, right out in the open on the coffeehouse counter. One of the men passed right by him, and it, on his way down the hall. Ahmet quickly grabbed the phone and shoved it into his pocket.

A shout came from the back courtyard. "There is a car!"

The tall one held out his open palm. "The keys."

Ahmet laughed nervously. "That old thing? That is certainly not a government car. And it has not run in years. That is not the kind of car a man of your stature would want to drive."

Rashif cleared his throat. "Is that what you are looking for? A car?"

"That is none of your business," the third man snapped as he emptied the contents of a drawer onto the floor.

"But surely there is a reason for you to be here inside our home."

"We come as saviors, the guards of Islam."

"And who is it, exactly, that you are saving us from?"

"Shut up, old man!" Rashif was shoved into a chair.

"Please," Ahmet said. "We are not anyone of interest to you. We are just Afghan citizens, like you, trying to do our jobs, trying to live our lives."

"I will be the one to decide who is of interest to us," the leader said as he continued to circle the room, stepping over the mess his men had made. Ahmet watched in silence as his huge shoes crossed over the part of the rug covering the hole where he was sure at least a couple of the girls were hiding.

"What's that?" The man spun around at the distinct sound of chirping coming from Ahmet's pocket. "Your phone." He curled his long finger toward Ahmet, indicating he needed to hand it over.

"But—"

"Have you been recording us, recording this?" He swept one arm across the coffeehouse.

"No! Of course not."

"I will take it," the man said, holding out his hand. "Unlock it."

Ahmet reluctantly pulled the phone from his pocket. He randomly poked at the numbers on the screen, guessing at Layla's passcode, silently praying that she had done what was asked and wiped the data from her phone. But none of the numbers were working.

The man snatched the phone from his hands. "Stop playing games with me. Tell me your code!"

179

"But I promise, I did not record anything. There is nothing to be seen here."

"Open the phone, or I will have my friend over there give you some help." He pointed with his chin to one of his beefy partners, who began to rub his weapon with anticipation.

"I can't—"

With a nod of the tall one's head Ahmet found himself with a rifle butt ramming him squarely in the face. He reeled back into a wall, his jaw bursting with pain.

"Now do you remember the code?"

"I am sorry—"

"If you were not filming us, then what is it you do not want us to see? Answer me!"

"I am telling you—"

Another blow to the head, and Ahmet was on the ground.

"Please!" Rashif shouted. "I beg you, let him be!"

Rashif's plea only resulted in a sharp kick to Ahmet's stomach. He couldn't help but cry out. The man had drawn back his foot for yet another blow when the closet door flew open and out dashed Fawiza, who grabbed the phone from his hand and continued running, straight out the coffee-shop door. The three men were behind her in a flash.

Kat was the first to emerge from hiding, from the space in the closet where she'd been huddled behind some boxes with Fawiza. "Where is she? Where did she go?"

Ahmet, battered and stunned, pointed to the open door. Kat approached cautiously and peered in both directions before entering the courtyard on tiptoe. That stupid girl. Kat had been able to keep her quiet until the noises on the other side of the door turned violent, and then just like that she was flying out of Kat's reach. What was she thinking? There was no one to be seen in the courtyard. The men must have followed Fawiza out into the street.

Kat ran toward the open gate. "Fawiza!" she called out. "Fawiza, where are you?" The street was empty, eerily quiet, save for a scatter of gunshot far in the distance. Kat's heart pounded against her ribs. "Fawiza!" she shouted again, peering first to her left, then her right. No sign of anyone, anywhere. She started back toward the house.

"Katayon," came a small voice from behind her.

Kat turned but could see no one.

"In here."

And there, in the empty guardhouse, she saw Fawiza curled up in a ball under a chair, shaking as if the hot summer breeze had suddenly turned to snow.

26

"Let me take that." Yazmina reached for the wooden box filled with dozens of spoons that Ahmet had pulled down from a shelf in the coffeehouse kitchen.

"I am fine," he insisted as the whole thing came crashing to the floor.

"You don't look so fine." She could almost feel the pain of the bruises on his jaw.

"What do you want me to do with these?" he responded, ignoring her remark. "Which pile?"

Yazmina pointed with a shaking finger to the one that was for items to be taken to the refugees in the park. The others were filled with appliances and housewares either to be used or sold by Bashir Hadi. Anything left behind, they knew, would be stolen by the Taliban or by looters. They were determined to leave them nothing.

She was still reeling from the night before, being stuck behind the closed door of the roof while below her nightmares turned real. Hearing those sounds coming from downstairs, it had taken everything she had not to rush to Ahmet's side. It was only the thought of her children, her babies, that had kept her silent. She had held both her daughters tight all night, and did not close her eyes once.

"Someone must have told them," she said out loud.

"Told who what? What are you saying?"

"The men who came last night. What if someone advised them of what we have been doing here? Perhaps an angered father or husband of one of the women. Or maybe it was that horrible man who lives next to the shelter, Jan Agha. I *knew* not to trust him," she hissed. "He must have said something. And now we are in their sights. They will come back, I just know it."

"It could have been a random visit. Maybe they knew nothing. And if it weren't for that girl running out like she did—"

"So you think they believed our story that you are a tailor?"

"All I am saying is that we would have been better off if you had respected our agreement not to bring any of the shelter women to our home. This girl could get us all killed."

"So this is my fault? I tried to help a child who went through something so horrible that she cannot even speak of it. You are saying I should have turned my back on her? If that is what you think, you don't even know who I am."

183

"She needs to go. Now. And what about Sunny? Imagine if they had found we had an American living with us. How would we have explained that?"

Yazmina just looked at him.

"Did you hear me?"

She turned to leave the room. "Fawiza will go when we are told it is time," she said over her shoulder. "And Sunny? This is her home. She will leave when she is ready to leave."

Ahmet grabbed her by the arm just before she reached the first step. "Forgive me, *azizam*. I am so sorry. I am not myself. Of course she will stay. They will both stay." Ahmet wiped the tears from Yazmina's cheeks.

She melted at the love in his eyes, yet was shaken by the fear that was there in equal measure. "Do you think they will come back?" she asked in almost a whisper.

"*Khuda na kona.*" God forbid, Ahmet replied. "We might not be so lucky next time."

"You call this lucky?" Yazmina gently ran a finger along the bandages plastered across her husband's forehead. "Perhaps we should find a way to stay in another house, somewhere they won't know to look for us."

Ahmet jumped at the sound of the wind rattling the windows. "Or maybe we should just leave. I have heard that there are plenty of people getting through the airport gates."

"You know what Candace said. It's too dangerous. The Taliban checkpoints are everywhere, and there are plenty who are trying, only to get beaten and sent away, or worse, shot. We need to wait until arrangements to get to the airport are made, until there is someone who knows we are coming, who can get us safely through and on a plane. We need to trust Candace."

Yazmina pulled out a small box from the back of a shelf and placed it in her lap. It was one of Sunny's old centerpieces, the ones she'd crafted from little toy Santas and reindeer, fake flowers and whatever else she could get her hands on for their annual Christmas celebrations in the coffee shop. Yazmina would never forget her first one—candles everywhere and a thousand twinkling lights, and a plastic tree that went all the way to the ceiling. Halajan wearing an elf hat over her scarf. "Ahmet?" she said in a hushed voice. "Do you really think we are going to be okay?"

Ahmet took his wife's hands into his. "Of course we are, *azizam*. We will be together, and that is all that matters. And just think of all we will see, what our children will experience. Imagine! It will be a new adventure."

Yazmina smiled weakly at her husband, appreciative of the valiant effort he was making to sound strong for her sake.

"And perhaps there will come a day when we will return to Kabul."

"But what if we can't come back?" she asked.

"We cannot think about that now. Come, let's get back to work. There is lots to do."

"You could hear them, downstairs with Ahmet and Rashif," Sunny recounted over the phone to Candace. "I don't think I've ever been so scared in my life."

"Jesus, Sunny." Candace sounded worn out.

"And who even knows *who* those guys were? The Taliban leaders said yesterday that they'd be granting amnesty to everyone who opposed them. They promised that nobody would be going door-to-door."

"Anyone can claim to be part of the Taliban now. I'm sure there are plenty who will use it to settle their own scores, or to suck up to the real Taliban."

"It's crazy, Candace. You don't know who to trust, or where to turn for help. It's like being locked up in a fortress with a ticking time bomb outside the door. We *have* to get them out of here."

"I'm trying everything I can. Texting everyone, calling in every favor. Hell, I even came *this* close to offering to sleep with a senator who's been stalking me for years."

"What, and you stopped yourself? Where's your team spirit, girl?"

The two of them shared a punch-drunk laugh that went on way longer than it should have.

"Seriously, Sunny," Candace continued, "to get the whole family out is a real challenge. It means convincing the powers that be that every single one of their lives is in extreme danger, and there are so many others at even more risk around. You've got twenty years' worth of Afghans who have worked with foreigners, tons of journalists and activists who've been free to speak their minds, a boatload of women who've been working as politicians and judges. People *are* getting out, but in most cases it's just the individuals who have been directly involved with that sort of thing. And many are having to leave their families behind. I may have some luck with Ahmet, Yaz and the kids, and Layla as a separate case, but Hala and Rashif are a different story."

"You know that can't happen. It won't happen. They won't go unless they all go together."

"Of course I know that."

"And you know Yaz won't go until she is sure the women in the shelter are in safe hands."

"She knows the plan. They'll all be transferred to the other location tomorrow. From there they'll eventually be evacuated, but it's all pretty secretive. Not even I know when or where."

"You sound exhausted, Candace."

"Oh my God, I'm a total wreck. I don't want to go to bed, because I feel like if I sleep I might miss a text or a call about an evacuation. And when I do fall asleep I have nightmares that I forgot to fill out a spreadsheet or that I misspelled a name on a manifest. The other night I nodded off at three am and woke up two hours later to my phone blowing up with messages. When word got out that I was helping with evacuations, holy shit! The calls, the texts, the emails, people everywhere pleading, saying they were going to be killed. It's beyond belief. I even received a video of one guy's relatives being beaten by the Taliban. And of course I can't say no to anyone. How could I live with myself thinking that people could die because I said no to making a phone call or doing some damn paperwork? What type of a person would that make me? And trying to keep track of it all? Organization is not my strong suit. I'm a schmoozer, not an accountant."

"Oh Jesus, Candace. I can't even imagine."

"Nobody can, except for those of us in the middle of it. It's unbelievable how many people around the world, from truck drivers to lawyers, are chipping in to do the job our government seems to be failing so miserably at." Candace paused to sigh but wasn't finished. "And with all those requests we're getting for help? Do you know how it feels to have to pick and choose who to prioritize? *Who is the most high risk?* is always the question. I hate playing God. But I swear to you, Sunny, I will get the whole family out. No matter what."

"I need to be here for them until you do, Candace. I need to know they get out safely."

Candace paused. "Just be ready to roll, my friend. That's all I can say."

Sunny ended the call and scrolled through her phone, checking her feeds for some news of what was happening outside their door. By the look of things the airport was just as chaotic as the day before. Now the Taliban were trying to prevent any Afghans from entering the compound, even those with the necessary documents, and the US embassy was saying they couldn't ensure safe passage for Americans needing to get on a plane. Yet what she came across next made her truly sick to the stomach. It was footage from an amusement park in Herat, not unlike the one they had visited just a couple of weeks before. But instead of the laughing, joyful children who should have been enjoying the sweetness of a late summer day, it was the Taliban who were sailing up and down atop the painted carousel horses, weapons still in hand.

Kat could feel Fawiza's eyes upon her as she folded her T-shirts and jeans, her hands still shaking from the trauma of the night before. She looked up at the girl sitting silently across from her on the floor. She could have gotten herself killed, Kat thought. What the hell had been going on in that head? Kat could not wait to get away from this place, where you now couldn't even step outside your door without fear of being harassed, kidnapped, or killed. She quickened her pace, as if the sooner she finished packing the sooner the evacuation call would come for her and Sunny. Thank God she had given away so much of her stuff to the women in the park. She paused to hold up a gauzy overshirt she'd intended to leave for Layla, who would now have to cull her belongings to a minimum as well.

"How long will it take?" Fawiza suddenly spoke.

Kat looked up from her chore. "How long will what take?"

"For you to be back. In your home."

"Oh. Well, normally it should take only about a day. Sixteen or seventeen hours in the airplane, and the rest to get to and from the airports. But now, who knows?" Kat didn't care how long it took, all she wanted was for those wheels to be off the ground and the Kabul airport disappearing behind her.

"Will they be waiting for you?"

"Who?"

"Your family."

Kat shook her head.

"Why not?"

Kat thought for a minute about how to answer. "My parents are no longer around."

Fawiza picked up a pair of sunglasses and tried them on. "Don't you have any sisters?"

Kat pushed her backpack away and leaned against the wall. This was the most the girl had spoken since she'd been at the coffeehouse. "I don't. I always wanted one, though. Do you have sisters?"

Fawiza lowered her eyes. "I did. But that was before."

"I see. What are their names?"

"Shaima and Razia. Shaima is the older one, just a few years younger than me. Razia is still almost a baby. She is probably starting to walk by now, though."

"Those are pretty names."

"I won't see them again. Ever."

"You can't say that," Kat replied, knowing full well the girl was probably right, especially since she would soon be on her way out of Afghanistan. "Can I ask you something, Fawiza?" she said softly, not wanting the girl to clam up again.

Fawiza shrugged.

"What was it you were thinking last night, when you ran from the closet?"

The girl hesitated before speaking. "I was thinking that I wanted them to stop beating him."

"You mean Ahmet?"

Fawiza nodded. "So I was thinking that if I ran they would chase me and leave him alone. The gate was not shut, so I ran out to the street and threw the phone into the gutter. I was fast, and hid behind a car until they were looking the other way. Then I ran back into the guardhouse."

"Do you know how brave you are?"

"Me? I am not brave. He has a whole family who needs him. I have nobody. So what is the difference if I live or die?"

Kat felt as though she'd been cut with a knife. "Oh, but you do have someone, *janem*. You have tons of people all working their

190

butts off to make sure you get the chance to live a decent life. Soon you'll be taken to somewhere safe, safer than here. And from there to somewhere else, somewhere even safer than that."

"Will I go to America, like you?"

"Oh sweetie, I don't know. Maybe."

Fawiza looked as though she were going to cry.

"And you talk about me having a family?" Kat said. "My family fell apart when I was just a girl, like you."

Fawiza looked at her, wide-eyed. "Really?"

"Really. And I will tell you something I've learned. Family can be where you find it. For instance, Hala. She's like a grandmother to me. My crazy grandmother."

Fawiza giggled a little.

"And Sunny is like my pushy aunt," Kat continued, "always telling me what to do. Then there is Layla. Layla is my sister. And now you will be too." Kat picked up a zippered bag and rifled through its contents until she found a thin gold bracelet that had been one of the pieces of jewelry her mother had left behind. "Here. Put this on." She clasped the chain around the girl's delicate wrist. "Now we are bound together forever. I will always be there for you. Remember that. I will hold you in my heart, for ever and ever."

"One bag. That is crazy. Who can pack up their entire life into one tiny bag?" Halajan leaned back on a pillow as Layla continued to hold up her belongings, one by one, for the old woman to decide yes or no. Just one look at the blood streaming down her son's face the night before had been enough for Halajan to change her mind. She would be leaving Kabul with the rest of them, off to spend what little time was left of her long life as a stranger in somebody else's land.

"What's this?" Layla retrieved a box from under the small table against the wall.

Halajan lifted the lid and pulled out two long, thick braids, severed from their roots in a private act of defiance over a dozen years earlier, when rumors began drifting through Kabul of a Taliban return to the hillsides in the south.

"Yours?" Layla stifled a chuckle. "Are you planning on wearing them again?"

Halajan ignored her remark. She prayed they'd get out soon, the sooner the better. There was the fear of the Taliban coming back to the coffee shop, but what Halajan was also fearing was that she'd change her mind about leaving. Better to get out before she had too much time to think about it. It was impossible to imagine that she might never again set foot on the streets she grew up in, where her parents and grandparents and their parents and grandparents had. She was even tempted to slip on the damn burqa Ahmet had bought, just to take a quick walk outside to smell the scent of baking *naan* wafting from the ovens of the women's bakery down the road, to hear the familiar sounds of her neighbors fighting, to make her way one last time to the tailor shop on the narrow alley in the Mondai-e, where Rashif used to sneak his letters into her waiting hands. But before she could do anything, she had to finish this dreadful task of deciding what parts of her life to leave behind forever.

Halajan let out a huge sigh. "Well, you know what they say. *Life is a balance between holding on and letting go.*"

"By *they* I assume you mean your fellow poet, Rumi?"

"Yes. But sometimes I think he gets things a little wrong."

"You'll be fine, Hala. There are some things in America that are not as different as you think."

"Oh, really? You don't remember crying to us about how everyone walked around practically naked over there, how the food made you sick? How you missed your *kharbuza* and *naan*?"

Layla laughed. "Yes, but I got over it. Honestly, there are a lot of good things there."

"Like what?"

Layla had to think for a moment. "Well, there are some very nice people." She smiled thinking about Kat's old boyfriend Sky. "And it is so green where Sunny lives. They call Seattle the Emerald City. Then there are the whales—creatures as big as, well, whales—swimming so close you can almost feel their spray."

"As if I want to feel the spit of one of those blubbery beasts on my skin."

"And *all* the women drive there, Hala. You will be able to drive anywhere you want with nobody batting an eye. Think about it. Seriously, the hardest thing about being there was missing my family."

"Then it should be easy for you this time."

Layla didn't answer.

"Am I right?"

Layla shrugged.

"What? Do not tell me you are not going."

"I'm not sure, Hala. Maybe not."

"Ach, is it because of that boy? If he is still playing games with you, I say good riddance."

Layla shook her head. "No. It isn't about Haseeb."

"You must go. We are all going."

"But it is because of that that I *can* stay."

Halajan raised her brows.

"Don't you see? With everyone gone, the only person I will be putting in danger with what I do is me. I need to be here, now more than ever. If not for people like me, then who will stand up for what is right? Who will protect the progress we have made and fight for more? How can I run away and still call myself a fighter for justice?"

"You will break your sister's heart, Layla. In fact, I do not even think she will go if you don't. This isn't just about you. It isn't just about me. We are a family." Halajan stuffed her ancient denim skirt into the suitcase. "You are a fighter. There will always be injustices. You can be who you are no matter where you are. It will be fine."

"If that is so, why does it seem so hard for *you* to leave?"

"Because I am old," was the only thing Halajan could think to say. She snatched a pair of shoes from Layla's hands. "You go pack your bag. I will finish this myself." Halajan stood, and after the young woman left, retrieved yet another, larger suitcase stashed between the wall and the back of her armoire.

"Have we gotten everything?" Yazmina closed the drawer with a thud. Candace had told them to gather all the family's personal documents—marriage certificates, birth certificates, medical records and the like—to photocopy and also photograph to save on the Cloud. She waited for her husband to answer. "Ahmet?"

She looked up to see him standing at the coffee-shop counter, a piece of paper held loosely in his hand. "Ahmet?" she repeated. She rose from her chair and went to his side. "What is it? Is something the matter?"

"It was all for nothing," he replied in a hush.

"What was all for nothing?" She took a quick look at the thick yellow document. From the shiny gold stamp she could immediately tell what it was—his diploma from the university. "Oh, Ahmet, that is not true one bit. Think of the good work you have done since those days, how many people you have helped."

"And now?"

"And now we will have to wait and see."

"See what? What have we seen so far? That we are to give up everything? That all I have worked for suddenly means nothing?" He wiped a sleeve across his eyes. "I am sorry, Yazmina."

"There is no reason to be sorry. We all feel this way, having to walk away from our lives. It is almost unthinkable."

"Yes. And how am I supposed to take care of everybody? I will be sweating behind the wheel of a taxi, or up to my elbows in dirty dishwater. Is that what I did this for?" He waved the diploma in the air.

She took the paper from his hand and slid it gently into an envelope. "We will do whatever it takes."

"Please forgive me. I don't like to hear myself sounding this way. All work is honorable, and of course I will do whatever it takes to provide for our family. But it is so hard to imagine myself starting over."

"We will start over together."

Ahmet pulled his wife close. "My darling Yazmina, how did this happen to us? We were good people, a strong family."

"We are still a strong family," she replied, holding him closer. She could feel his clammy skin and trembling limbs through his clothes. "We are still good people."

"But to leave? I love my country, and everything about it. Even now. I would have never imagined leaving my land, my home like this. We were happy, Yazmina."

"And we will be happy again. Who knows? Perhaps we will be able to return some day and take back what belongs to us," she said as her husband's tears rained down upon her shoulder.

27

The sting of her sister's words remained with Layla as she rushed to join the others near the presidential palace. *You are selfish,* Yazmina had said, once her pleas for Layla to stay home had failed. *If you want to put yourself in danger, that is one thing. But what you are doing puts the rest of us in even more danger than we are already in.* Layla understood the stress Yazmina was under, worrying about her children, waiting for the women in the shelter to be taken to a safer place, trying to get the house in order, preparing everyone to leave. Never before had she seen her sister like this. But that couldn't stop Layla. Nothing was going to stop her today. She'd explained to Yazmina that the protests were happening all over the city, all over the country on this Afghan Independence Day. People were taking to the streets everywhere to demonstrate against Taliban rule. There was no way she was going to stand silently aside.

Layla could hear the crowd even before she saw them, the roar of the chanting sending shivers up her arms. She quickened her pace. When she caught up with the others she was greeted with a cheer. There were perhaps one hundred people gathered, equal parts men and women, all young, loud, and determined. Someone unfurled a huge red, black, and green Afghan flag and draped it over Layla's shoulders. "*Bairaq ma, Hoyat-e ma ast!*" Our flag, our identity! came a shout from behind.

Layla raised a fist in the air. "To the palace!" she yelled, and they were off, their chants competing with the sound of fighter jets roaring over the city. Layla shaded her eyes and turned them toward the sky.

"*Saag shoi.*" Dogwashers, foreigners! said a man who had been keeping pace beside her. "Scrambling to evacuate their own, before it is too late."

Layla nodded and pulled the shiny cloth closer around her shoulders. "Our flag, our identity!" she shouted.

The voices behind echoed back.

Yazmina was still fuming when Sunny came running downstairs, breathless with the news. "Candace says your call may come within the next two hours."

Yazmina swore she could feel her heart stop for a few beats. "So soon? But—"

"It's now or never, Yaz. You'll need to be totally ready to go on a moment's notice. Remember, one small bag each. Don't forget your documents. And the phones should be hidden on you or Hala, as you're less likely to be searched." Sunny was talking a mile a minute. "Ahmet got the dummy phone, right?" The dummy phone was to be the one he carried to the airport, a phone with few contacts and no incriminating information on it should the Taliban find it. "We'll use your phone to communicate, but if you're using WhatsApp make sure you log off every time." She paused to take a breath. "Got it?"

"But what about you? And Kat?"

"Don't worry about us. Ours will come soon as well. We will for sure get out. Just hurry. Oh, and when the call does come, it will be on your phone. They say *apple*, you say *orange*. That's the way you'll know each other is legit. Don't give any information to anyone without the password."

Yazmina's mind was reeling. Apples, oranges, dummy phones.

"And make sure everything is charged. I'll go tell Hala and Rashif."

Yazmina didn't know where to turn first. Outside the window Najama and Aarezo were playing quietly in the courtyard. Their bags were ready. Ahmet had taken Fawiza to her pickup point earlier that morning and was now delivering the last of what they were donating to the refugees in the park. He would be home any minute now. And Layla—Layla! Yazmina began to punch in her number. It was then she remembered that Layla's phone was gone.

Layla made one last sweep of the street with her eyes before giving the nod. The guy next to her cupped his hands and squatted down to give his pal a boost up the flagpole. In one quick motion the white banner of the Taliban came floating to the ground, and in its place the Afghan tricolor that Layla had been wearing was raised.

Our flag, our identity!

There was a roar as they continued their march toward the palace. Layla drank in the feeling of power coming from the crowd. She couldn't help but have hope for her country, witnessing the conviction of those around her. Whether she left now or not with her family, Layla knew her future was right here in Kabul.

Our flag, our identity!

They sat with their bags lined up at their sides, as if the bus was going to pull up right there to the coffee-shop door. Yazmina had packed one knapsack with water and snacks, as they'd been told that their wait at the airport might be for some time. Only the children, left to play in the courtyard, were talking. The rest of them were silent, checking their phones, watching the door waiting for Layla to appear, counting down the minutes they had left in their home. Only a half hour had passed since Sunny's announcement. It felt like two days.

Yazmina had secretly made up her mind. She would send Ahmet ahead with the others, should Layla not return in time. He would make sure they all got to the airport safely, and she would figure out some way for them to follow. Leaving her sister in Kabul was unthinkable. She'd sooner cut off a limb and leave that behind for the Taliban to find.

"I will go look for her," Ahmet said, as if he knew what she was thinking.

"You will not!" Yazmina leaped from her chair.

"I will be quick." He patted his pocket. "And you can call me the minute that word comes."

"But there won't be enough time! You know what Candace said. A moment's notice."

"No, Ahmet," Halajan said. "You must go with your family. I will stay should the girl not return in time. I will watch after her."

"What are you thinking, *maadar*? A son does not leave his mother behind. I will go find where people are gathering. I'll bring her back."

"*I'll* go." It was now Rashif who was offering. "You stay with your children, Ahmet. I can do this."

"Then I am going with you," insisted Halajan.

"Stop! Would all of you just *stop*? Nobody is going." Yazmina glanced nervously at the door. "Perhaps Layla will get back in time."

"But how can we know that, Yazmina?" Ahmet slipped on his shoes.

And then Yazmina's phone rang.

"I can't believe you are here."

Layla turned to see her friend Needa walking beside her. "Of course I am here."

Needa slowly shook her head. "I don't know how you are doing it."

"We have to do something, don't we? I don't see *you* hiding at home behind the curtains."

"But you are handling it so incredibly well."

Layla gestured to those marching around them. "Well, I'm not the only one. We are *all* a little worried, but we all showed up."

"I meant because of Haseeb."

Layla stopped dead in her tracks. "Haseeb? What has happened to Haseeb?"

"Oh no, he's all right." Needa took her arm and continued to walk.

"Then what? What about him?"

Needa looked at her feet. "I guess you haven't heard then."

"Heard what?"

Needa pulled her friend to the side, away from the rest of the group. "Haseeb is getting married."

Layla felt her knees buckle. The sound of gunshots suddenly rang out as a truckful of Taliban fighters, their weapons pointed high into the air, rumbled down the middle of the street, scattering protesters to each side like the wake of a boat.

Long live Afghanistan! shouted one bold person as they passed.

Long live Afghanistan! echoed the rest.

28

Friday, August 20, 2021

The call never came that day. Everyone had been waiting on pins and needles for Layla to return, and when she did their relief way overpowered any anger toward her for making them worry so much. Not even Ahmet had admonished her, had instead embraced her in a huge hug. After that they sat ready and waiting for four hours, just in case the person who was to give them instructions had been delayed. The phone call Yazmina received had been from Feba, to let them know that Fawiza and the other women from the shelter had arrived safely at a new location. But the next day an evacuation call did come—for Kat.

I am calling from the American embassy. You are to be at Qasaba Khana Sazi, near Abdul Jaweed High School at 4 o'clock this afternoon. We have a planned pickup to escort you to the airport.

"But it's not just me. There are two of us, two Americans waiting to get out. Sunny Tedder. She's on your list as well, right?"

One moment. Let me check.

The man hesitated. Kat could feel her heart racing.

Okay, I do see a Ms. Tedder here. It will be fine. It looks like she'll get her call in the next few hours, tomorrow at the latest.

"But we need to go together. Why can't she come with me?"

Again, the man hesitated.

I don't have that information. Do you want to take this evacuation?

"I don't understand why . . ."

I have space for only one person, and you are it. Do you want the seat?

"Can't I wait and go on her flight?"

No. We cannot guarantee that. Again, do you want the seat?

Kat took a deep breath. "Okay. I'll take it. Where do I go? What do I do?"

Good. Now, listen to me carefully. Do you have a red scarf, or a red hat?

"Yes, I have a red scarf."

I need you to wear it. You will be picked up by a man wearing a red hat. He will identify himself when he sees you by touching its brim. That's how you will know he's a safe contact. Please be calm, and when you see him, pretend he is your uncle, or your brother. He will tell you what to do. And try not to draw any attention to yourself. This needs to be fast. Do you understand?

"I do." Kat ended the call and immediately went looking for Sunny. She found her standing near the edge of the roof, gazing out through the hazy sky toward the mountains in the distance.

Sunny jumped at the sound of the door banging closed behind her. "What's up? You scared me."

"They called. The ones arranging rides to the airport."

"So everyone is ready?"

Kat shook her head. "No. It wasn't for them. It was just for me."

Sunny took hold of Kat's shoulders. "Thank God. You're ready, right?"

"Are you kidding me? Of course I'm ready. But I can't go without you. And what about everyone else?"

"You have to go. I'll get out. I'll be fine. You know they won't leave any Americans behind. And, honestly, I'm glad to still be here for them." She pointed to the coffee shop below.

"But what if the Taliban come back? What if Candace can't get them out? What if something happens and you can't get out?"

Sunny covered her ears to mute the chop from a pair of Chinook helicopters crossing overhead. "What if, what if. Somebody is going to have to get out first," she said once they had passed. "Why not you? I'll be right behind you. Go home to C.J. He'll be so thrilled to see you."

Kat next went to tell Layla. She found her friend alone in her room, her bag packed and ready, leaning against a wall. "It won't be too long now for you," Kat said after she broke the news of her departure. "We'll be seeing each other again soon."

Layla burst out crying.

"What?" Kat said. "It's going to be okay." She took Layla's hands in hers. "You'll be fine. At least you've lived in America, you know what you're getting into. You've got this, Layla."

Layla shook her head. "It's not that," she insisted.

Kat looked at her quizzically. "It's a guy. Am I right?"

Layla nodded.

"I knew it! So you're in love with a guy, and you don't want to leave him. Is that it?"

Again Layla shook her head.

"I don't get it," Kat said.

"He got engaged."

"Wait, what? You guys got engaged, or he got engaged?"

"Not us, just him."

"You mean he dumped you? For someone else? What an asshole."

"I'm not sure what the situation is, who she is." Layla began to cry even harder.

"Well, what did he say when he told you?"

"He didn't tell me. My friend Needa did."

"What? Fucking coward. That is unbelievable."

"I knew something was going on with him, but he kept denying it. And he didn't even show up today."

"You need to confront him."

Layla looked up at Kat, her eyes still wet with tears. "What good would that do? It's not as if I can change his mind, or even want to. Why would I ever want to be with someone who obviously doesn't want to, or who can't, be with me?"

"It's for you, Layla. You can't let him get away with this. Think about your pride. At the very least you are owed an explanation. It's called closure. It's the only way you can keep from being crushed by what he's done."

"But I—"

"Here, use my phone." Kat placed it in her hand. "Send him

a message. Tell him it's you. Tell him you need to talk. See what he says."

"I'm not sure—"

"Do it. Trust me. It will work."

Layla's thumbs danced across the screen. Then they waited.

"See?" Layla said. "He cares nothing for me. Not even enough to reply."

Kat took back her phone. "Let's give the guy a chance. Come on." She pulled her friend up from her seat on the ground. "I need to get going soon."

There were tears all around as Kat said her goodbyes.

Halajan wrapped her in a hug. "The only good thing about where we are going is that we will see you again, Katayon."

"Gee, thanks a lot, Hala." Sunny laughed.

"Keep an eye on her," Kat said to Rashif. "And good luck with that."

To Yazmina and Ahmet she offered a million thanks for all they had done for her. "You've taught me so incredibly much," she told them. It killed her to see them so anxious, like two scared rabbits on the side of a highway. "And soon it will be my turn to maybe teach you a thing or two. It will be okay," she tried to assure them. "It will be better than okay."

To the kids she promised pony rides and many trips to the beach. "We will have so much fun in America. You'll see."

She checked her phone and gave Layla one last hug. "Not yet," she whispered in her friend's ear. "I promise I'll get word to you through Sunny if I hear anything."

Kat turned and gave the coffee shop one last look, then followed Ahmet and Rashif out into the car.

*

The minute Rashif and Ahmet dropped her off and drove away, Kat had the sense something was wrong. She thought she might be in a car with other Americans, but so far it was just her and an Afghan driver in a red hat, and he wasn't speaking a word. He'd driven off as if they were being chased, winding through the streets of the city like a bat out of hell. By the time she realized they were headed in the opposite direction of the airport, she was beginning to panic a little.

"Aren't we going straight there?" she asked.

"We need to go meet the others," was all the driver said.

Kat peered through the darkness, struggling to get her bearings. She thought she recognized her father's neighborhood out the window, but it was hard to tell. No matter where they were, something did not feel right. Finally the man slowed to a stop at the top of a steep hill. Kat rattled the door handle, only to find it locked.

"You need to give me your phone," he said, looking at her through the rearview mirror.

"Why? Where are you taking me?" As she spoke she slipped her shaking hands inside her bag and began to blindly type out a call for help.

"Your phone," he repeated, holding out a hand. "We cannot have people communicating our locations. It is too dangerous."

Kat pinned her location and hit send, then gave the guy her phone. As she did, she felt her panic turning into full-fledged terror.

29

Saturday, August 21, 2021

The next day was torture. With Fawiza and Kat gone the coffee shop seemed empty. Perhaps it was just that so many of the family's belongings had already been stowed or given away, that everything was so neat and tidy in preparation for their departure. Whatever the reason, the coffee shop no longer felt like a place where people actually lived.

Another twenty-four hours had passed with no word about their evacuation. Everyone was on edge, anxious to leave before the Taliban chose to pay another visit. But so far things had remained quiet. Almost too quiet. Sunny sat slumped on top of a *toshak*, pecking at her phone.

"Anything?" Yazmina asked.

"Nope. Not yet."

Their heads turned in unison at the sound of a scream coming from the front courtyard.

"It is just the children. Playing games with Rashif." Halajan was standing at the coffee shop counter, a soft rag in one hand and a lemon in the other.

"What are you doing?" Sunny asked.

"What does it look like I'm doing? I'm polishing the espresso maker."

"For who, the Taliban?" Ahmet rolled his eyes.

"Always the smart one, my son is. No, it is for us. I want things to be nice, for when we come back."

"It's good to keep busy." Yazmina rose to straighten what few dishes they had left on the shelves.

Sunny remained glued to her phone.

"Do you think Kat is there yet?" Halajan's hand rubbed hard in circles against the copper vessel, as if a genie might appear to grant her wishes.

"It's too soon," Sunny replied.

"Has anyone heard from her?" Yazmina asked.

"Not that I know of. But imagine how these things must go. The mess at the airport, and who knows what kind of a connection she had to make in God-knows-where. And maybe she hasn't been able to get a signal, or her phone ran out of charge." Sunny didn't add that she'd been texting C.J. like mad, searching for answers to put her mind at ease. He had promised to let her know the minute Kat surfaced.

"Quickly, quickly!"

Sunny looked up from her phone to see Rashif frantically shuttling the girls inside.

"There is someone near the gate," he said between breaths.

Ahmet jumped up and locked the door behind them. "Did they say who it is?"

"I grabbed the girls quickly and ran when I heard footsteps approaching."

Ahmet dashed to the closet where, in a locked box, he had hidden his AK-47, the one he used to carry across his shoulder when he worked as the coffee-shop guard, so many years before.

"Girls! Run upstairs!" Yazmina yelled. "Ahmet! Please." She tried to take the rifle from his hands. "Do you really think it's the time for such heroics? They're looking for people with guns! They'll charge you with rebellion. I beg you, do not go out there."

"I am supposed to just stand here and let something happen to my family?" He held fast to the weapon and bounded out the door.

Sunny and the others peered out from behind the curtains as he crossed the courtyard. "It'll be okay, Yaz. It could be anybody, right?"

Now Ahmet was speaking to someone through the gate. They held their breath until they saw his arms relax, the rifle coming to a rest at his side.

"Thank God," Sunny whispered.

"*Shukr Khudaya*," Halajan echoed.

"Look," Rashif said. "He is coming back."

They circled Ahmet as he came through the door. "Who was it? What is going on?"

"It was the neighbor from next door."

"What did he want?" Halajan asked, her eyes narrowing.

211

"To ask if we were okay. He heard the screaming." He pointed toward the courtyard. "At least that is what he said the reason was. I think he might have been trying to find an excuse to talk to me."

"What did he ask?" Rashif took the gun from his son-in-law's hands and returned it to the box in the closet.

"If we are staying, or thinking of going."

"You didn't tell him anything, did you?" Yazmina asked.

"Of course not. We have no idea who is on what side now, or who is looking for information to trade for their own purposes."

"Or who will be jealous, thinking we have special connections. We do not need that kind of trouble. We have enough already," Yazmina said.

"That's for sure," Ahmet agreed.

"No one is to be trusted." Yazmina returned to her dishes.

"No one." Halajan picked up her rag.

Ahmet began to pace the room, back and forth, back and forth.

"Please, can you just stop?" Yazmina snapped as a plate slipped from her hands and shattered into pieces on the marble floor.

"Let me get that." Rashif scrambled for a broom, knocking over a pitcher of water on his way.

"I'm sorry, Ahmet, my love." Yazmina reached for a towel. "It is just that I'm so nervous. Perhaps we should move to a different house. Just until it is time to go."

"There is nowhere to go," he answered.

"What about the shelter? It is empty now."

"It is probably already under the Taliban's watch. We're safer here, don't you all agree?"

Nobody spoke, but Sunny knew what they were all thinking. They weren't safe anywhere.

Yazmina let out a huge sigh. "When *will* that call come?"

It had been a torturous night for Kat, starting from the minute the driver yanked her out of the car and into the street. She'd stood, blinking at the cinderblock house perched, like all those around it, on the edge of a hill. She knew that house. It was the one she had lived in as a child. But why had she been taken here? And why was this man, whose grip on her arm was as tight as a vice, being so rough with her? The driver had led her up the stairs. As they reached the top the door swung open and there he was.

"Welcome home, *dokhtar*." Her father cocked his head and squinted, as if trying to size her up. "We will talk in the morning." He nodded toward a room behind him, where the man who had brought her there swiftly deposited her and pulled the door shut.

Kat had heard the turn of a key before all went silent. She'd dropped to her knees, bowed her head, and begun to pray.

Now, along with the first daylight, came the sounds of children squabbling. Kat banged against the locked door with her fist. She spoke in Dari. "Let me out! Someone! Please. I need to use the bathroom."

The bickering stopped, and the door opened a crack. It was a woman around Kat's age who took her by the arm and led her silently down the hall. Kat's eyes darted around the house. It looked pretty much the same as she remembered, with pillows

213

and toys strewn across the carpet, the smells of cumin and coriander coming from the kitchen.

"Where is he?" she asked.

The woman silently pointed to a pair of plastic shower shoes outside the bathroom. Kat slipped them on and went through the door. The lock was slid shut, and Kat was left alone inside. At the sink were four toothbrushes, two of them emblazoned with action figures. And then it sunk in. That woman must be his wife. The mother of his precious new boys.

After a few minutes she was led back to the little room and again the door was locked tight. A plate of fruit and naan had appeared on the floor. Kat pushed it into a corner with her foot. She unlatched a small window high on the wall and pried it open, peering on tiptoes through the bars only to be facing the solid blue wall of the house next door. She slid onto the floor and closed her eyes.

Without her phone, she'd lost all track of time. She had no idea how many hours had passed before she was startled awake by the sound of a slamming door and then her father's voice, booming through the house.

"She is awake?" A key turned in the lock. "Katayon." He held out a hand.

Kat scooted back against the wall.

"It has been so long, *dokhtar*."

Kat's eyes flew to the open door behind him.

He reached to push it shut. "What? You are not happy to be with your father after all these years?" He lowered himself to a seat across from her on the floor and folded his arms, regarding her with an air of curiosity, as if he weren't quite sure what to make of her.

She found herself doing the same.

Finally he spoke. "You know, when your cousin Hanifa told me you were in Kabul I was saddened that you had not come to see me. My own daughter. But then, I told myself, if you were not going to come see me, I would make certain to be the one to reach out. So I asked your cousin for your number. How could I live with myself, knowing you were so close and not making the effort?"

Kat's mind flashed back to the blank look in her father's eyes when they'd come face-to-face that day outside the mosque. "So why didn't you contact me earlier? And why didn't you just call me? Why trick me into coming here? And why am I being locked in?" Kat struggled to stop her voice from trembling.

"So many questions. Relax, *dokhtar*. Would you like some *chai*? Are you hungry?" He waited for her answer. "No?" he finally said. "Okay. So let me tell you what I have been thinking." He leaned back against the wall and looked up at the ceiling. "You see, at first when I heard you were in Kabul, I hoped you had come home for good, that you had realized your faith and your country meant more than all that so-called freedom America had to offer. But your cousin told me otherwise, and that your stay was to be only temporary."

Now he turned his eyes to Kat. "I was disappointed. And then, with everyone trying so hard to leave, I knew I would only have this one last chance to talk with you. And, as you hadn't come to see me on your own, I knew I would have to bring you to my home myself."

"So you have me *kidnapped*? And what is it that you have to say to me that you can't just say it, instead of locking me in here overnight like an animal? You're a sick, twisted man."

"Katayon!" He jumped to his feet, the color rising up his neck.

Kat scooted back against the wall.

Her father seemed to be working hard to restrain himself, breathing loudly in and out before continuing. "Perhaps you have become used to saying what you want, doing what you want. But that is *not* the way to speak to your father."

"My father?" she responded despite her fear. "How can you call yourself that when you completely blew up my life and walked away? Is that what a father does?"

"I had no choice after what your mother did to us. I was supposed to allow myself to be taken to prison for the rest of my life? How would that have helped you, can I ask?"

"After what *she* did to *us*? Are you kidding me?"

"And you, you are apparently just like her, thinking only of yourself, not even bothering to find me."

"*I* was supposed to run after *you*? I was only a child!"

"I am your *father*."

"You are a murderer!"

Her father slapped a hand hard against the wall. "Quiet! That is enough." His eyes shifted to the door and back again. "You are in *my* house, and I absolutely forbid you to talk like that."

Kat fought back her tears. "I am in your house because you forced me to be here. And you gave up your right to tell me what I can and cannot say years ago."

"You are my daughter, my property, so it will always be my right."

"A murderer has no rights!" she yelled at the top of her lungs.

"I said to be quiet!"

"What, you're scared they'll hear the truth? I've seen you with your new children, the boys you've always wanted. And her." She pointed toward the door. "She's your new wife? You throw one family away and get yourself another one just like that?"

"You have been spying on me?"

Kat pushed herself up off the floor and reached for the door. Her father grabbed her arm and pulled her back.

"Let me go!" she shouted.

"You are going nowhere. It is time for you to live up to your duty as my daughter. You dare to disobey me and you will pay for it," he hissed through clenched teeth.

"I've already paid enough for what you've done."

Her father flung her back toward the wall and stomped out the door, turning the lock behind him.

Kat must have again fallen asleep. Her eyes flew open at the sound of someone clearing his throat. Her father's looming figure filled the doorway. He tossed a ball of clothing onto her lap and gestured for her to put it on. A scarf fluttered down from inside a long, dark dress as she pulled it over her T-shirt and jeans. He gestured again and waited as she stood and wrapped it around her head, flinching as he leaned in to tuck it in place.

One word came from his lips. "Come."

There was no sign of the family. The house was quiet, the toys out of sight. He led her into what must have been their room for guests. There she saw an older man and a woman in a burqa seated side by side on *toshaks*. Even from behind the veil, the woman's gaze seemed to travel up and down Kat's body, making her feel as though she were an item for sale. Which, she soon realized, she was.

"Allow me to present my beautiful daughter, Katayon." Her father turned his palms upward, as if he was proudly unveiling a creation solely of his own making. "As I have told you, she has finished with her studies, and she is very good at house chores. She loves cooking and receiving guests." He turned to the woman. "I am sure your son will be pleased with our arrangement. Do you not agree?"

Kat whipped her head around. One look at her father's face told her she shouldn't dare say a word.

"My sister does not speak to strange men," the old man said, explaining the veiled woman's silence.

Just then her father's young wife entered with a tray. He gestured for her to set it down, then nodded for her to leave the room. "Katayon, you will serve our guests their tea." He turned to the man and rubbed his hands together. "My daughter will make a fine wife for your nephew. You will see."

Kat felt the acid rise from her stomach. She swallowed hard as her father pushed her forward with a gentle shove to the back.

The woman whispered something to her brother.

"My sister says there is much work to do around the house, with her son and all his brothers."

The woman nodded.

"The tea, Katayon!"

Kat reached for the pot with a shaking hand. The woman watched silently. Kat wanted to fling the hot liquid straight at her, but instead obediently passed the steaming cup. Another cup was poured. Then Kat had an idea. She raised her left arm before setting down the tea, as if she were swatting away a bug. The woman let out a little gasp. Her brother followed her gaze. Then they leaned in toward each other and began, again, to whisper.

"Is something the matter?" Kat's father asked in a wobbly voice. "I have guaranteed that my daughter will make a good fit for your family. Our deal is still good, is it not? Khawar jan, I promise, my daughter is a strong girl. And she is younger than she appears, I swear."

"I am sure she is a good worker, but it is not that," the man said. "It is those."

The woman pointed a finger at Kat's arm, which was now hanging down by her side and completely covered. Kat's father looked confused.

"Under her sleeve," the man added.

Kat's father grabbed her arm and yanked up the sleeve, exposing the rose tattoo in all its glory. He eyed it in horror, then raised his eyes to Kat's face. He stood frozen in place with an expression that terrified her. "A thousand pardons, Khawar jan. I meant no insult."

"I appreciate your pardons, but I think that will be all for today, brother."

Kat's father scrambled to keep up with the pair as they made their way to the front door. "It is just that I didn't—"

The man turned to face him and offered a tight smile. "We thank you for your hospitality, brother. Our family will be getting back to you. We will give you an answer soon."

30

Sunday, August 22, 2021

It was Halajan who was the first to break, fed up with the waiting and the fear that went hand in hand with it. After another restless night they were all short-tempered and jumpy. Nobody could keep still, yet there was really nothing to do. Sunny tried to engage the others in conversation to help pass the time, but her attempts went nowhere.

Then Sunny's phone rang, the noise bouncing across the silent room like an alarm. All eyes were on her as she listened to the person on the other end. After a couple of minutes she placed the phone down. "My evac is supposed to happen today."

"When? What time?" Yazmina asked.

"Not sure. He said to expect a call in the next few hours."

"That is good news," Ahmet said with a nod. "Finally."

"It doesn't feel so good to me," Sunny said. "I'm not even remotely comfortable leaving before you guys do."

"Don't be ridiculous." Yazmina placed a hand on Sunny's knee. "You said yourself Candace was certain our call would come soon. You must go while you can."

"We are sure to be right behind you," Ahmet added, not really sounding so sure about it.

"We'll wait and see what happens. Hopefully your call will come too."

"Even if it does not, you have to leave. Promise me, Sunny."

"I can't do that, Yaz. You have to understand."

The coffee shop fell back into silence. Then Halajan disappeared for a while. Sunny assumed she had gone over to her rooms to rest, but when she reappeared with black streaks across her bony fingers and a smudge of dirt on her forehead it was clear something was up.

"It's all ready to go," she said as she grabbed a towel.

"What are you talking about? Are you all right, *maadar*?" Ahmet went to her side and picked up one of her hands for examination. "Are you feeling okay?"

Halajan pulled her hand away. "Of course I am. I have reconnected the battery in the car, like they taught me in driving school. We are going to the airport. My bags are already in the trunk. I have called Bashir Hadi to drive us there. There is to be no more waiting for nothing to happen."

Sunny looked up from her phone. "Oh, I don't know—"

"It has to be, Sunny jan. We will go, and you will go. We can no longer be sitting here with targets on our backs, jumping at every little sound or movement on the street outside. I cannot

221

witness my son beaten again by those animals. I cannot spend another day worrying for my grandchildren's lives. And if anything happened to you because you stayed here for us, I would never forgive myself. No, it is time to go."

Yazmina stood. "Halajan is right. If we can just get there, to the airport, they will put us on a plane. It is happening for others, so why not for us?"

"We at least have to try," Ahmet added. "If we need to turn around and come home, so be it. And then we will try again. Do you agree, Rashif?"

"I will do what my wife wishes." He took the towel and gently wiped at the grease stains on her hands.

"But it's so dangerous!" said Sunny.

"Sitting here in our house is dangerous, Sunny jan," Halajan said. "This is no time for your bossiness, not now. It will do no good. We are going."

Sunny knew there was no sense in arguing against all of them. She could only hope that their call would come before they left on their own. But around her a flurry of activity had already begun. Sunny stabbed at her phone, trying to reach Candace.

"Go tell Layla to get the girls ready," Yazmina said to Halajan as she headed to the door leading out to the back courtyard and across to her house. "Tell her to dress them in layers, to bring as many warm clothes as we are able. We may need them where we are going."

"We will put these in the car." Ahmet pointed to the pile of knapsacks and suitcases that had been waiting by the door for four days already. "I will make sure that everything is in order, nothing left behind that should not be, all in place for Bashir Hadi to watch over while we are gone."

"Promise me you will turn around at the slightest hint of trouble," Sunny said to Yaz as she nervously followed her around the room.

"Yes, of course."

"Your phones are charged?" Sunny asked, even as she watched Yazmina unplugging the devices from the sockets. "Those will be hidden on you, Hala and Layla, right? In case you are searched. Remember, use only the dummy phone that Ahmet bought. The one without anything that might get you into trouble."

"We know, Sunny."

"And keep checking your email. In case something comes through from Candace, right?"

"Right."

"Do you have enough food and water for everyone?" Sunny stuffed a box of tissues into the nearest bag. "All your documents?"

Yazmina stopped and turned to her friend. "Yes, Sunny. You know we have been prepared for days."

The two of them stood facing each other, their eyes filled with worry.

Less than an hour later, and still with no phone call, the family was standing by the car with Bashir Hadi, ready to go.

"Be careful." Sunny embraced Layla first. "It will be so nice to have you in the States again."

Next was Ahmet. Sunny hesitated, yet couldn't help but hug the man, who didn't fight it.

"Thank you, Sunny jan." Sunny could feel his body shudder with sobs.

"Stay out of trouble," she told Hala through tears that refused to stay hidden.

"Listen to your parents." She kissed Najama on the top of her head, and bent to hug little Aarezo, along with the giant pink elephant she was apparently refusing to leave behind.

"As we say at home, I'll see you on the other side."

Sunny and Yazmina held each other tight.

"I'm not so sure I like the sound of that," Yazmina replied, laughing through her tears.

And then they were through the gate, gone.

31

After two long nights alone in the locked room, Kat was hungry and exhausted. She'd refused to touch the food her father's wife kept sliding through the door. All she wanted to do was get out. But how?

The high window was firmly locked behind bars. That she knew. She could perhaps try to force the door open and make a run for it when the woman tried to bring her next meal, but she feared her father would easily catch up with her. She could listen for him going out, and perhaps then tell the woman she needed to use the bathroom. The problem with that was she hadn't heard him leave since that first morning. Surely he'd have to go out somewhere soon.

Kat scooted along the floor toward a spot near the door and struggled to stay awake for as long as she could manage with her ear pressed against the wood. She never heard a door slam, or a shouted goodbye, but after some time had passed she began to catch wind of an argument.

"Why should she have been given the opportunity to get out, and not us? Where is the fairness in that?" It was a young woman's voice. Her father's wife.

"You know I have tried," he replied. "The Taliban will never let us go once they see that I worked with the police."

"If we are to stay here in Kabul, you need to do something to make sure we'll be safe, to make them believe we are on their side."

"And what is it that you think I have been trying to do?" he snapped. It was the same terrifying voice Kat remembered him using with her mother.

But his new wife didn't seem to be so terrified. "Obviously not enough," she replied. "You cannot even control your own daughter."

Kat could not make out her father's reply.

"And now what are you going to do with her?" his wife continued. "Let her go, and give up on trying to trade her for protection for the rest of us?"

"I don't know. Perhaps this family will accept her as she is, but I honestly doubt we will even hear from them again. Maybe I will try one more time. I will ask my connection to send someone else looking for a bride."

"And have the same thing happen again? What Talib will want her with that thing on her arm? And there are sure to be more of those elsewhere on her body. Don't you know how they feel about tattoos? It is clear that your daughter does."

There was silence for a moment.

"Well, then perhaps we must do something to rid her of those ungodly stains."

In the quiet of the empty coffeehouse the ghosts came alive. As she waited for her call, Sunny wandered the room thinking about all the crazy things that had happened there, both good and bad. She could almost hear the conversations bubbling up in Dari, English, French, and Arabic, and could imagine the aromas of coffee and grease, bacon and fresh-baked bread coming from the kitchen. The buzz, the life that pulsated through this place, had been like nothing she'd ever experienced before, or since. Sunny had changed here. *Everything* about her had changed here. It was a place where anything was possible, and anything could happen.

She stood with her back to the counter, her hands on her hips, and breathed in deeply. There was the doorway where she first saw Candace, with that bleached platinum hair and those knee-high boots, the skin-tight jeans and ridiculously expensive designer bag. Sunny had been immediately put off by Candace's air of entitlement, but that didn't last long. Once she detected the fellow Southern girl buried under Candace's chichi persona, all bets were off. They'd been fast friends for too many years to count now.

Out the window she could see the patio where Jack had surprised her with Poppy, a "car dog" he had insisted on for her protection while driving. Sunny, until that moment, had hated dogs. She would never forget laughing at the petrified look on Ahmet's face as he held one end of the German shepherd's leash. Of course, the two of them eventually became fast friends as well, Ahmet throwing a ball for hours just to keep the pup amused.

As her eyes circled the walls around her, Sunny couldn't help but remember how they'd all transformed the coffeehouse for Yaz and Ahmet's wedding. She pictured the draped fabric and hanging lanterns, the flickering candles on every surface, and could feel a smile come to her face. How they had all struggled to keep this place open, both during Sunny's time in Kabul and after, when Yazmina and the others took over. Would she ever see the inside of these walls again? Would any of them?

She checked her phone for messages. Nothing from the family. They were probably still trying to get through the traffic around the airport. The whole of Kabul seemed to be heading there. Nothing from Kat, who could be high in the air over who-knows-where about now, *inshallah*. How Sunny loved that word. And no news on the time for her own evac, which could come any minute. She was ready, she thought, as a tear began to slide down her cheek.

When she first heard the crunch of shoes on the gravel she thought it might be Bashir Hadi, returned from the airport. But not that much time had passed. Even without the crazy traffic and Taliban checkpoints, it should have taken longer. The footsteps approached, heavy footsteps. Sunny grabbed a broom that was leaning against the wall and held it in front of her with two hands, like a horizontal shield.

There was a rap at the door. A male voice rang out. "*Bale, enja kas e ast?*" Hello? Is anybody there?

*

"It looks like this is as close as they will allow us to get." Bashir Hadi stopped the car by the side of the road. Around them others were pulling luggage from their vehicles, throwing bags over their arms and hoisting children onto their hips. There were empty cars and abandoned bicycles everywhere.

The family piled out of the Mercedes and into the blazing sun. Bashir Hadi helped Ahmet, placing their bags in a heap on the street. The children's backpacks were strapped onto them. Layla and Yazmina each grabbed a small suitcase on wheels and slung their handbags across their chests. Halajan and Rashif were the last to emerge.

"I thought we were told to bring only small bags," Ahmet said, pointing to a large piece of luggage still on the ground.

"I can take care of it myself," Halajan insisted. She picked up the handle and began defiantly walking away, the suitcase bouncing on its wheels behind her. After some tearful goodbyes and hurried thank-yous to Bashir Hadi, the others raced to catch up with her for fear she'd get lost in the crowd.

Indeed there were Taliban present, making sure no cars got through.

"Why do you want to leave?" one of them shouted at the mass of people passing him by. "We are good people, trying to keep peace! We forced the Americans out of our country!"

But nobody was listening. Ahmet couldn't believe how many people were descending on the airport. It was an endless flow that got denser and denser by the minute, restricting their pace to barely a shuffle. They stuck close together, Ahmet in front pulling two suitcases, Layla in the rear making sure everyone was accounted for.

They had only been walking for a few minutes when Ahmet spied another Taliban checkpoint. There were only about ten or fifteen of them, not enough to stop every Afghan determined to reach the airport gates. "Go back! Go back! Where are you going?" they'd yell, using wire and sticks against some of those managing to slip by.

Ahmet watched what others were doing, weighing his options. Those who obeyed and stopped were showing passports or green cards, or other sorts of documents, real or not. Afghan passport holders were told to go home, as were those who had no papers at all. Others were being waved through. The Talib soldiers looked tired and worn down, exhausted and overwhelmed by the attempt to stop and check the thousands and thousands of people coming at them. Ahmet decided to not chance his family getting beaten. If they were turned back, they would try another day. He pulled out the letter Candace had written, along with the spreadsheet with all their names on it, and came to a stop in front of a young Talib. He was banking on the very real possibility that the boy could barely read, that he would not be able to make sense of the words on the letter, that the fact that it was in English would be enough to get them through.

He was right. One brief look at the papers and the Talib told them to keep moving. Ahmet gathered his family around him and they shuffled forward into the hot, swelling mass. The airport gates were still almost two miles away.

When she heard the key turning in the lock Kat scrambled backward across the floor, as far away from the door as she could get. From a corner of the room she watched her father enter. When she saw that his hands were empty she relaxed, but just a little. She had heard of the lengths people would go to around here to erase tattoos, or to disguise telltale scars from suicide attempts, both, she knew, were considered un-Islamic by many. Acid was used, or boiling water. And sometimes even knives. The man would certainly be capable. Look what he did to her mother, or at the very least what he made her mother do to herself. She began to rub at her forearms without realizing she was doing it.

Her father slowly circled the small room and then sat down cross-legged on the floor across from her. "Let me ask you something," he finally said. "Did you not learn in your life about how to be a good daughter? To love and honor your father? Or did America brainwash that out of you?"

Kat didn't dare answer.

"To show that thing." He pointed at her arm. "Knowing you are putting us in danger. That is something I cannot fathom. What do you have to say to me about that, I ask you?"

Again Kat bit her tongue.

"Don't you see what I am faced with, what I have to do for my family?"

Kat jumped to her feet. "*I* am your family!" she exploded. "My mother was your family!"

"If you are my family, then you would help us and do what is right."

"What is *right*? I'd rather die than marry a Talib. I'd rather set myself on fire and die like my mother did."

"Do not speak of that in my house!"

"Do you know what you are? You're a coward. If you're threatened by the Taliban then fight back like a man."

He let out a patronizing snort. "You know nothing about how this world works."

"And you know nothing about courage, or decency, or compassion!"

Her father suddenly rose from the floor and drew back a hand. Kat stood there, defiantly looking him straight in the eye.

"You are my daughter." His words were now quiet, seething. "And you will do as I say."

The door had barely shut behind him when Kat heaved the morning tray—still covered with food—against it with all the strength she had left.

"Who are you? What do you want?" Sunny shouted through the door in her best Dari.

"My name is Haseeb."

"And?"

"I am a friend of Layla's."

"She is not here. Please go away."

"I am worried about her."

"We are all worried about everyone right now. There's nothing I can do for you."

His response was too fast for Sunny's rusty Dari.

"Slower please. I don't understand."

"Are you Sunny?" he asked in decent enough English. "I have heard about you from Layla."

"And?" Sunny asked, still a little wary.

"She has told me everything about her visit to America, about picking grapes, about a kind old man named Joe."

Sunny relaxed a bit. Nobody would know those things if they were not a true friend. "And what is Layla's favorite soft drink?" she asked, just to be sure.

The guy didn't hesitate. "Mountain Dew. She told me she even has it for breakfast with some sort of sugar cereal from America."

Sunny opened the door a crack. There stood a good-looking young man with a chiseled face and the beginnings of a beard, and eyes brimming with concern. She ushered him into the coffeehouse and locked the door behind him.

"I received a message from Layla," he said as he slipped off his shoes. "I am very worried."

"When?" Sunny asked. "What did she say?"

"It was two days ago," he began breathlessly. "She wanted to talk."

Sunny cocked her head. "So?"

"We had been—friends. But I have not been such a good friend lately. And I avoided answering right away. When I did finally answer, Layla didn't respond."

"Well, I'm sure she's not paying much attention to things like that right now. She is on the way to the airport with her family."

He ran his hands through his thick hair. "But I got a second message that night. Asking for help. At first I was suspicious. The message was in English, and Layla and I never spoke English together. I thought it had to be some sort of a setup. Things like that are happening all over right now. So I blocked the number."

"You think someone got Layla's phone?"

Haseeb shook his head. "It wasn't from her phone. Neither message was. But later I began to think that perhaps Layla got a new phone, and that it might really be her. What if it was, I thought, and she was in some kind of trouble?"

"They did get a dummy phone for the evacuation, but I'm not sure—"

"And there was a location that was sent along with the message."

"Let me see your phone." Sunny held out her hand and took a look. "That number, I know it."

"Is it Layla's?"

"No," Sunny said. "It's someone else's." She ran to the front closet and grabbed one of the burqas Ahmet had bought. "I think I'm going to need your help."

32

The crowd near the airport became too thick to navigate. The family, suffocating under their multiple layers of clothing in the relentless heat, had lugged their belongings behind them for the entire two miles only to find themselves in worsening chaos with every step they took. Their walk from the car had felt like some sort of gruesome procession—men and women, the old and the young, marching tighter and tighter together the closer they got to the gates that would either lead them to safety or slam shut in their faces. When they finally reached a standstill it was as though they had arrived in the center of a gathering storm, with nowhere to turn and no room to spare.

"This is as near as we can get!"

"What did you say?" Yazmina asked, unable to hear above the shouting around them, desperate pleas in English, Farsi,

Dari, and Pashto competing for attention from the American military on the other side of the barbed wire. *Let us in! Some of my family are inside! Hey, mister, help us! I work for an American company!* The shouts, along with the papers held high in the air as if they were golden tickets, were ignored.

They were at the third checkpoint where, on their side of the barricades, Taliban militants were standing on cars, waving their weapons in an attempt to move people away from the gate. Aarezo yanked her hand from her mother's to cover her ears as gunshots rang out. Yazmina grabbed both girls and pressed them against her pounding chest. The crowd continued to swell, crushing those in front tighter and tighter against the barricade. One of the Talib began to scream at people to sit. Ahmet frantically gestured for his family to comply as the militant's whip crashed down on a woman in front of him, tearing her skin right through her clothes. Yazmina shielded her girls' eyes. *Sit! Or you will be shot!* Some obeyed, others continued their surge forward. There was pushing, shoving. Those who came too close to the wall were lashed or beaten with cattle prods. The family huddled close together as bullets whizzed overhead, so near that Yazmina's ears began to ring. At the wall, some were trying to climb over, or hoisting others over before them.

Then, in an instant, they found themselves surrounded by a smoke so thick that they could barely breathe. Yazmina rushed to cover the girls' mouths with the edges of her scarf. She could hear Halajan hacking and gasping, but could not even see the old woman through the dense haze. Her head began to spin. "What is it?" she yelled to her husband. "They will kill us!"

"Tear gas! The Americans are throwing cylinders over from the other side of the wall!"

As a noxious layer of fog settled around them, they could see people turning and fleeing, leaving their luggage behind. Others lay prone on the ground, trying to escape the overpowering fumes. A second round of canisters were lobbed into the crowd. "Stop! Please!" someone near them yelled. "We have children!" Their cries went unheeded, lost in the pandemonium.

And through the deepening madness came a sound so familiar that for one split-second Yazmina was able to close her eyes and summon the comfort she had once felt from its clashing melodies. Across Kabul came the call to prayer.

33

Sunny and Haseeb had the taxi driver take them to the location that had been shared via Kat's phone. The small cinderblock houses were perched tightly together on a hill, curtains drawn as if nobody would dare be seen. All of Kabul, at least those not swarming to the airport, seemed to be in hiding. Sunny tugged at her own camouflage; the blue burqa that was making her sweat like a pig. She turned to Haseeb, who was adjusting the scarf she'd fashioned like a turban around his unruly hair, thinking it might help if they came across any trouble.

Sunny turned in a circle. "Which one do you think it is? She could be in one of these houses right around here, right? Or anywhere, for that matter."

Haseeb nodded as he awkwardly adjusted Ahmet's rifle on his shoulder. Then Sunny noticed a sudden movement in a window above them. A curtain had been pulled back and dropped again. It was a few beats before the front door swung open. A man appeared, his face breaking into a nervous grin. Haseeb stood up tall. Sunny was clenching her fists so hard she could feel her nails digging into her palms.

"*Khush amaden befermayen khana,*" the man said. Welcome inside my home.

"Who *is* that guy?" Sunny whispered. "And why is he inviting us in?"

At the top of the stairs the usual greetings were exchanged with Haseeb. *Salam khob asten, khush amadin, fahmil hamagi khob astan.* To Sunny he nodded politely. He stood back and allowed them to enter, gesturing to the guest room as they passed. Sunny peered awkwardly through the mesh grill that covered her eyes, searching for any sign of Kat. All she saw were closed doors, and some toys strewn around the hallway carpet.

"*Befarmayen.*" Please sit, said the man, the tight grin still plastered on his face.

They sat. Out of nowhere a young woman in a green chador silently appeared and set down a tray with tea and sweets before them. This was not, at all, what Sunny had expected.

But Haseeb was good at playing his role, and even better at playing along with whatever this man had up his sleeve. He fixed a stern look on his face and waited for the other man to speak first.

"I did not expect you to come back so soon, in just one day." He nodded toward Sunny, invisible under the burqa. "I was not quite—quite ready for you."

Haseeb didn't answer.

"I mean"—the man shifted in his seat—"it is fine that you are here. Very fine. I am happy to meet you."

Sunny's ears were desperately hunting for a sound, any sound, from around the house. If Kat were here, why was everything so quiet? And exactly who did this man—who thankfully seemed to find Sunny invisible—think she and Haseeb were? She felt a sudden buzz in her pocket and froze. Her call. *The* call. Candace would kill her. She fumbled to silence it. Shit, shit, shit. Her call, now missed. The man looked at her quizzically, then turned his attention back to Haseeb, launching into a conversation that Sunny, with her lousy Dari, couldn't follow, though she did detect the name Katayon coming up a few times. So this *was* the right place. The man gestured wildly as Haseeb nodded his head. Then the man abruptly stood, rubbed his hands together nervously, and left the room.

"What's going on?" she whispered frantically to Haseeb. "Who is he?"

"He is Kat's father," he whispered back. "He is assuming I am a Talib, and that you are my mother. He is trying to give her as a bride, to buy himself protection."

"Holy shit!"

"He thinks I am the groom, that we are here to finish the deal. He seems to be very desperate to make this happen, as if maybe he is in a very bad situation with the Taliban that can only be fixed in this way."

"Okay, okay." Sunny took a deep breath and wiped her damp palms across her burqa. "Maybe that's to our advantage. Maybe that's good. But listen, whatever happens, we need to take Kat with us now, today. We cannot leave her behind, no matter what. Think you can handle that?"

Haseeb reached down and touched the rifle he'd placed on the floor between the *toshak* and a pillow. "Do not worry. I will do whatever it takes."

"Get up!" Kat's father yanked her by the arm. "He is here. The man you are to marry. You are to come with me, now. And if you try any funny business this time, I will show you no mercy."

From the look of him, Kat's father seemed more frightened than angry.

"I don't need your mercy," she muttered.

"What did you say?" His grip on her arm tightened.

"I said I don't care what you do!"

"Keep your voice down!" he hissed as his eyes darted toward the closed door.

"Why should I? There is no way I will allow myself to be married off to some asshole Talib."

"Shut up! And I swear, if you dare to do anything to risk this you will not live to see another day."

And with that, he opened the door and shoved her through it.

The two of them sat there like lumps, the stupid Talib and his mother. Oh, what a big, strong man, sitting quietly by his mama's side. Kat was sickened by the look of him.

Her father was all smiles. "This is my daughter, Katayon," her father said to the young man.

241

Kat just stood there.

After a few awkward seconds the man in the turban spoke. "Your daughter, she does not know how to serve tea?" he asked with a nod to the pot.

Kat remained immobile, basking in her father's discomfort. He was stuck. He couldn't very well ask her to wait on the two of them, because she would refuse. And if he left her alone with these horrible people to summon his wife, Kat was bound to do something even worse.

"Of course she does. As I told your mother and your uncle yesterday, she is an excellent cook, a very hard worker. She is just being a little shy."

The Talib rolled his eyes. His mother sat there in silence. She must have been as stupid as her son, Kat thought.

"I am pleased to see you have considered overlooking the unfortunate issue from yesterday," her father said.

The Talib simply nodded. Was this loser so desperate that he and his family had decided the tattoo was okay?

"Now, would you care for some tea?" her father asked.

The old woman quickly shook her head. "No, I guess not. Thank you," said her son, following his mother's lead.

Her father took a seat, clasped his hands together, and leaned in toward the young man. "So," he cleared his throat. "Our deal, is it complete?"

The Talib seemed to be thinking. "She appears to be rather scrawny." He looked at his mother, who nodded in agreement. "I prefer a healthier, fuller girl. And she does not seem to have the spirit of someone who will be a help to my family."

Again the mother nodded, this time more forcefully.

"You will be surprised," Kat's father said. "She is very strong, and extremely obedient."

Kat couldn't help but laugh.

The Talib raised his eyebrows. "I think this one could be trouble. But nevertheless, yes. The deal is done."

Her father placed a hand over his heart and gave a little bow. "I thank you, you and your uncle and your mother, for your kindness."

"But we have come far from the provinces, and it would be a great hardship for us to return once again to Kabul. So it is a deal only if you allow us to take your daughter with us now. Today."

Her father was nodding like a dashboard bobble-head doll. "Of course, of course, brother. That is very understandable. You will not be sorry. I give you my word." He shot Kat a glare that held a thousand threats, and then he stood.

Kat looked from her father to the man with the gun by his side and weighed her options. She could make a run for the door, but there was no way she'd get far. She could grab the rifle, but they'd be sure to overpower her quickly. Then came the thought of turning the gun on herself—a thought that flooded her with both anger and fear, and with the sorrow she'd carried like a stone since her mother's death.

Suddenly she saw something that made those thoughts disappear. Those shoes. Peeking out from under the old lady's billowing burqa, over a pair of thick socks, were two brown suede Birkenstocks that she would recognize anywhere.

"It's you, right?" she said in English. Her father's head whipped around at the sound of Kat using a language he couldn't understand.

But the woman still didn't speak.

"Silence, Katayon!" her father hissed.

"Sunny," Kat continued, "if it is you under there, tap your toe three times."

Three times the rounded, clunky tip of one of the Birkenstocks hit the carpet. Kat smiled, and the Talib seemed to as well.

"What is happening here?" her father asked, looking back and forth between Kat and his visitors.

The young man shrugged his shoulders. "Perhaps your daughter is happy to be my bride."

Her father smiled nervously. "It may be so. Please, allow me to gather her belongings. I know you must be in a hurry to return to your home." He scurried down the hall, obviously anxious to get her out the door before things turned south.

Kat fought to contain herself in his absence, feeling the same.

But they made it. After a few cursory goodbyes between the men, and one final look from Kat at her father, they were out on the street. Kat was dying to throw her arms around Sunny, but didn't dare, knowing her father might be watching from his window. Instead she turned to the stranger next to her and said, "So, my new husband. Tell me, where will you be taking me for our honeymoon?"

34

Monday, August 23, 2021

Daybreak brought no relief from the misery of spending a sleepless night on the rock-hard ground outside the airport gates. The growing crowd had been subdued by threats and weapons into a relative calm, an uneasy quiet that was interspersed with desperate attempts to breach the lines of Taliban on one side of the perimeter, and the Americans on the other. Now tempers were rising along with the sun as it climbed higher into the sky. Any little movement was cause for another surge against the gates, more shots fired into the air, more tear gas, more sticks and whips brought down with a crack. Amid the havoc were a few moments of mercy, American soldiers taking pity and tossing bottles of water over the wall, encouraging people to drink, to stay hydrated. *Stay calm*, they shouted.

Just sit down! No noise! Some obeyed, others could not control their impatience. Yazmina did her best not to show her fear and frustration in front of the children, but inside she knew none of them could tolerate this situation much longer. She was most worried about Halajan, usually so hearty but now slumped over, her tiny frame sagging between the support offered by Rashif and Layla on either side. It was clear that the hours spent in the sweltering heat and suffocating crush were taking their toll.

"I'm *hungry*, Mama," Aarezo whined, one hand clutching her elephant.

Yazmina rifled through her bag for some crackers. What if they ran out of food? Then what? Would they be forced to turn away like some of the others before them who she'd seen shuffling back against the tide with tears in their eyes, their shoulders slumped in defeat?

"Keep your eye on Hala," Yazmina said to Layla. "Make sure she takes some water."

Then, in a flash, every single person around them seemed to rise in unison. *The gate is opening!* The words traveled like lightning through the crowd. People were pushing, shoving forward, waving papers in the air. The military people were shouting. *Move! Move! Move!*

Ahmet grabbed hold of the children's hands. "Stay close!" he yelled to the others.

In the stampede Yazmina turned to see Rashif struggling with Halajan's huge suitcase. "Leave it behind!" she shouted to her mother-in-law, who didn't seem to hear above the roar of the crowd. Things were becoming even more frantic, the crowd tightening around her, making it hard to breathe, even harder to move. The distance between Yazmina and Halajan, Rashif, and Layla grew wider as others pushed their way in. The next time she was able to find enough space to pivot to check on them she saw a woman in front of Halajan trip, taking Halajan down with her. Rashif grabbed her in his arms, but her suitcase was trampled. Yazmina watched as the familiar bundles of papers tied in colored ponytail holders were strewn across the dusty ground. Rashif's love letters, written in his fine penmanship so many, many years before. Yazmina's heart broke at the sight.

But the moment was fleeting. The military continued to scream and wave their guns. The children were petrified. The crowd swelled, and Yazmina felt herself being lifted through the gate. Everything was out of control. Yazmina heard Ahmet scream the children's names and looked up to see his two empty hands waving frantically in the air. Behind them Layla was calling out for Halajan and Rashif.

"The gate, it has closed!" Layla grabbed Yazmina's arm.

"The children!" Their daughters were gone, lost in a sea of people.

"Najama! Aarezo!" Yazmina shouted across the hordes on the tarmac.

"Aarezo! Najama!" Ahmet echoed.

Layla grabbed the arm of an American soldier standing nearby. "Two of our family have been left behind!" She pointed to the gate. "They are old. Please, you need to let them through!"

The man held out his rifle sideways and used it to push her away.

"I beg you! Please!"

He turned his back on her and began yelling orders at the crowd.

With one quick glance at the shuttered gate, Layla pushed her way through to join her sister and Ahmet in their search for the children. The chaos inside the gates was as bad as it was on the outside. Despite the soldiers' attempts to get everyone to line up, scores of people were running across the tarmac.

Yazmina and Ahmet and Layla remained not far from the gate, reluctant to leave Halajan and Rashif behind. Yet they still had not spied Najama or Aarezo. They continued to call out their names, venturing farther and farther away from the gate. Before they even realized, they'd been herded into what was becoming a line of people as long as the Kabul River.

"I will go look for them," Ahmet told the others. He handed Layla his phone. "Try to call my mother and Rashif. See if they are all right."

But the minute he stepped out of the line he was shoved back into place by a soldier. "You leave the line, you leave the airport," the man threatened.

"My children!" Ahmet shouted in English. "Don't you understand? I need to find them!" But the man had already moved on. Ahmet grabbed the phone from Layla and frantically punched in a number. "Perhaps Candace has connections here, perhaps she can help."

Layla shook her head. "No signal."

"Do something!" Yazmina jumped up and down, desperately trying to see over the heads of others.

"I'm trying!" The blood had drained from Ahmet's face.

He reached out for the arm of another passing soldier. "Help us! Please!"

But the man pulled away before Ahmet could explain.

"*Najama! Aarezo!*" he shouted with all his might. "*Where are you?*"

Sunny was pacing across the coffeehouse floor.

"Do not even think about going out there. At least not without me by your side." Bashir Hadi had returned from driving the family to the airport the day before to find the coffeehouse empty. He had assumed Sunny had gotten a last-minute evacuation call, until he noticed her suitcase still sitting by the door. That's when he began to panic, worrying that the Taliban had returned to the coffeehouse, or perhaps that she'd encountered some other type of danger. But then, to his great relief, she had shown up, and with her were Kat and a young man, Haseeb, who had insisted on staying with them until Kat and Sunny were safely out of Kabul.

Through the window Sunny could see Kat and Haseeb seated across from each other in the front courtyard, engrossed in conversation. They were all on edge—worried about further trouble ahead, anxious to hear from the family, waiting to get word about another plan for Kat and Sunny's evacuation, since Sunny had missed the call from the day before.

"Any word on your situation?" Sunny asked Bashir Hadi, who was busying himself behind the counter.

"Nothing yet. There seems no way for me to get back to Delhi. At least not now. And Sharifa, I think maybe she is better off where she is. She should not be here at this time. Neither of us should be. You are aware of how they treat people like us. They hate the Hazaras."

"I am aware."

"You know the last time the Taliban took over Kabul, back in '96, they had a saying. 'Tajiks to Tajikistan, Uzbeks to Uzbekistan, and Hazaras to *goristan*—graveyard.' And the fighters, they made good on that threat."

"Well, for what it's worth, they're saying they'll protect all ethnic groups this time around."

"And you believe that? You've heard about the massacres in the provinces, have you not? I am too frightened even to go to the mosque. And driving to the airport yesterday? My heart was in my throat the whole time, thinking I might be stopped and questioned."

"I know. You're right." Sunny plopped down in a chair. "It's just all so unbelievable. Who would have ever thought back then that twenty years later we'd be sitting here hiding out like this, like a bunch of scared mice? It's as though none of it made any difference. All that effort, all that hope. Did any of it mean anything?"

Bashir Hadi wiped his hands on a dishtowel and came to join Sunny. "Of course it did. It meant that I got the chance to meet so many people from so many different backgrounds, with so many different ideas. That, for a time in my life, I was doing something far beyond what I had ever imagined. It meant that over those years, in this coffeehouse, I became a part of a family. And it meant that I found a friend like you."

*

Kat could see why Layla had been attracted to this guy. Haseeb was definitely hot, with a Brad Pitt jawline and Bollywood hair. But that didn't mean she was about to let him off the hook for pulling a fast one on her friend. "You know, Layla is a truly awesome girl. You are aware of that, aren't you?"

"She is the most amazing woman I have ever met in my entire life," Haseeb agreed.

Kat nodded. "I consider her my best friend. And you know what that means."

Haseeb looked confused.

"It means," Kat continued, "that I will always have her back no matter what. That if anyone dares to hurt her they'll have me to answer to."

Now Haseeb shifted in his seat, his eyes concentrating on the pebbled ground below.

"I've seen her hurt before. That time, I was partially to blame. I'll never forgive myself." Kat knew that what had happened between Layla and Sky, Kat's boyfriend at the time, was simply an unrequited infatuation on Layla's part. A childish crush. "She was just a kid, a teenager. But that doesn't mean she's any less vulnerable now."

Haseeb still didn't respond.

"Well, are you going to explain yourself, or what?"

"There is no way on earth I'd want to hurt Layla." The words came gushing out. "What happened, the way I handled it— I was wrong. I'm nothing but a coward."

"Well, I don't know about that, based on you rushing in for my rescue the way you did, without even knowing me."

"That's different. I was a coward not to come forward and tell Layla the truth. And now she's gone, and I'll probably never see her again. I will never have the chance to explain." The poor guy looked as though he were about to cry.

"So how about you start with me?" Kat sat back in the chair and folded her arms, waiting.

Haseeb looked at the sky. After a moment he began. "So, when I was younger, really just a boy, my family had discussions about an engagement between me and the daughter of their close friends. I never took it too seriously. I figured that by the time I was grown it would be forgotten, that it probably wasn't very meaningful in the first place. But it seems that now Afghan families everywhere are scrambling to marry off their young daughters, worried about the dangers they might face with the Taliban. Apparently these friends felt the same way, so the pressure was on. My parents felt obligated to honor their word, and I felt bound to be a dutiful son to my parents. It all happened so fast."

"So you've agreed to marry this person, and you haven't told Layla?"

Haseeb dropped his head into his hands. "I should have said something right away, but I was ashamed. And when I didn't, it just became harder and harder. I couldn't find the words."

"When's the big wedding?"

Haseeb looked up at Kat. "That's just it. There is no wedding. This girl, she apparently had her own ideas. She didn't want to be married. Imagine my surprise." He laughed a little. "All she wanted was to leave Afghanistan, to go live her life elsewhere. And now she is gone, just like Layla."

Kat reached for his hand and then withdrew, remembering where she was. "You'll get your chance to explain everything to Layla. And you never know; fate can be a funny thing. Maybe someday, somewhere, your paths will cross again."

35

Yazmina could barely speak. Was this what they call being in shock? All she knew was she wanted to die, right there on the tarmac. Warned by the military that if they left their spot they'd be forced to exit the airport, they'd spent the entire night huddled in place with hundreds of others outside a hangar. And still no sign of the children, or of Halajan and Rashif. Perhaps those two had turned around toward home, but how could they even think of leaving the airport without finding their children? She had seen a number of planes taking off. What if her daughters had been forced onto a flight without her? Would Najama know enough to be able to find a way to connect with them from a foreign country? *Why* hadn't she thought to write phone numbers on her children's clothing? *Why* had she led them into this horrendous situation? When she closed her eyes all she could see were her daughters' faces, scared and confused. But when she opened them there was the reality: hordes of Afghans sitting on the hot ground around her, none of them Najama or Aarezo.

It was a complete nightmare. They'd been directed to settle in the middle of what was clearly an area meant for garbage—metal, wood, plastic everywhere. The dust was thick in the air, stirred up constantly by the passing military vehicles and by the planes starting their engines for takeoff. Yazmina could feel her cheeks burning from the sun.

Next to her Ahmet, once again, stood and shouted out for his children, his voice hoarse and weak. He'd begged every passing soldier, every translator for help, had provided descriptions of the children, of their clothing. But still nothing. Again he was barked at to sit—or else. He slumped back down and handed Yazmina a bottle of water, insisting she drink. Earlier he had tried to get her to eat, but gave up after a few bites of a cracker left her gagging. Ahmet had still not been able to reach his mother and Rashif, or Sunny or Candace, or anybody for that matter. Service was spotty. Nobody around them seemed able to get a phone signal. Yazmina stayed close to her husband and sister, praying for a miracle.

Zarween placed a hand on her belly and was met with the jerk of a tiny limb. She could only hope that the growing life inside her did not feel the stress and discomfort of its mother. It was now becoming so hot in the hangar that it felt like an oven on high, with the breath of so many people, hundreds of them, filling the air. The night had been even worse—so cold on the concrete floor, with nothing for cover but a sheet of dirty plastic they'd found among the empty boxes and used water bottles, the paper trash that was piled high around them. And the smell! There was the stench of the garbage, yes. But on top of that there was the stink of human waste, with many unwilling to be escorted by the military to the washroom for fear of missing their opportunity to get on a flight.

The littler of the two girls was, thank goodness, still asleep with her head on Zarween's lap. She had cried long into the night, despite Zarween's assurances that they would find her mother and father. Now the girl was curled on her side, holding fast to a toy pink elephant that was almost half her size. The older one—Najama was her name—had been trying hard to keep a brave face, but Zarween had caught her crying too when she thought nobody was looking.

"I should try to ask for help again," said her husband, Sayed. Both their hearts had broken at the sight of the two children the day before, scared and alone as the crowd swirled around them, nobody giving them even the tiniest glance. Though Sayed and Zarween had just been told to stand in preparation for entering the hangar after sitting outside for two days, they knew they had to do something to help these little ones locate their parents. But the military was trying to keep everyone in place. They were advised not to leave their spot. Yet how were they supposed to abandon these children who so desperately needed someone's help?

Sayed had lifted the smaller girl onto his shoulders to see if she might be able to spy her family, and used what little English he knew to ask the passing soldiers for their help. None seemed to have the patience to even try to understand. One soldier did point them in the direction of a translator, but he was too busy helping control the crowds to be of any assistance. Their only hope was that perhaps the girls' parents were behind them and would be ushered into the hangar as well.

So far, though, they'd had no luck. Inside the hangar they were surrounded by soldiers who told Sayed and Zarween just to sit—don't move, don't stand. They had, along with everyone else, been asked to show their documents, and even though they tried to explain that the children were lost, not theirs, nobody knew quite what to do with them. They were all issued bracelets and told to stay put. And now the night had passed, and they were still there, waiting to be told what to do next, hot and tired yet grateful to at least be shaded from the rising sun.

Sayed lifted his arms and stretched, his body aching from another night on the ground. Zarween used the tip of her scarf to wipe the sweat from Aarezo's cheeks. All night she'd listened to planes taking off, escaping from the hell that had come knocking at their door. She and Sayed had fled to Kabul from the north, after the Taliban had forced people from their homes in retaliation for cooperating with the Afghan government. They'd seen their house looted and burned to the ground. Staying in Afghanistan meant being trapped in the clutches of the Taliban forever or, worse yet, murdered. Leaving meant freedom to start a new life, with a new baby. Zarween prayed they hadn't missed that chance.

"Don't worry," she whispered to Najama. "I am sure that your mother and father are somewhere behind us." The truth was,

Zarween was beginning to doubt that the children's parents had even made it through the airport gates in the first place. If they had, surely they all would have found each other by now.

Hours passed. The couple parceled out the water and packaged food they had been given by the military to the children, Sayed insisting that Zarween take his share. "For the baby," he said with a sad little smile. They were all exhausted, worn down by the heat, the stress, and the anxiety, and by the sheer horror of the nightmare that was unfolding before their very eyes.

Suddenly they found themselves swept up in a surge of activity. Everyone was being directed to rise and move toward the front of the hangar. They gathered their things and joined the others. Zarween's heart was racing. The line began to move forward. What would happen to these children? Could she and Sayed afford to take the chance of missing a flight for the possibility of reuniting them with their parents? Or should they, could they, go ahead, and take the girls with them? Her baby began to kick, as if trying to send her an answer in an unspoken language only the two of them shared.

36

"The line, it's moving." Ahmet held out a hand for Yazmina and helped her up from the ground. Layla took hold of her and her sister's bags. The three of them stood frozen, all thinking the same thoughts. There was no way they could continue toward the planes without Halajan and Rashif, yet neither could they turn back home without first finding the children.

The line inched forward toward the hangar. Again the three of them were calling out the girl's names. "We can't leave them." Yazmina spoke as if to herself. "We cannot leave our children," she repeated, over and over. Then the line stopped moving. A group ahead of them had been shepherded inside. The rest were told to wait.

"And my mother? What do we do about my mother and Rashif?"

"We need to get out of this line and find the girls and go home," Yazmina said.

"If we get out of this line they will make us leave the airport. And we can't leave the airport without our children." Ahmet jabbed at his phone. "Still no signal." He slammed the phone against his leg. "If only we could get someone to pay attention to our situation!"

"Najama! Aarezo!" Yazmina felt her knees buckle.

Ahmet reached out to keep her from falling. "We will find them, *azizam*. Please stay strong."

Keep your families together! Have your documents ready! Inside the hangar a man in a chair was checking papers and distributing bracelets. Ahmet led Yazmina and Layla forward until, once again, they found themselves at a dead stop. Still no sign of the rest of the family, still no phone service. When they were moved again, it was toward a second hangar, where they were to be fingerprinted.

It was two hours before they got through that process. By now Yazmina was numb, so sick with worry that she felt as though she would die. Outside once again, she shaded her eyes from the blinding sun bouncing off a huge hulk of a plane not more than fifty yards away.

It was stop and start, stop and start. They were sandwiched in, being carried along by the force of others. Yazmina struggled to get free, screaming her children's names. And then she saw it. A giant pink elephant and, almost buried beneath it, her daughter.

"Aarezo!" she shouted.

Her daughters dashed across the tarmac into their mother's arms.

Yazmina held them tight, tears running down her dusty cheeks. "My babies, my loves."

Following the children were a man and a woman, with tears in their eyes as well.

"You found my children?" Ahmet asked the man as he approached.

"We did. We have been trying to locate you since yesterday. *Khoda ra hazar bar shokor.*" A thousand thanks to Allah.

Ahmet reached for the stranger's hand, then pulled him in for a tight hug.

They began to move forward together as the pace picked up once again. Then a uniformed arm appeared as if out of nowhere, blocking their way. "Stop!" A man as big as a horse gestured for the couple who had found the girls to leave the line. They looked back at him, confused. He called over a translator.

"He says you are not in this group."

"But we have already passed through the hangars." The man held out his bracelet for inspection.

The translator shook his head. "Your plane, it has left."

Again the line stopped moving.

"But our home, it is gone. We have nothing. Please, we beg him to have a heart. We will not survive here." He pointed to his pregnant wife.

"Tell them they have to get on the bus," the soldier told the translator. He placed one hand on his rifle and with the other pointed to a bus parked on their left. "Over there."

"But where will it take them?" Ahmet asked.

"Out," the soldier said. "They'll have to leave the airport." He called over a fellow soldier, a woman, to escort them away, as he continued down the line with the translator.

"But they have nowhere to go!" Ahmet called out.

The woman burst out crying and Yazmina rushed to console her. The soldier approached, her eyes weary beneath her dusty helmet. She reached out to take the woman by the arm but hesitated, her gaze dropping to the hand the woman held protectively against her belly. Then she took one furtive look over her shoulder and quickly gestured for the couple to move forward with the others, toward the waiting plane.

Bashir Hadi handed Sunny a steaming latte. "Bless you," she said after taking a sip. She was the first one up, besides him. Kat had yet to appear, nor had Haseeb, who had insisted on staying the night. Halajan and Rashif were still sleeping, exhausted by their ordeal at the airport. They'd arrived back at the coffeehouse the evening before, looking as though they'd been dragged through the streets. They shared the story about what had happened to them, how they'd been cut off from the others when the gates shut. They'd stayed put for a while, pressed in among the desperate crowd, waiting to see if they'd open again. But when Halajan fainted, Rashif knew it was time to get her back home.

A taxi driver had taken pity on them, denying others his services in order to help Rashif usher Hala into the cab. Halajan had arrived at the coffee-shop door pale, her usually sharp eyes hollow and dim. The trauma had clearly taken its toll.

Sunny picked up her phone and called Candace. "Did I wake you?"

"Are you kidding me? I haven't slept in weeks. You okay?"

"Fine. They made it through the gate. Except for Hala and Rashif." She'd already filled in Candace on Kat's kidnapping and rescue the day before.

"Shit. Where are they?"

"Here. They'll be okay. But you're gonna have to add them to whatever plan you're cooking up to get me and Kat out."

"Shit. That is not going to be easy."

"What ever is?"

"You don't understand, Sunny. It's become impossible to get *anyone* out. Believe me. I've called in every favor in the book. Even your friend Brian is trying to help by leaning on the academic community to make waves. We're all trying, but nothing is happening. The family simply isn't considered high risk enough."

"That's crazy! What the hell else needs to happen to them before anyone cares?"

"I get it. But they're not eligible for special immigrant visas. They didn't work with the troops or with diplomats or government contractors. They're not news anchors or judges or parliament members. And even some of *those* guys are having trouble getting out. Yaz and the rest, they're simply not a priority for our government, or *any* government for that matter."

"That sucks, Candace. What can we do? Hala and Rashif *have* to get out with me and Kat."

"I won't give up, Sunny. But I have to be realistic."

"Well, then, you'll just have to work your magic. You've got this, girlfriend."

"Ha! I've got something, all right, but I'm not sure what."

"At least the others are through the gate. Fingers crossed."

"Honestly, Sunny? It will be a miracle if they actually get out. I really wish they hadn't gone ahead without any plan."

"I know."

"And you, missing that call."

"What? I was supposed to leave Kat to be married off to the Taliban?"

"That's not what I'm saying. This whole thing is just so damn frustrating. One minute I'm told that someone inside the airport will help me, that I'll get a call. I wait up all night, and nothing. I reach out to people at all hours, from all parts of my past. I even approached the mother of an old high-school friend, hearing he'd become a big military contractor, thinking they might want to help out a hometown girl. Nothing. I'm calling on Democrats, Republicans, even hard-core Trumpers—I feel like I've been selling off my soul, bit by bit. I've sent out tons of photos of the kids—anything to garner some sympathy. You would not believe the hours I've put in trying to get info on *anyone* organizing charters. It's always *check back tomorrow*, or *I need to wait until I hear from my person on the ground*. The whole thing is so unbelievably fucked up. It's like the wild west out there."

"Oh, Candace. I am so sorry."

"I'm not the one to be sorry for, Sunny. Look, I need to go. Keep your phone on, and charged. And make sure you guys are ready to move fast. If everything goes right, it's all supposed to happen tonight."

Tonight. That would mean that within a couple of days at most, she'd be back on Twimbly Island. It was hard to fathom, returning to somewhere so far removed from all this. How would she be able to help from afar should the others not get out?

She didn't even want to think about going home, except for one thing. She missed Brian, in a way that made her happy and confused, excited and guilty, all at the same time.

Sunny took her cup and headed toward the back courtyard and Hala's house. She was greeted by laughter and the smell of smoke.

"Want one?" Hala held out a pack of Marlboros.

"What on earth could you two be finding funny?" Sunny asked, her eyes going from Hala to Kat and back again.

The old woman chuckled. "You know what Rumi says."

Sunny waited as Hala took a pull from the cigarette, exhaling into the morning sky.

"*Laugh as much as you breathe.*"

"You two keep smoking those and you won't be doing either much longer." Sunny took the pack from Hala's hand and helped herself.

"What else are we supposed to do?" Kat passed her the lighter. "Any news?"

"Not yet. But don't worry. Candace is working on it."

"And nothing from the airport?"

"Nope. It's possible that their phones are dead. But from what I understand, the signals might have been jammed."

The three of them inhaled in unison and then exhaled as a helicopter churned overhead. Halajan offered a wave to the sky.

Suddenly Haseeb came barreling through the door. "Quick! You must hide!"

Sunny's blood turned to ice in her veins. "What's going on?"

"Someone is at the gate. I am going with Bashir Hadi to see." He glanced nervously over his shoulder. "Go!"

The three of them headed swiftly and silently across the courtyard to Halajan's house, where a sleepy-eyed, rumpled Rashif hurried them through the door.

"You know I must turn back," Ahmet was saying to Yazmina as they neared the ramp leading up into the belly of the plane. "I must make sure they are safe at home."

Layla watched as her sister nodded sadly.

"It is my duty as a son to take care of them."

"Of course."

"You will still go?"

Yazmina hesitated, her eyes brimming with tears. "How can we allow our children to be raised in a place like this?" She turned toward the continuing chaos on the tarmac. "To live in constant hiding, to have to pay the price for the choices we made with our lives."

Now it was Ahmet who nodded.

"But I will have to believe that you will be following us soon, all three of you. Without that belief, I—"

"Of course, *azizam*. Of course. Candace will help. It will all be okay."

But Layla could tell that neither of them were convinced of that. Who knew what was going to happen day by day in this place, even hour by hour? They both had to be living with the devastating possibility that they might not ever see the other again.

Layla was also well aware of the risk of staying, especially after that night the Taliban came to the coffee shop. And she couldn't help but feel as though she might have been to blame. She knew she'd been careless online, too outspoken. She hadn't said a word to anyone about the death threats she'd been receiving on Instagram. She also knew how hard it was to lose a parent. She'd lost both. She looked at her nieces—clinging to their mother, accepting kisses on the head from their father as he struggled to say goodbye—and made a decision.

Together, the five of them were edging closer to the plane, Ahmet reluctant to leave his family's side. Now her sister was full-on sobbing, Aarezo hugging her waist and Najama doing her best to comfort her mother.

Bring it in! Bring it in! A soldier with a rifle was herding the crowd into tight, single-file order. Layla hung back to allow a family of six to squeeze themselves into a space between her and the others. Ahmet gave the children one last hug and took a long look at his wife. Layla watched as her sister neared the ramp and took a step up before directing her daughters to board ahead of her. Ahmet, still by her side, hesitated.

"*Move! Let's keep it moving!*" shouted a soldier.

Ahmet turned to leave, locking eyes with Layla, now fifteen feet behind.

"Go!" she shouted to him. "I am staying. I will watch over Hala and Rashif. Just go!" As she backed away from the line she saw her sister freeze on the ramp. Layla blew her a kiss, then ran.

37

In a blink the coffee shop was full of life again. Bashir Hadi rushed about making sure everyone was properly fed; Halajan and Rashif were resting in the house across the courtyard; Kat was busy with her phone, no doubt texting with C.J.; and Haseeb and Layla were huddled over a table on the front patio, deep in conversation.

It had been Layla whom Bashir Hadi and Haseeb had found standing at the gate earlier that day. The description she gave of the situation at the airport had been beyond belief. Sunny couldn't imagine how terrifying it must have been for Yazmina and Ahmet, losing their children amid all that madness. What a relief it was that they'd boarded a plane, even if none of them knew where it was headed.

"Could be Abu Dhabi, Kosovo, Doha," Candace was saying as Sunny took her phone out to the back courtyard to speak in private. "Those places are the lily pads, waiting spots for processing, vaccines. I'm sure we'll hear from them soon."

"I hope so. And from there? What will happen?"

"They'll probably end up at a military base here in the US for more processing. I've already been working with an immigration lawyer on their humanitarian parole. Hopefully they won't be stuck there for too long. I'm on top of it."

"Have I told you lately how awesome you are?"

"Nope. I don't believe so. Tell me again."

"Don't get greedy."

Candace sighed. "I can't wait to see your face again."

"Likewise." Sunny paused at the sound of gunfire in the distance. "Any progress on Hala and Rashif? And now Layla— she would be considered high risk, am I right?"

Candace paused. "You're going to have to get used to the idea of going without them, Sunny. I'm doing everything I can. Everyone is. C.J., Brian—hell, even my ex-husband the ex-ambassador is on the case. But things might not happen fast enough. The clock is ticking. And if you don't take this next evac, I don't know how long it will be before you get another chance."

Sunny entered the front patio through the coffeehouse door looking as though she'd aged twenty years in a day. She approached the table where Layla sat across from Haseeb, what looked like a forced smile etched on her face. "You're all set, right?" she asked Layla.

"I haven't even unpacked. So, yes, I'm ready."

"Candace said it could happen at any time." Sunny's eyes moved from Layla to Haseeb and back again. "I'll leave you two alone."

"She is a very brave woman," Haseeb said once Sunny was inside. "Getting your friend Kat away from that place? Brilliant."

"In America they'd call her a 'piece of work'."

"A piece of work," Haseeb repeated. "And you, what will they be calling you?"

"That Afghan girl, probably."

"Come on, Layla. Surely your voice will be as strong in America as it is here in Afghanistan."

"And what am I supposed to be fighting for over there? More extra-skinny cappuccinos?"

Haseeb smiled. "Every place has its issues, its need for those who speak out for justice. And what is wrong about fighting for people here from over there?"

"I would just be one more of those talking heads. Blah blah blah. No, I need to be in the *middle* of things, in the same shoes as those whose rights I'm fighting for, with my heart feeling the same pain. That can't happen while I'm lounging at the beach waiting for the sun to set. Trust me, I know. I've been there."

"Well, you are going to have to figure it out. No matter what you do, I know that you will never truly leave all this behind."

And you, Layla thought to herself. I will never truly leave you behind, either. "What about you? Your family?" she asked. "What will you do?"

"We are trying to make our plan." Haseeb shrugged. "There are so many of us, with all the aunts and uncles and cousins.

My mother won't go unless every single one of us can leave together." He laughed a little. "We'd take up a whole plane, just my family."

"And you would never go without your parents, am I right?"

Haseeb thought about that for a minute. "I guess if I had some way to go ahead and make things ready for the rest of them, I would. But I haven't figured that out. At least not yet."

"I know you will, *inshallah*."

Haseeb's eyes turned to the sky. "Layla, do you ever wonder what it would have been like, had we met in another time, or another place?" His hand had inched its way across the table toward hers, as if it had a mind of its own.

Layla could almost sense his skin against hers. "It's a useless exercise." She sighed. "Besides, we wouldn't be who we are without this time, this place. And the man that you are, he is the Haseeb that I l—"

Haseeb smiled in a way Layla had never seen before. He gave a quick glance over both his shoulders and leaned in toward her. "I love you too, Layla," he whispered. "And I will never forget you, I will never forget us."

38

"Why hasn't Candace answered?" Sunny paced back and forth across the coffee-shop floor.

"You know you're making me crazy, don't you?" Kat pushed a chair toward Sunny. "Sit."

"How can I sit? I'm a wreck!"

"We're all wrecks. But you wearing a groove into that floor isn't doing anybody any good."

Darkness had fallen. Sunny had received the call with instructions for her and Kat's evacuation. In less than an hour, the two of them were supposed to get themselves to the designated location—a gas station fifteen minutes north of the airport. Just her and Kat, and nobody else. She was assured that if she followed instructions, all would go well.

She'd told Bashir Hadi to have the car ready and immediately fired off a flurry of texts to Candace.

What's happening with the others?

Any progress?

What do we do about everyone?

It was an hour before she finally heard back. *PLEASE just follow the instructions, Sunny.*

Now Sunny stood at the coffee-shop counter with her phone in her hand, watching the seconds go by. "What if she can't do anything for them? Then what?"

"I don't know," Kat replied. "I don't even want to think about it."

Sunny heard the door from the back courtyard open. "I think it is time to go, Miss Sunny."

She looked up to see Bashir Hadi dangling the car keys from his fingers. And behind him stood Hala, Rashif, and Layla, dressed and ready. With one quick glance at Kat, Sunny clapped her hands like a drill sergeant. "Let's do this! Now!"

Kat was out the door in a flash, with Layla following stoically behind.

Rashif turned to his wife. "Where are your things, *ishqam*, my love?"

Halajan pointed to a small satchel sitting by the door. "That is it. All I need is my family; all I need is you." She took his hand. "Come," she said to Sunny. "Bashir Hadi will have the engine running."

"I'll be right there." Sunny turned to give the coffee shop one final farewell. She saw a room simmering with the warmth of friendships that crossed all borders, of people from every corner of the earth united by the bonds that come quick in the face of danger. She heard the babble of a dozen languages,

273

felt the spirit of love and the pain of loss, smelled the smoke of battle and the sweetness of hyacinths bursting in the spring. And there, in his favorite spot against the wall, sat the ghost of Jack, his million-dollar smile lighting up the place as if it were noon instead of night. She offered a smile back just in time, before the image faded slowly from view.

"Thank you," she said out loud. "Thank you," she repeated to no one and everyone before closing the door behind her.

There was silence in the car as they wound their way through the dark streets. With one stop by the Taliban, all could be lost. As they neared the airport the traffic became denser. Even at this late hour the streets were full of people descending on foot, dragging their belongings with them. But on the north side of the airport, things were somewhat quieter.

"There it is." Sunny pointed through the windshield at the gas station.

Directly across from it was a corridor that seemed to have been slapped together out of barbed wire and Hesco barriers. Bashir Hadi pulled over and turned off the engine. From the other side of the street Sunny saw a bearded man in camo approaching, looking back and forth from his phone to her.

"Are you the bride?" the man called out.

"No, she is with the groom," Sunny answered, using the code she'd been given. She jumped out of the car with Kat close behind.

The man grabbed a flashlight from a holster on his hip and shined it straight at them as he neared. Sunny shaded her eyes with one arm.

"Whoa, whoa, whoa!" the man shouted as he stopped dead in his tracks, his free hand going for his rifle. "What the hell?"

Sunny turned to see Hala stepping from the car. "She is my friend! My family!" she shouted back.

"Stay right there!"

A second man in uniform, rifle in hand, ran into the street to join him.

"The orders are for two people only. Two Americans!"

"They are not taking us, Sunny jan?" Hala gripped her arm. "But I thought—"

"It has been arranged!" Rashif appeared by Sunny's side. "We are on a list! Our friend Candace—"

"Take the Americans!" the second man said to his partner, pointing his gun toward the old couple. "No Afghans!" he shouted toward them. "Do you understand?"

"I'm trying to get a hold of Candace!" Layla yelled from inside the Mercedes.

"Try C.J.!" Sunny shouted to Kat.

"We need to hurry!" the man in camo barked. He pulled out a two-way radio from his vest. "Get them out of here!"

"Just give us a minute!" Sunny pleaded.

"What is going on?" Now Bashir Hadi was out of the car.

"Get back in the car!"

"Please, I am just the driver. I am only trying to—"

"I said back in the car! Or I'll shoot!"

Bashir Hadi backed up.

"Candace is trying!" Layla cried out.

"Please," Sunny tried. "I beg you. Can't you see that these two are old and fragile? Can't you find just a little space on the plane? The rest of their family are already on their way out. You wouldn't want to separate a family, would you?"

The man, trying to get through to someone on his radio, ignored her plea. Kat was frantically explaining the situation to C.J.

"They *cannot* be here!" the man shouted. His radio crackled. He checked his watch. "You two." He pointed with his chin at Sunny and Kat. "Let's go."

Sunny turned to her Afghan friends with tears in her eyes. "I don't know what to do. I can't—"

The man's radio crackled again. This time he spoke. "I have the two Americans. But there are some others here, some Afghans."

They all stood quietly while he listened to a jumbled reply.

"Yes, sir. That's right." Another jumbled reply. "Copy that. Are you positive, sir? There are three of them."

Sunny held her breath.

"Yes, three," the man repeated.

"There are two," came a small voice from inside the car. "There are only two."

Sunny turned and peered into the back seat of the Mercedes. "Layla, you can't—"

"We need to move, and we need to do it now!" The soldier took hold of Halajan's bag.

"*Khoda hafiz!*" Halajan called back as the man began to shepherd the old couple across the street. May God protect you.

"Layla!" Kat took a step toward her friend.

Layla held up a hand. "Go. Please. I'll be fine."

"Hurry!" the soldier shouted from the other side of the road.

Sunny grabbed Kat's hand, and together with Halajan and Rashif they hurried toward the airport, and home.

39

Saturday, December 25, 2021

Sunny cranked up the music, singing along as she placed the red-and-green plaid napkins around the table set for eleven. *That's the jingle bell rock!* Her brand-new Christmas apron sparkled with sequined snowflakes, and in the reflection in the window she could see the red-and-green bulbs hanging from her earlobes blinking on and off along with the rhythm of the song. She had always loved Christmas and everything about it. In Afghanistan Sunny was famous for her Kabul Christmas parties, where everyone who was anyone vied for a seat in the coffeehouse for a sumptuous feast of turkey with all the trimmings. Her Christmases since then had been fine—some better than others—but Sunny had never quite managed to recreate the vibe from those days in Kabul. This year, however, was a different story.

"Think this is enough?"

Sunny turned to see Kat and C.J. at the front door, their arms laden with freshly cut logs. Behind them Brian was scraping the mud from the bottom of his boots. Sunny took a bundle of wood from Kat and placed it on the hearth next to the fireplace below the two giant stockings hanging from the mantle. "That should do it. And if not"—she pointed out the window— "there's plenty more fallen trees where that came from." Brian took off his heavy wool jacket and knelt down to arrange the logs. Sunny loved how at ease he seemed to be in her home, how he quietly went about pitching in to do whatever needed to be done.

"What time is Candace arriving?" Kat asked as she pulled off her stocking cap, allowing her two-tone hair to fall into place.

Sunny looked at her watch. "Should be soon. Her plane landed a while ago."

"I can't wait to meet the famous Candace face-to-face," Brian said.

Though they'd spoken often by phone—sometimes fifteen to twenty times a day during the height of their evacuation efforts—Brian and Candace's visits to Twimbly Island had never quite been in sync. Candace had started accusing Sunny of keeping the guy hidden from her. Today, Sunny thought, should be fun.

Outside the huge window an overcast sky hung over Puget Sound like a heavy winter blanket. Sunny didn't mind. It added to the ambience and made the huge Douglas fir growing on the sloped lawn leading down to the water sparkle even brighter under the hundreds of lights she'd paid an arborist to string.

In Kabul she'd had a bulky plastic tree that had taken up almost a third of the room. Here, in a house surrounded by pine, it would be ridiculous to chop down a perfectly good tree just to drag it inside. The twinkling giant in her yard looked just like the one at Rockefeller Center.

"We are here!" The front door swung open again. With Halajan in the lead, one by one they entered, carrying more trays, platters, and bowlfuls of food than Sunny could have ever imagined.

"I told you that you could do the side dishes. What the—"

"And that is what these are. Dishes for the side." Halajan patted her hips and directed the girls and Rashif to place their loads on the long table. Yazmina and Ahmet followed closely behind with a potful of *qabili palau*. Although Sunny had always insisted on all the traditional dishes, this Christmas she decided to allow things to be done a little differently to make her Afghan friends feel more at home. Though Yazmina and the family were well aware that they were better off than most in their situation—like the poor refugees struggling to find housing, crammed into tiny hotel rooms, desperate for jobs, or worse yet still stuck in limbo on military bases, like Zarween and Sayed, the couple from the airport, were in Doha—the adjustment to life in the US had been challenging. The money, the street signs, shopping for food, everything was strange and new. The children were thriving in the wide-open spaces, but the rest of them seemed to jump at the slightest sounds that came from the still woods that covered the island. And then there was always that feeling of being the other, singled out instantly by their clothing and language. It didn't help that Fox News and

Trump tried their best to make everybody wary of the Afghan refugees. *How many terrorists will Joe Biden bring to America?* Trump had asked. But around Twimbly Island the locals had been mostly welcoming. And on top of that the Seattle area had become one of the top destinations for families fleeing the Taliban.

Yazmina, Ahmet and the girls had arrived at Sunny's in late October. From Kabul they'd been flown to Qatar, then Germany, then onto a military base in Wisconsin for processing. Already Ahmet was finding support from others at his mosque, though he never stopped complaining about having to take a boat just to get there. And Yazmina had recently—once the girls were settled in school—started volunteering at the nonprofit Kat was working for, where they provided services for immigrants and refugees to help them become self-sufficient. Kat said Yazmina spent hours patiently soothing others less fortunate than she had been, those who were scrambling for money, a home, and some small sense of security. But Sunny knew Yaz also found solace in talking with them about the one thing they did share: fear for those who had been left behind.

Layla had broken everyone's hearts when she made that final, wrenching choice to remain in Kabul. Yet there she was, four months later, secure in her decision to stay behind. Living with Bashir Hadi, reunited with his wife and staying in the old coffee shop, she was committed to focusing her efforts on helping others secure safe passage out of the country. She'd taken extreme measures to cover her tracks, making it appear on social media as though she'd gone to the US with the rest of her family, even going so far as photoshopping herself into pictures of New York and Disney World. Now she was keeping the lowest of low profiles in Kabul, working day and night and relishing each and every success. It was great what she was doing, but that didn't keep everyone on Twimbly from worrying to death, even with Bashir Hadi pledging to watch over her. Yet, as Sunny constantly pointed out to Yazmina, at least Layla was learning enough to get herself out, if and when it became necessary.

Haseeb and his family had managed to get to Pakistan, with the hopes of obtaining sponsorship from family they had living in Canada. Being the hopeless romantic she was, Sunny wished things had worked out for Layla and Haseeb. If only Yaz and Ahmet had gotten the chance to meet him, like she had. Seeing what a caring, sweet, and capable man he was might have gone a long way in getting them to accept Haseeb as a match for Layla. If it had worked out for Halajan and Rashif, why not those two? Sunny smiled at the sight of the old couple standing hand in hand at the big window, admiring the giant, shimmering tree.

"Far cry from our old one, right, Hala?"

"Hah! And at least you're not making us listen to those stupid singing chipmunks this year."

"The night is still young, my friend."

"Who would like a beverage?" asked Brian, pointing to a cut-glass bowl of iced fruit juice dotted with cranberries and orange slices floating on top. Kat followed with a couple of bottles of Pinot she'd picked up from her favorite wineries on the island.

"Should we wait for Candace?" Yazmina asked.

"No. We should *prepare* for Candace," Sunny answered as she poured herself a glass of wine.

The kids were quiet but antsy, trying hard to contain the excitement they felt about this magical holiday Sunny had been hyping for weeks.

"Oh," she now said. "It looks like Santa left you something in those big socks over there." She pointed toward the fireplace. "I wonder how he knew you were here?"

Najama, older, obviously knew better than to believe in those things, but the smile on her face was worth every stop in every shop Sunny had made in the last three months. The kids attacked their stockings with glee.

"He doesn't know *I* am here?" Hala asked with a cackle.

"You? You are more naughty than nice." Ahmet laughed at his joke.

It was good to see him happy. Of all of them, he seemed to be having the hardest time adjusting. Being with the other men at the mosque had helped, as had the long walks around the island he took to help soothe his nerves. And there was a great Afghan restaurant in Seattle where he loved to hang out. But the pressure had to be difficult. Yes, they were living rent-free in old Joe's house next door, and, yes, they had Sunny to help smooth the bureaucratic hurdles and explain how things worked, and, yes, the children were happy, rushing to climb aboard the yellow school bus each morning to be with their new friends, their English improving in leaps and bounds. But as settled as their life might appear from the outside, they were still living with uncertainty, not knowing what the future was for their country, and not knowing what the possibilities might be for them in this one. Like all the other Afghan evacuees, they lived in legal limbo in the US. They could seek permanent residency if they chose, but the immigration system was incredibly slow-moving and backlogged. It might take years until their applications were approved, and even that wasn't guaranteed.

Sunny sidestepped the girls to reach the mantle. "Candles, please?" she said, handing the lighter to C.J.

The sun had started its slow descent over the water. The room began to glow with dozens of tiny flickering flames. Sunny took a sip from her glass and sighed.

And then, woosh! With a sudden gust of wind in blew Candace, looking every bit as Hollywood as she had when Sunny first met her twelve years before. Her blond hair was windblown, her nose red from the cold. But the woman had clearly dolled herself up for the occasion.

"What an ordeal!" Candace dropped her bags to the ground and tossed her white down coat over the back of a chair. "Seriously. Who the f—" Her eyes darted to the kids. "I mean, that boat! This place *is* pretty, but come on!"

"Right?" Ahmet rushed to carry the bags for her.

"And the princess has arrived," Halajan laughed.

"Nice to see you too, Halajan." Candace wrapped the old woman in a hug. And then there were greetings all around, until Candace came to Brian. "And the famous Brian, in person," she said with a twinkle in her eye.

"That would be me," he replied.

"Huh." She stood back a little, assessing him with her head cocked, a smile on her lips.

"*Huh?* What does that even mean?" Sunny asked.

But Candace had already moved on, pulling shiny wrapped boxes out of one of her bags and depositing them in a pile in front of the girls. The sky grew dark as chatter filled the room, the heat from the fire mixing with the warmth of friendships old and new. Yazmina and Sunny snuck off to the kitchen to bring out the food.

Candace stood over the spread covering the long table. "So it's just us and whose army?"

There was turkey and gravy, and Sunny's cranberry sauce, the *qabili palau*, and also *mantoo, alshack, chapli kabob, ferni*, and a pile of bread nearly a foot high. They'd apparently gone nuts in Joe's gourmet kitchen, putting every pot and pan to work for this amazing feast.

They all sat, including Phil the elephant who had a chair next to Aarezo, and for a while the only sounds to be heard were forks against plates and more than a few satisfied groans. It wasn't until the feeding frenzy died down that Sunny stood and tapped a spoon against her glass.

"Uh-oh. Here comes the schmaltz," Hala said, using a word she'd learned from their old friend Isabel—*Rohash shad bashat*, may she rest in peace.

"You don't like my speeches, Hala?" Sunny feigned hurt.

"Oh no, Sunny jan. You are a great orator. Just like your Abraham Lincoln."

"And what do you know about Abraham Lincoln?" Ahmet asked his mother.

"I know plenty. I read, remember?"

Sunny banged her spoon against the glass again and cleared her throat. "So, as some of you know, I used to give a speech every Christmas."

Candace groaned, making the kids giggle.

"Come on, it was always a short one, right?"

"Speech! Speech!" Brian urged her on.

Sunny shook her head. "This year I thought we might do things a little differently. So I'm going to bring what is usually a Thanksgiving tradition to Christmas. We're gonna go around the table, and one by one each of us will share something we're grateful for. I'll go first." She closed her eyes for a second, thinking of what she might say to start things off on just the right note. The last thing she wanted was for Christmas to turn maudlin. She opened her eyes and smiled. "I'm grateful for the tasting-room customers who keep Hala out of my face every day."

Everyone laughed.

"You should be grateful for *me*, who is the reason the customers come to your tasting room in the first place," Hala said.

She was probably right. Hala had been holding court almost every afternoon since they'd reopened. It reminded Sunny of their days at the coffee shop, where Hala had ruled with a sharp tongue and a quick wit.

"Okay, so you can go next," she said to the old woman.

"I am grateful for that television show here where the men dress like they are women, Ruples Dragon Race, or whatever it's called."

"And I am grateful to hear your beautiful laughter every time you watch it," Rashif responded.

285

Kat stood. "Okay. So, first of all, I am grateful for the family in Kansas who will be sponsoring Fawiza once she gets out of the camp in Kosovo."

"Soon," Candace said. "Hopefully soon."

A chorus of *inshallah* echoed across the table.

Kat couldn't stop smiling. "And," she added, "I am grateful for Yaz, who has agreed to make my wedding dress." She gave a little bow to Yazmina. There was applause, some woo-hooing.

"And I am grateful to be having a wedding," C.J. added, beaming at his bride-to-be.

Sunny almost gasped. At that moment he looked so much like his father, Jack.

"I am grateful to have so much love in the air," Brian said with a glance at Sunny, who could feel her cheeks burning.

"And I am hopeful to find some of that for myself," Candace added.

Sunny laughed. "It's not *hopeful* we're talking here, it's *grateful.*"

"Okay, so I'm grateful that there are men in the world." She pointed to the mistletoe Sunny had hung in the kitchen doorway. "Leave that there, Sunny. I'll be back."

"And you two?" Sunny asked, turning to the girls.

"I am grateful for my teacher, because she is funny and nice," Aarezo said.

Najama turned to Sunny. "I am grateful for the puppy Auntie Sunny promised to get me soon."

Yazmina rolled her eyes. "Me, I am grateful for my phone, as it is my lifeline to my sister."

Sunny thought she saw a tiny tear roll down Yazmina's cheek.

Now Ahmet stood. The man looked serious. Everyone quieted. "I am grateful, like Candace. But instead of for the men in the world, it is the women in the world I am grateful for. The women in *my* world. Candace, without you I do not think we would all be here today, together and safe. Sunny talks about how you pull strings, and whatever that means, I thank you from the bottom of my heart."

He turned to Kat. "To you I am forever grateful for the influence you have been on not only our Layla, but on our daughters as well." He held up a hand. "I know. At first, when Layla came to visit America, I thought she would be ruined by the way of life here by being around teenagers who showed no respect for anything or anyone. But she came back strong, and curious, and filled with new ideas that will forever help others. And Kat, with Layla and you as their aunties, Najama and Aarezo will be unstoppable."

Now he turned to Halajan. "*Maadar*, I am grateful to be your son. Though you have often made me crazy with your stubbornness, you have also helped me grow into a man who learned to think for himself, which is a gift I will always cherish."

Despite Sunny's attempts to keep things light, the room was becoming rather weepy. She dabbed a napkin at the corners of her eyes.

"My Yazmina." Ahmet smiled. "I am the luckiest man in the world to have you as my wife. I know it is not always easy, and I hope you feel that your patience is paying off. Just know that I am trying, and will continue to try for you forever. I am grateful for your strength, and for your guidance."

Yazmina reached for his hand.

"And you, Sunny," Ahmet continued. "So many things would never have happened without you, without the Kabul coffee shop. Our lives were forever changed with your arrival in our country, and will continue to change with our arrival in yours. My daughters have always been surrounded by strong women, the women at this table. Women who taught them that they could do anything and be anyone they want. But then came those who thought otherwise. Those who would say my daughters have no value, those who would steal their futures away from them. Those who would try to prove that the women who showed my daughters the way were wrong. And that is something I will not stand for. I am witness to the power of women, and will never be a part of a world that tries to extinguish it. So, here I am. Grateful for a future that may be uncertain, but that is one that will allow my daughters to live the lives they desire. And no matter where that may be, it is my promise to them, forever."

There was silence in the room as Ahmet took his seat. Outside, a light snow had begun to fall. Sunny swallowed the lump in her throat and pushed back her chair.

"I *knew* Sunny wasn't going to let us get away without a speech."

Candace's comment was met by giggles.

"A little toast. That's all, I promise." Sunny tapped a spoon against her wineglass. "Tonight I just want to talk about one thing, and that's family. Some of us have known each other a long time now, for others the connection is newer." She offered a little smile to Brian. "But old friends, new friends, human friends, even elephant friends, it really doesn't matter, because we've all been through something together that makes us way more than just friends."

There was nodding around the table.

"You—each and every one of you in this room—are more than I ever could have hoped for as my family. The love, the laughter, and, yes, even the arguments"—at this she pointed a finger toward Hala and Candace—"are what make me feel whole, like I belong to something bigger, more important, more lasting than myself."

"Here!" Candace lifted her glass.

"Wait. I'm not done yet! One more thing. Or maybe two. You know, life isn't always predictable, as most of us have learned the hard way. But . . ." Here Sunny had to pause. "No matter where we find ourselves in this big, wide, crazy world, we will forever be united, we will always be there for one another. Together, we are unstoppable."

Author's note

I went to Afghanistan for the first time after the Taliban's 2002 defeat, as a volunteer with a humanitarian medical group. After one month there, I knew my work in the country would be to teach hairdressing. To many people it seemed like a crazy idea, doing this in a land where women covered with burqas. But most were unaware that hair and makeup were a massive part of Afghan culture. Being a hairdresser myself, I understood the freedom learning this skill could give, and I was determined to share that freedom with my newfound Afghan sisters. That journey was recounted in my first book, *The Kabul Beauty School*.

After three years of teaching at the beauty school—and three years of drinking instant coffee—I decided I needed a new challenge, and a place where I could get the cappuccino I'd been craving. The result was the real coffeehouse that inspired *The Little Coffee Shop of Kabul*.

Fast forward to August 2021, when the Taliban succeeded in taking over the country once again and Afghans began running for their lives. The progress of the previous twenty years vanished in one swift moment. Hopes and dreams were dashed. And, in what seemed like the blink of an eye, a humanitarian crisis began.

The thought of my friends being imprisoned in their homes simply because they were women, and the fears that they might suffer at the hands of the Taliban or that their daughters might be forced into a Talib marriage, spurred me into action. I dove in to help with evacuations.

What was happening in Afghanistan was terrifying. It was a life-and-death situation, and many people were depending on me to find a solution to get their families to a safe place. I had never experienced that level of responsibility and pressure in my life, but I knew it was nothing compared to what the families in Afghanistan were going through. I couldn't sleep, afraid I would miss a phone call or text message about an evacuation opportunity for one of them. I feared that someone might die if I shut my eyes for even a moment. Though I was exhausted, sleep became my enemy, as the nightmares I would have were worse than the extreme tiredness. When I did sleep, more often than not I'd wake to my phone going wild with videos of Taliban beatings, and requests from strangers for help. It was almost more than my broken, sleep-deprived heart could take. I felt so unqualified to be doing what I was doing. I am sure many other volunteers working to help the evacuation efforts felt the same way. I could not understand how the ball had been dropped so badly, leaving people like us to find smuggling routes and create code words. In what world is that right? None of it made sense to me.

With the support of Oasis Rescue, and friends and foundations from around the world, I helped more than seventy people, including some of the old Kabul Beauty School staff, get safely out of Afghanistan. Some made it to the United States, but the majority, along with many vulnerable Afghans who were not able to get on the initial emergency evacuation flights, fled to neighboring countries, where they found themselves in limbo waiting for a visa that would allow them to start a new life elsewhere.

With this, my worry shifted. Now what? There they were, without jobs to support their families and without the language skills needed to gain employment. How would they survive this waiting game, and how would they survive once they had the ability to relocate to somewhere else? What would happen to the women who had fled on their own, now alone in a strange country?

Now, I may not be an expert in the world of secret codes or smuggling routes, but I do know hairdressing. And I knew I could open an emergency beauty school anywhere in the world. That is how the Afghan Refugee Beauty School was born. The first class began in September 2022, and as I write this, in March 2023, forty-five students have graduated, and many of those have been able to secure work. A new class of twenty-five students has just started. The school is packed with incredible women, but my favorite part of this story is that many of the teachers, all refugees, are from the original Kabul Beauty School. And some of them are working side by side with their daughters, who they had trained to be hairdressers as well. Together, these women are working to give hope to others in this very complicated world they've all been thrust into.

As you can imagine, over that tumultuous year I did not have much time to think about anything other than the evacuations and the launch of the school. But in a quiet moment, as I was traveling, something happened. I began to hear the voices of the Little Coffee Shop of Kabul characters asking, 'What about us?'

I had never planned on writing a third book in the Little Coffee Shop of Kabul series, because in my head all my characters had lived happily ever after *Return to the Little Coffee Shop of Kabul*. But now the perfect life I had planned for all of them was gone. What would the future hold for Yazmina's daughters, with girls no longer allowed to attend university? And Layla—what would her experience be like, as a twenty-something who had gotten a taste of American freedom? How would she manage in this world? The idea of Halajan having to endure the Taliban yet again brought tears to my eyes. I cried with Yazmina as she feared for the future of her sister and daughters, and for all the women in jeopardy. I worried with Ahmet about the entire family, feeling the weight of the world that had landed on his shoulders. I listened to my characters and started writing down their stories. That is how *Farewell to the Little Coffee Shop of Kabul* came to be.

Things in Afghanistan have only gone from bad to worse since my real and fictional friends were forced to leave their country behind. Now, girls are banned from attending school past the sixth grade, women have vanished from politics and female civil servants have been told to stay home. Women have been ordered to cover their faces in public and are not allowed to travel more than seventy-five kilometers from their homes without a male escort. In some areas, rules forbid women from seeing a doctor or hailing a taxi unless they are accompanied by a male relative. Even in the shop windows of Kabul, bags cover the faces of feminine mannequins. But I have witnessed the strength and resilience of Afghan people firsthand. The Afghans I know personally are doing everything they can to find a path forward. And even in the midst of so much uncertainty, one thing is for sure: they will never give up hope for their futures, and for the future of the country they love.

Acknowledgments

When I started writing my acknowledgments for *Farewell to the Little Coffee Shop of Kabul*, I couldn't wait to tell everyone about all the wonderful people around the world who worked with me or supported me while writing this book.

First of all, I would like to thank my agent, **Marly Rusoff**. I have always loved and respected you, but when you dove right into the middle of the Afghan evacuation crisis to help, I was especially proud to have you as my agent and friend. We have always shared a lot of common ground, but this experience bonded us in a way that is hard to describe. I can't believe how many hours we spent on the phone, not talking about books, but instead about how we could safely get Afghan people out of Afghanistan. After seeing your drive, selflessness, and commitment to help, I was in awe. Marly, thank you for believing in me, supporting me on all the books, and encouraging me with this new one. Thank you for all the sleep you missed due to our midnight phone calls. I'm sure that when your husband and business partner **Michael Radulescu (Mihai)** would hear you talking in the wee hours of the night, he must have wondered what was going on, and who was on the other end of the call. It was just me. Mihai, thank you for supporting Marly and me during the evacuation period. I know we kept you awake far too often. Thank you for being such a wonderful part of the **Marly Rusoff Literary Agency** and for having my back for nearly nineteen years. OMG, that is a long time! I'm thrilled you have been a steadfast part of my life for so many years. I appreciate you and your support for me and my books.

I would like to thank **Lizzy Kremer** at **David Higham Associates** literary agency for all your efforts with my books. Lizzy, you have truly been a partner on the journey, and I am so grateful for your tireless efforts on my behalf.

Ellen Kaye, you have made such a lasting impact on my life. Your writing talent enriches the world, and I am grateful to work with you. I know working on this book was challenging and often kept you awake at night because you care about the real people of Afghanistan. I know it was hard digesting the true accounts of people who have suffered and lost so much. I can't imagine telling this story without you, and it was comforting to know you were by my side through the entire process. You were often the only person who could untangle the thoughts and emotions in my head. You have always been my rock. I don't want to tell stories without you, because you always guide me in the right direction and your writing wisdom is always spot-on.

We have worked on many projects together, but this one seems to be one of the most important. Thank you, Ellen, for being you. I will forever cherish your friendship and your extraordinary talent with words.

I would like to express my appreciation to **Penguin Random House Australia** and **Little Brown Group UK** for everything your exceptional teams have done to bring this book to life. Throughout the entire process, you have been a supportive presence. Thank you for believing in me and my work. I am so grateful to be part of your publishing family.

Beverley Cousins, my wonderful publisher at Penguin Random House Australia, you are indeed remarkable. You make the editing process a bit less painful. (Thank you for that.) I can always count on you to make each book the best it can be. You have a great eye and ear for story, and I am always so shocked at how fast you can read! Thank you for approaching my manuscript with care and sensitivity, while preserving my voice. You always catch the book's vision, and I am thrilled you believe in me and my stories.

Thank you **Ruth Jones**, my brilliant editor at Little Brown Group UK, for providing insightful comments and suggestions that helped me refine my work. Your feedback was so crucial to making the book come alive. Thank you for everything you do.

Kathryn Knight, Lauren Finger and **Cristina Briones**, I am so thankful to you for your exceptional work on my manuscript. Your skillful attention to detail has transformed my writing and helped create this beautiful book.

Muhammad Saddique, you are one of the most remarkable people I have ever met. I first saw your generous and kind nature appear during the Afghan evacuations in how you constantly worried about other refugees, doing everything possible to help people. You are an inspiration. Thank you for working with me from beginning to end with this book. Your perspective and insight as an Afghan working and living in Kabul during this challenging time were so important to getting the story right. Thank you for dedicating so much time to ensuring the details were right. Thank you, Muhammad, for answering my endless questions and embracing my characters as if they were real people. But, most of all, thank you for doing this all while you and your family were in crisis, learning to make your way as refugees. You are amazing, and I am so proud of how you care for everyone. You are truly a good human, and are now one of my best friends. Meeting you has been one of the highlights of my life.

Zarwin Mujaddidi, I don't think I've ever met a woman so strong and confident in the middle of a storm. Your real-life perspective of modern women living and working in Afghanistan was a beautiful window into a time in Afghanistan when everything felt hopeful. Your knowledge of Afghan women's affairs and attention to detail makes this book so powerful. Thank you and your husband, **Rabeullah Mujaddidi (Rabe),** for advising me on current Afghan matters. You both have done so much to make this book speak the truth. I love how you and Rabe would tag-team and help me understand every detail. I know that the book is better because of you both.

Brian Williams, I believe you are one of the most intelligent people I have ever met. I cannot tell you how comforting it was to talk to an expert during the Afghan evacuation. And when I say expert, I mean it. Let me share just the tip of your iceberg: Brian's scholarly credentials include a PhD in Central Asian Islamic history, a tenured full professorship in Islamic History at the University of Massachusetts Dartmouth, and a stint teaching Muslim history at the prestigious University of London. On top of being smart, Brian also has a heart for the Afghan people and spent time in Afghanistan researching his own books and working as a CIA field analyst. Honestly, I gleaned so much information from you, and appreciate you breaking everything down into bite-size morsels so that I could understand this real-life game of thrones. I had to have a character like you in the book, whose name also happens to be Brian. Thank you for being a part of my life, and for holding my hand all hours of the day and night during the Afghan crisis. I am not sure if I could have made it through without you. Most importantly, thank you for introducing me to all your people who have helped to save lives. I will be forever indebted to you. I am honored to know you, and you will always be my hero.

Aimal, I loved your insight into the lifestyle of a single, trendy Afghan who was living their best life and enjoying every minute of it. (Of course, this was pre–Taliban takeover.) Most people only know about the Afghanistan they see in the news, and your Afghanistan was so much bigger and richer than that. Thank you for spending countless hours sharing your Afghanistan with me while you were trying to sort out what you were going to do next.

Saboor Hanifi, thank you for sharing your story with me. Our families have been friends for a long time, and my life in Afghanistan was better with you and your family in it.

Your family's experiences during the evacuation were harrowing, and I can only hope I've done justice incorporating some of them here.

Humaira Ghilzai, you have no idea how much I love and appreciate the recipes you provide. It makes me wish that I could cook! You are an amazing, talented woman and I am very proud to know you.

Ingrid Ostick, your keen eye for detail is always so helpful. I think you read the manuscript of this book at least five or six times. I love our friendship and am very happy you are a fast reader.

Judith Pollock, thank you for being a first-time reader. It is clear that language is your passion, and your insight went a long way in helping make this story tto make sensc. You're good at this!

Linda Bine, thanks for helping get this one off the ground. Your editing talents are always appreciated.

Denis Asahara, we've come a long way, baby, and I'm happy that you are my life partner. I always tell my friends that you are low maintenance—kind of—and that I think it all works because perhaps I'm a little on the higher side in the maintenance department. You make it easy for me to write and be creative. You knew this book was different from all the rest. When I would get overwhelmed, you were always there for me. You understand and respect my love for Afghanistan and its people, and allow me the space to process things in my own way. I love you. Thank you for stealing my heart.

I have two incredible sons, **Noah** and **Zach Lentz**, and two wonderful daughters-in-law, **Aretha Lentz** and **Martha**

Villasana, along with seven wild, beautiful, and fun grandchildren aged between 17 and 3—**Didier, Derek, Italya, Kai, Silas, Luna** and the youngest, **Lucas.** Everyone in my family has inspired or supported me in some way or another while writing my books. When I watched and read about all the horrors that were going on in Afghanistan, my family was my comfort. Thank you all for allowing me the freedom to be creative, quirky, and the best version of myself.

To the beautiful **Afghan people.** You are kind, generous, and like no other people on earth. Your culture is rich and your history is complicated. I am so blessed to have met so many wonderful, gracious Afghan people. I will never pretend that I understand what you are going through or the heartbreak you are feeling, but know that I will always stand alongside you, and that you can count on me as your sister.

I am grateful to **Afghanistan** for adopting me and loving me unconditionally. I fell in love with you twenty-one years ago; our passion has been fantastic and complicated. You changed my life the moment I set foot on your soil. I never saw things the same way again. I never ate fruit that was sweeter or met kinder people. My family knew they could not compete with this strange love affair. My heart stopped when you lost your freedom on August 15, 2021. The only thing I knew to do was to keep telling your story, and I hope you are pleased with it. I don't want people to forget about Afghanistan, its beauty, and its pain. You will always be the love of my life.

About the author

Deborah Rodriguez is the author of the international bestsellers *The Little Coffee Shop of Kabul*, *Return to the Little Coffee Shop of Kabul*, *The Zanzibar Wife*, *Island on the Edge of the World* and *The Moroccan Daughter*. She has also written two memoirs: *The Kabul Beauty School*, about her life in Afghanistan, and *The House on Carnaval Street*, on her experiences following her return to America. She spent five years teaching at and later directing the Kabul Beauty School, the first modern beauty academy and training salon in Afghanistan.

Deborah also owned the Oasis Salon and the Cabul Coffee House, and is the founder of the nonprofit organisation Oasis Rescue, which aims to teach women in post-conflict and disaster-stricken areas the art of hairdressing.

She currently lives in Mazatlán, Mexico, where she owns Tippy Toes salon and spa.

For your reading group party

Reading group questions

1. When Sunny arrives back in Kabul after eight years, she can't believe how much it has changed. Were you at all surprised by the descriptions of the city? If so, in what ways?

2. Imagine that your country was suddenly faced with a takeover by an oppressive force whose ideas went against everything you believed in. Would you stay? If you did stay, do you think you'd try to fight for your beliefs? Or, if you think you would choose to leave, where would you go?

3. Halajan discovers poetry as an outlet for her outrage. Is there something you turn to as a way to vent your own anger or frustration?

4. What was the most shocking moment in the book for you? Was there one particular element or detail that brought home to you the fate the citizens of Kabul, and women in particular, were facing?

5. The family in this story is faced with impossible choices. Have you ever had to make a decision that felt impossible in your own life (that you feel comfortable sharing)?

6. Imagine that you were being forced to leave your home and your country, and could only take one small suitcase of belongings with you. You have no idea if and when you might ever return home. What would you pack?

7. Much has changed in Afghanistan since the Taliban seized power in 2021, including a ban on female education and restrictions that prevent women from working and traveling independently. Do you think Layla would have continued to live in Kabul? If so, what do you imagine her life would be like?

8. How do you imagine the lives of Ahmet, Yazmina and their children would be five years after they left Kabul?

9. The refugee situation has reached a tipping point in many parts of the world today. The characters in this story have a relatively easy time finding sanctuary, but in real life many do not. How do you think the issue should be addressed?

10. How do you think refugees who have made their way to your country or community might best be helped?

Some delicious Afghan dishes to share

Summon up the tastes and smells of Kabul with these delicious recipes, kindly supplied by Humaira Ghilzai from her inspiring website Afghan Culture Unveiled. You can visit it here: afghancultureunveiled.com

Khasta e shereen

Cardamom almond brittle

This flavorful almond and cardamom treat is easy to make, great for potlucks and a great accompaniment to a cup of black or green tea.

Serves 8–10 people
1½ cups granulated sugar
1 pound (450 grams) unsalted roasted almonds*
1½ teaspoons ground cardamom

Cover a baking sheet with parchment paper. Spread the almonds in a single layer on the baking sheet, grouping them together with no spaces between the nuts.

Heat the sugar in a heavy-bottom saucepan over medium heat, stirring regularly. The sugar will eventually turn to liquid. Continue to cook, stirring all the while, until the sugar is golden brown. Add the cardamom and cook a little longer until it reaches a deep amber color and smooth texture. The whole process of caramelizing the sugar will take about 15 to 20 minutes.

Drizzle the sugar in a thin stream evenly over the top of the almonds, covering them all.

Cool completely. Break up the almonds with your fingers into two-bite pieces. Store in a jar with a tight lid or a Ziploc bag.

*If you have raw almonds, you can toast them in the oven at 325 degrees Fahrenheit (180 degrees Celsius) for 10 minutes before making the recipe.

Options:

You can use many other ingredients to lend different flavors to your nuts. In place of cardamom (the traditional Afghan flavor), try the following:

- stir ⅓ cup cocoa nibs into the melted sugar in place of the cardamom

- add ½ teaspoon ground cayenne or ground black pepper to the melted sugar in place of the cardamom

- sprinkle ¾ teaspoon *fleur de sel* over the top of the caramelized sugar after you've poured it on the almonds. The salt will be delicious with or without the cardamom.

Qabili palau

Afghanistan's national rice dish

No Afghan gathering can be called a party without the aromatic scent of this meat and rice dish topped with raisins, carrots, and almonds. While challenging, this dish offers many unique flavors as well as a taste of traditional Afghan cuisine.

Serves 6–8 people
4 cups basmati long grain rice
5 skinless chicken legs
5 skinless chicken thighs
3 medium yellow (brown) onions, peeled and quartered
½ cup plus 2 tablespoons olive oil or vegetable oil, divided
5 teaspoons salt
1 cup chicken broth (stock)
3 large carrots, peeled
1 cup black raisins
½ cup slivered almonds
3 tablespoons sugar
¾ cup water
2 teaspoons ground cumin
1½ teaspoons ground cardamom
½ teaspoon ground black pepper
12 cups water
2 tablespoons browning sauce such as Kitchen Bouquet
  (optional)

Immerse rice in a bowl of water and drain in a colander. Repeat this step 3 times.

Wash and dry the chicken. Set aside.

Chop the onions in a food processor using the pulse button. Don't puree the onions. You can do this by hand if you prefer.

Choose a sauté pan that is at least a couple inches deep and large enough to fit all the chicken. Pour ½ cup of the oil in the pan and sauté the onions over high heat, stirring quickly, until brown (5–10 minutes). Don't burn them. Cook until the onions take on a deep, rich brown color.

Add the chicken to the pan and sprinkle with 3 teaspoons of the salt. Cook the chicken over medium-high heat for 6 minutes, turning from time to time so all sides turn golden brown. The onion will start to caramelize and turn into a thick sauce.

Add ¼ cup of the chicken broth, and continue stirring to keep the chicken from burning. Once the liquid has been absorbed, add another ¼ cup of chicken broth, bring it to a boil, cover with a lid or aluminum foil, and simmer for 10 minutes. The sauce should turn a dark brown. If your sauce does not take on a dark color, you can add the Kitchen Bouquet to give it color.

Preheat the oven to 500 degrees Fahrenheit (250 degrees Celsius).

While the chicken is cooking, cut the carrots into long thick matchsticks, about 4 inches long and ⅛-inch thick. Make sure that they are not too thin. In a large frying pan add ¾ cup of water and bring to a boil, add the carrots and cook until they are tender and a deep orange hue (5 to 7 minutes). Keep a close eye on this to make sure you do not overcook them.

Once the carrots are done, drain any leftover liquid from the pan. Add the remaining 2 tablespoons of oil, raisins, almonds, and sugar to the carrots. Stir quickly over medium-high heat and keep stirring for about 3 minutes. The raisins will look plump; the carrots will take on a nice sweet flavor. Remove from heat and package the carrot mixture into a sealed aluminum foil pouch about the size of a small paperback novel.

Remove the chicken pieces from the broth and set aside. Stir the cumin, cardamom, and black pepper into the broth. Continue to cook on low for 5 minutes to allow it to thicken.

Meanwhile, measure 12 cups of water. Add water and the remaining 2 teaspoons of salt into a large Dutch oven or pot with a fitted lid. Bring water to a boil. Add the rice to the water and cook until it is al dente (nearly cooked, though still slightly crunchy). This will take just a few minutes depending on the rice you use. You will have to taste it to check for doneness. Do not overcook it.

Immediately strain the rice through a colander. Put the rice back into the cooking pot and add the sauce from the chicken. Mix well. Arrange the chicken pieces on top of the rice. Set the aluminum package of carrots on top of the rice. This will keep the carrots warm and deepen the flavors without mixing with the rice yet. Cover the pot with aluminum foil and then place the lid to make a tight seal. This way all the flavors and the steam will stay inside the pot.

Bake the rice for 15 minutes at 500 degrees (250 degrees Celsius) then drop the temperature to 250 degrees (120 degrees Celsius). Cook for another 20 minutes.

To serve, arrange the chicken pieces on a large platter and cover with the rice. Sprinkle the carrot, raisin, and almond mixture on the rice. Serve with a fresh green salad.

Chapli kabob

Juicy Afghan burgers

These Afghan kabobs are shaped like burgers, but are way more flavorful with a hint of coriander and paprika. You can use plant-based beef, beef or ground turkey. This recipe is easy to double or triple and will satisfy the pickiest eaters.

Serves 6 people

1 pound (450 grams) plant-based ground meat, ground beef
    or ground turkey

¾ cup finely diced green onion
    (both white and green parts)

¼ cup finely chopped cilantro (coriander), including stems

1–2 jalapeño peppers, deseeded and finely chopped

1 teaspoon finely chopped garlic (around 2–3 cloves)

½ teaspoon salt

½ teaspoon black pepper

2 teaspoons ground coriander

½ teaspoon paprika

½ teaspoon red pepper flakes (optional)

1 cup of avocado oil or vegetable oil (or less, if you choose
    to cook on a lightly oiled skillet; see instructions below)

Add all ingredients except for the oil to a large bowl and mix by folding the meat (rather than kneading like dough) while pressing the ingredients in the meat and making sure that it's evenly distributed. It's very important that the ingredients are mixed well and the meat takes on a smooth texture. This should take 3–5 minutes.

Let meat rest for 10 minutes.

Place a large frying pan on a medium-high flame, add oil, and let it get piping hot. In the meantime, divide the meat into eight balls. Pat each ball into a thin, round disk and add to the frying pan. Cook each side for 2–3 minutes or until the disk is cooked all the way through and juicy. While there is no "medium rare" in the Afghan vocabulary, be careful not to overcook them. You can skip the frying by simply cooking the kabobs in a lightly oiled skillet for about 5 minutes per side.

Serve with warm pita bread, green salad, and a dollop of plain yogurt.

Bolani with yogurt chutney sauce

Afghan potato and spinach flatbread

Bolani is Afghanistan's answer to the long tradition of stuffed flat bread snacks such as quesadilla, pupusa, or fried calzone. This recipe tweaks the original by baking instead of frying. (There is a video of Humaira cooking bolani on her website, afghancultureunveiled.com)

Makes 15 servings
Bolani:
2 large potatoes, boiled
½ cup cilantro (coriander)
½ cup finely diced green onions
1 cup finely diced spinach
1½ teaspoons salt
1 teaspoon black pepper
1 teaspoon paprika
1 teaspoon ground coriander
15 uncooked tortillas
olive oil spray
cookie sheet
parchment paper

Yogurt chutney:
1 cup of cilantro
1 teaspoon salt
½ teaspoon black pepper
½ teaspoon pepper flakes
¼ cup white vinegar

½ cup fresh mint
1 cup yogurt

To make the bolani stuffing; in a bowl, take the cooked potatoes with skins still on and mix with cilantro (coriander), green onions, spinach, salt, black pepper, paprika, and ground coriander.

Let the stuffing be a little lumpy as you mix all the ingredients with the potatoes for a better structure.

At this time, set your oven to broil (grill).

Once you have mixed the potatoes and ingredients, set aside.

Clear your workspace in order to assemble the tortillas. For each tortilla, scoop 1–2 large tablespoons of the bolani stuffing. Wet the edge of the tortilla (if needed) and fold in half with your stuffing inside to close. Repeat with all the tortillas you have.

Once complete, grab a cookie sheet and line with parchment paper. Place your bolani pieces evenly on the cookie sheet. Spray them lightly on both sides with the olive oil spray.

Place them in the oven for 3–4 minutes. Watch closely, as each stove has a different broil strength. When time is up, flip them, and broil for another 3–4 minutes on the other side. Take out of oven and let them cool.

To make the yogurt chutney, place all ingredients except the yogurt in a blender and mix until creamy. Once smooth, add the yogurt. However, do not blend now – just pulse. 4–5 pulses should give the desired consistency of a dipping sauce.

To serve, cut the bolani in half, if desired, and put the sauce in a bowl.

DEBORAH RODRIGUEZ

The Little Coffee Shop of Kabul

INCLUDES EXCLUSIVE
10TH ANNIVERSARY EDITION
AUTHOR MATERIAL

One little café.
Five extraordinary
women . . .

Go back to where it all began . . .

THE LITTLE COFFEE SHOP OF KABUL

Deborah Rodriguez

One little café. Five extraordinary women.

In a little coffee shop in one of the most dangerous places on earth, five very different women come together.

Sunny, the proud proprietor, who needs an ingenious plan— and fast—to keep her café and customers safe . . .

Yazmina, a young pregnant woman stolen from her remote village and now abandoned on Kabul's violent streets . . .

Candace, a wealthy American who has finally left her husband for her Afghan lover, the enigmatic Wakil . . .

Isabel, a determined journalist with a secret that might keep her from the biggest story of her life . . .

And **Halajan,** the sixty-year-old den mother, whose long-hidden love affair breaks all the rules.

As these five discover there's more to one another than meets the eye, they form a unique bond that will forever change their lives and the lives of many others.

'The idea behind this book was a beautiful one, and I can say without a doubt that the sheer genius of the idea has come across to the reader through the pages. To write about a warzone, to humanize it for one's readers, give it life and an identity beyond bloodshed is a feat that deserves more appreciation than I could ever articulate into sentences.' *The Guardian*

AVAILABLE NOW

DEBORAH
RODRIGUEZ

Return
to the Little
Coffee Shop of
Kabul

THE LONG-AWAITED SEQUEL TO
THE INTERNATIONAL BESTSELLER
The Little Coffee Shop of Kabul

With a little magic,
anything is possible.

The
Zanzibar
Wife

DEBORAH
RODRIGUEZ

Author of *The Little Coffee Shop of Kabul*

THE ZANZIBAR WIFE

Deborah Rodriguez

Set both in Oman and on the Tanzanian island of Zanzibar, *The Zanzibar Wife* is the story of three different women, each at a turning point in her life . . .

Oman. The ancient land of frankincense, wind-swept deserts, craggy mountaintops and turquoise seas. A place where tales of evil spirits and eerie phenomena abound.

Into this magical nation come three remarkable women, each facing a crossroad in her life.

Rachel, a troubled American war photographer who is struggling to shed the trauma of her career for a simpler, gentler life. Now she has once again picked up her camera and is headed to Oman to cover a quite different story – for a glossy travel magazine.

Ariana Khan, a bubbly British woman struggling to keep up with the glitz of Dubai and ready to give up on love. She has rashly volunteered as Rachel's 'fixer', a job she's never heard of, in a country she knows nothing about.

And **Miza**, a young woman living far from her beloved homeland of Zanzibar. As the second wife of Tariq, an Omani man, she remains a secret from his terrifying 'other' wife, Maryam. Until one day, when Tariq fails to come home.

As the three women journey together across this weird and wonderful land, they are forced to confront their darkest fears and their deepest wishes. Because here in Oman, things aren't always what they appear to be . . .

AVAILABLE NOW

AUTHOR OF
The Little
Coffee Shop of
Kabul
In Haiti, nothing
you see is what
it seems . . .
Island on the
Edge of the
World
DEBORAH
RODRIGUEZ
INTERNATIONALLY BESTSELLING AUTHOR

ISLAND ON THE EDGE OF THE WORLD

Deborah Rodriguez

A captivating tale of four very different women on the hunt for a lost child.

Haiti. A poor country rich in courage, strength and love. As these four women are about to discover.

Charlie, the rootless daughter of American missionaries, now working as a hairdresser in Northern California. But the repercussions of a traumatic childhood far from home have left her struggling for her way in life.

Bea, Charlie's eccentric grandmother, who is convinced a reunion with her estranged mother will help Charlie heal.

Lizbeth, a Texas widow who has never strayed too far from home. She is on a daunting journey into the unknown, searching for the grandchild she never knew existed.

And **Senzey**, a young Haitian mother dealing with a lifetime of love and loss, who shows them the true meaning of bravery.

Together they venture through the teeming, colorful streets of Port-au-Prince, into the worlds of do-gooders doing more harm than good, Vodou practitioners, artists, activists, and everyday Haitian men and women determined to survive against all odds.

For Charlie, Bea, Lizbeth and Senzey, life will never be the same again . . .

'This wonderful story of courageous, obstinate women transports you straight to the beating heart of a colourful land.' *People's Friend*

AVAILABLE NOW

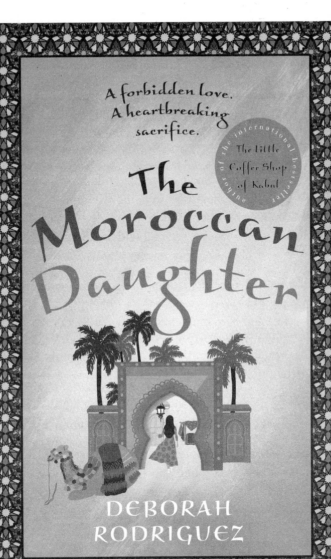

THE MOROCCAN DAUGHTER

Deborah Rodriguez

From the twisted alleyways of the ancient medina of Fès to a marriage festival high in the Atlas Mountains, an entrancing modern story of forbidden love set in the sensual landscape of North Africa.

Amina Bennis has come back to her childhood home in Morocco to attend her sister's wedding. The time has come for her to confront her strict, traditionalist father with the secret she has kept for more than a year—her American husband, Max.

Amina's best friend, **Charlie**, and Charlie's feisty grandmother, **Bea**, have come along for moral support, staying with Amina and her family in their palatial *riad* in Fès and enjoying all that the city has to offer. But Charlie is also hiding someone from her past – a mystery man from Casablanca.

And then there's **Samira**, the Bennises' devoted housekeeper for many decades. Hers is the biggest secret of all – one that strikes at the very heart of the family.

As things begin to unravel behind the ancient walls of the medina, the four women are soon caught in a web of lies, clandestine deals and shocking confessions . . .

'Rodriguez brings Fès' ancient medina to vivid life, complete with bustling streets, sandstone walls, lush citrus trees and sparkling mosaic tiles. Rodriguez's writing sings, and as I read, I felt myself immersed in the sights and smells of Morocco; I could feel the uneven stones of the medina beneath my feet, and my mouth watered with the scents of orange, ginger, and cinnamon.' Better Reading

AVAILABLE NOW

Join us at

For competitions galore,
exclusive interviews with our lovely
Sphere authors, chat about
all the latest books
and much, much more.

Follow us on Twitter at
🐦 @littlebookcafe

Subscribe to our newsletter and
Like us at **f**/thelittlebookcafe

Read. Love. Share.